Disclaimer

This story is completely fictional. The characters in this story are fictional. The names, locations, businesses, establishments and organizations in this story are either the product of the author's imagination or are used in a fictitious manner. This book is intended for an adult audience. Anyone under the age of 18 should not read this book.

This is dedicated to Verna, my number one fan, whom I love so very much. Happy Birthday! ☺

*A new heart also will I give you,
and a new spirit will I put within
you: and I will take away the
stony heart out of your flesh, and
I will give you a heart of flesh.*

Chapter One

Perched at the corner of the bar, she stirred her lava drink. She was surveying the room, studying her options. From this strategic vantage point she could view with one sweep of her eyes every single person all around her, every single patron here at the tiny old, badly paneled hot spot in town dubbed by some as The Tiki Bar.

Her current buzz was a welcome relief. She was on her third drink if you counted the two glasses of Moet at the hotel room. But who was counting? Simone Sanders was on a mission. Out of the 30 or so people giving this place "atmosphere," she was carefully considering every male a potential prospect. And while it didn't matter if he was a local or a tourist, not just anyone would do. Tonight she had a very important decision to make.

Whom would she choose to go to bed with her? Which one of these guys would give it to her good?

The fireman in the corner? He was off-duty now, obviously, but earlier she'd seen him at the little grocery store when he was still in uniform. *Hmm.* She'd always wondered what it would be like to do a fireman. Firemen were *hot*, and this one definitely fit the chivalrous, studly mold that most women found irresistible. She imagined the feel of strong, hungry, fireman hands all over her body. Maybe he'd kiss her neck or nibble her earlobe. *Mmm.* He seemed to be looking over at her, too. But then, *everything* with a penis seemed to be looking over at her. And why not? She looked smoking hot. Plus she was all alone.

What about the two business types? They must've come in right after work because they looked a bit dressed up for the likes of *this* place. Maybe one would watch while she screwed the other one. *Hmm.* She contemplated that for a moment then decided *no.* One guy would be much easier to control, and Simone *always* had to be in control. *Maybe if I wanted their money,* she thought, shaking her head a little.

How about that studious-looking, nerdy guy over there with his girlfriend? She always did go for the quiet, sexy type with glasses. She could probably teach *him* a thing or two. Or maybe they could be a threesome? She'd never done *that* before. On second thought, she mentally shook her head. *No. Absolutely not!* Simone was not a sharing soul. Definitely not tonight. And definitely not with an intellectual.

There was a table of surfers by the window. The North Shore certainly didn't lack for any of those. But did she want a *young* guy? *Well, if they're in here, they have to at least be 21, right?* The blonde one was kinda cute. *He* might make her feel young again. He smiled a little when he caught her staring at him. *Hmm, pretty confident,* she thought. *He SEEMS non-discriminating. Probably screws anything that walks in front of him.*

She definitely didn't want the sailor, sitting two seats down from her. He'd already made eyes at her, but Simone hadn't returned his enthusiasm. He, too, was scoping out the joint, his back to the wall, elbows on the bar. The shelves behind him housed a collection of at least fifty million shot glasses. This little establishment in all its bamboo-paneled glory certainly didn't lack for personality! *But no.* No sailors for

Simone. Her dad was a sailor back in WWII, and that would just be too weird. Although, her chances of nailing a sailor were pretty good, based on how aggressive these guys had been since she'd first arrived in Oahu a week ago. What did Brenda used to call them? *Oh yeah. Jarheads.* But no. She didn't want a Jarhead. Or was a Jarhead a Marine? Her drinks had officially kicked in and she couldn't even think right.

It was only 9:00 p.m. and already the place was filling up. This was good. She'd have more and more options. Especially once the band started to play. Then she'd get out on the dance floor and break out some of her moves. Simone was a great dancer—everyone always said so. She swiveled her chair back around.

"It's my birthday!" she told the dark-haired, oversized bartender with the loud Hawaiian shirt. Her sudden, happy outburst seemed to startle him as much as it startled *her*. His name was Liko, and he was native as native could be. His family had lived here since forever, he'd told her when she'd first sat down. At the moment, he held up a finger and walked backward toward the wall. His puffy hand clumsily fumbled around for something in a big glass jar, and he returned with a light green, neon button. He placed it in her hand. It had a palm tree on it with the words KISS ME IT'S MY BIRTHDAY.

"Thank you!" she said, trying to find a place to pin it on her shirt. No easy task since her neckline was super low-cut. She finally stuck it to her spaghetti strap. The bright green really stood out next to the whiteness of her top and the darkness of her tan.

"How old are you today?" Liko asked her.

"Well, there went your tip!"

Simone smiled and sipped her drink.

Liko laughed. "Let me guess. Thirty-five?"

"You come here!" She stood up and planted a little kiss on his cheek. "I think I love you, Liko," she said, and he laughed again. *Hmm. Maybe I'll do the bartender!* Then *she* laughed. *No.* He was too big around. And too old.

Not that she was one to talk! Today was Simone's big 5-0. She was half a century old, and *she* intended to party. She'd certainly dressed the part.

Her outfit was from the junior's department— gladiator sandals, short white skirt and short white tank that showed off her mid-drift—but Simone could get away with it. She was in the same great shape she was in back when she really *was* 35. Maybe even more so, since she'd practically trained for this here Hawaii trip, working out and dieting the past two months.

She had shopped *very* carefully for tonight's ensemble. The idea was to *not* dress her age.

But that was fine. Her body could rival most any teenager's. True, her skin might be a bit saggy in places, but she felt her overall presentation wasn't so bad. And she still maintained a youthful glow.

"Hey, it's *my* birthday, too."

Simone turned to see who was talking to her. It was the blonde surfer guy from the table, holding a bottle of beer in his hand.

"How old are *you* today?" she asked, looking up at his clean-shaven face.

"Twenty-one." He stared down at her boobs.

"Have you ever fucked a fifty year-old?"

He quickly looked up at her eyes. "Nope."

Simone turned to face the bartender. "Liko!"

She pointed at her new friend. "He needs a pin!"

She sat down and patted the barstool next to hers as Liko fulfilled her request. "Have a seat," she told the blonde birthday boy. "I won't bite."

"I wouldn't care if you did," he said, sitting down.

She raised her eyebrows in response and sipped her drink through her straw. They stared at each other.

She smiled, playfully, and with perfect, comedic timing asked, "Would you *like* to fuck a fifty year-old?"

He raised his eyebrows and finished his beer. He set the empty bottle on the counter.

The surfer it is, she thought, as she pinned his neon button to his mint green t-shirt. And it was *that* easy. At least… it *would* be.

They did the preliminary chit chat. They had a few lava drinks. Then when the band started up they hit the dance floor. She could see that he had a few good moves of his own, most of which involved his hands, sliding up and down her hips and sides.

"What's your name again?" Simone asked, inhaling the cotton fabric on his shoulder during a slow song. Not that he'd already told her his name.

"Finn."

Of course it is.

"What's yours?"

"My name's Simone." She looked up at his face. With both hands she combed his hair behind his ears, twirling the long, dangling ends with her fingers. "But you can call me Rambo."

*　　　*　　　*　　　*　　　*　　　*　　　*

On their way to her hotel, they stopped at the local 24-hour grocery store to buy themselves a birthday cake. Finn's friends had given them a ride and dropped them off although Simone would've been happy to splurge for Lyft again.

As they made their way to the entrance of the store, they saw some drunk, old man, urinating on the outskirts of the parking lot. Finn, who'd played the role of Simone's personal tour guide on the car ride over said, "And that there is Papa Leaky Caca." Simone had to grab on to Finn's arm after that one, lest she fall on her butt, laughing at the corny, age-old humor.

They couldn't find much in the way of a spectacular cake this late at night—or was it considered morning? So they got the white quarter sheet with princesses in pale pink dresses. Simone even thought to purchase candles and a book of matches. They walked across the street to her hotel, through the lobby and up the elevator to her room. She flipped on the light, and Finn set the goods on the dresser.

"Do you care if I finish this?" Finn held up the bottle of Moet she'd left chilling in a gold and silver bucket next to the TV.

"Knock yourself out," she said. "I'll be back in a minute."

She grabbed a few things then went into the bathroom and closed the door. First, she peed. Then she brushed her teeth.

She removed all but her gladiator sandals and squeezed into the little camo outfit she'd bought at the costume store back home. The hip-hugger shorts were so dang short, it looked like she was wearing a skirt.

She turned her body to view her backside in the mirror. Her white, half-moon butt cheeks showed just a little. *Nice!*

The top was nothing more than a bikini, so she tied the string in the back. It, too, was a camouflage print, not that anyone could tell. Once she put the bullet necklace on and criss-crossed it over her chest, the bathing suit top completely disappeared from view. *This is so hot!*

She tied the camo headband on the side of her head so that the strings dangled down with her hair. She frumpled her highlighted, shoulder-length locks to give herself the "messy" look. Had she thought of it, she might have applied eye black.

All that remained was the bullet garter, which she slipped up near the top of her thigh. Perfect! She was ready. In more ways than one.

When she walked back into the main room, Finn was reclining up against the pillows on the headboard. He'd turned on the TV and was drinking the champs he'd poured into Simone's used glass from earlier. When he saw her, his mouth dropped open.

"Dude!" he said. She took this as the highest, most supreme compliment. He held up the glass in her direction to offer her a sip.

"Set that down," she said.

He set the glass on the nightstand, never once taking his eyes off of her body.

She stepped up onto the foot of the bed and put her hands on her hips. No smile at all, she stared down at him. He looked up in apparent awe and wonder.

"You really *are* Rambo!"

Sweet thing, you have no idea, she thought. She

was straddling his legs now, undoing his pants.

Simultaneously, he pulled his t-shirt up and over his head. His flip flops were already off his feet and resting on the floor.

"I have a raincoat," he said, gesturing toward his jeans, which she'd just flung aside.

"I don't care," she said. It's not like she could get pregnant, heaven forbid. And as for STDs, she really *didn't* care. Not anymore.

Simone reached between her legs and unsnapped the crotch of her short shorts. She lowered herself onto Finn's protruding shaft and surfed him better, she guessed, than he could ride any wave. Much to her delight, he lasted longer than she thought he would. They climaxed at the same time then she collapsed next to him on the pillows. All he could say was *damn!* But she wasn't anywhere near finished. No, not yet.

After a 10 minute rest, she got up and walked over to the dresser in front of the bed. She carried the cake to the little table by the sliding door. Finn did not take his eyes off of her.

"I'm going to light our candles," she said. "Watch."

Turning away from him, she leaned over and stuck her ass way out, as far out as she could while she lit the two candles she'd placed on the cake. She turned around to face him.

"One for you," she said, seductively blowing out the match, "and one for me."

She carried the cake to the bed and presented it to the birthday boy.

"Happy birthday to *me*," he said.

"Make a wish," said Simone.

"I think it already came true."

"You get a lot more than one wish tonight."

He closed his eyes and started to blow out the candles, but Simone stopped him.

"On second thought…." she said.

She set the cake down beside him on the bed and grabbed one of the candles. She held it over Finn's chest and let the wax drip on him, three little dots.

"Ow. Ow. *Ow*!" Finn was grinning.

"*Now* blow it out," she said, putting the candle near his mouth. He did.

"Okay, your turn," he said, and before she had a chance to respond he sat up and flipped her onto her back. She smiled, admiring his aggression.

He tugged at the center of her bullet necklace. "But first, we need to remove this." She arched her back in full cooperation as he reached around and untied her bikini top. He pulled the top along with the bullet necklace completely off of her. Then he grabbed the other candle from the cake.

"I don't know if I'm going to like this," she said. Simone didn't get into pain. Not even minor pain.

"Don't worry," he said. He circled her right breast with the fingertips of his free hand. "I promise I won't put it here…" he said, lowering his face to give the center a little kiss. He did the same thing to her left breast. "Or here."

Damn! This isn't his first road trip, she told herself. He'd given her the two biggest goose bumps.

She said *ooh!* each time the hot wax fell to her skin, the place where her cleavage *would* be were she standing up and wearing a bra. *So kinky*. But she still didn't get why anyone would like this kind of thing. Other than it made a branding mark, maybe? Like a sick symbol of ownership? But she didn't really want to belong to Finn. Well. Maybe just tonight.

When she decided she'd had enough torture, she sat up on her knees. "Want some cake?" She slid the cake a little closer to the two of them.

"Sure," he said, repositioning himself against the headboard. "Why not?"

"Oh, darn!" she said. "We forgot to get plates. And utensils." Finn watched as she tore off a corner of the cake with her hand. He laughed and said *what are you going to do with that?* And slowly, she smeared frosting on Finn's chest. She stuck her finger in it and brought it up to his face. She outlined his lips all in white and laughed. He laughed, too, and then she proceeded to kiss it all off. He put some frosting on his index finger as though he were going to dab her with it. She intercepted the attack, grabbing his wrist with two hands. She swirled her tongue around and around his finger, never once taking her eyes off of his. She closed her lips and sucked his finger clean. Finn looked *very* impressed. Then she licked up some of the mess she'd made on his chest.

He, in turn, did the same to her, only worse. By the time he was done, that poor cake was smeared all over Simone's body. She was quite sure it would take *days* to get the frosting out of all her oral cavities although Finn's tongue gave it its best shot.

Of course, all that birthday cake inspired another round of sex. And then another. And then another. Finn did her in ways she'd never been done before and vice versa, she was sure. Finally, they showered together. In the morning she'd leave an extra tip for the unfortunate housekeeper who'd get to clean *this* room, but for the time being she just tossed aside the cake-laden sheets and fell asleep in her playmate's arms.

They awakened long after the sun came up. Finn was zipping up his jeans when Simone squinted up at him as he stood near the sliding door.

"You leaving me?" she asked.

"Yeah, I gotta work, later," he said. "You gonna be around tonight?"

"Naw," she said. "I have to catch my flight."

"Think you'll come back here again some time?" he asked.

She shook her head.

"Want my number, anyways?" he asked, starting to take out his phone.

"Nope," she said. "Don't need it." Then she told a lie. "But I promise I will think of you every year on our birthday." She smiled.

Now it was his turn to smile. "It wasn't really my birthday."

"I didn't think so," she said.

She frowned as another thought occurred to her. "Just tell me you're at least 18."

A few hours later, Simone boarded her plane. Had she thought of it, she'd have bought a book to read from the gift shop if only to distract herself from the myriad of thoughts that tormented her. But Simone wasn't in her right mind. She was *far* from her right mind. She *must* be because she'd deluded herself into thinking perhaps her wild night with Finn might have brought her some kind of personal satisfaction. That it might have eased her pain, or changed her mind, or deterred her from her purpose. If only a little.

But it hadn't. If anything, she felt worse.

Simone felt completely empty inside.

At least she wasn't crying anymore. Simone had shed all of her tears back at the hotel after Finn had left.

Once her carry-on bag was secured in its place, she sat down, grateful the seat next to hers was unoccupied.

She took out a pen and a pad of paper from her Kate Spade bag. She supposed now was as good a time as any to write a letter. Besides, it would kill some time on the long flight back to Cleveland. On the long journey back to her dark destiny. On the long and agonizing flight home to her husband.

Chapter Two

Manicure. Check.
Pedicure. Check.
Skimpy bikini. Check.

She smiled at herself in the mirror. Travis was going to *love* life. She'd finally taken the plunge and endured the torture session otherwise known as a Brazilian wax—just for him. Just for her man! And Simone felt mighty damn sexy.

She peeled off her bikini bottoms to admire the esthetician's handiwork. *Ah, smooth as can be.* Maybe Heidi and Jodi were right. *Maybe those Millennials DO have some valuable information to impart.* Maybe after two whole years these same coworkers (that Meredith had hired against Simone's better judgment) were finally demonstrating their worthiness to work under her if only by virtue of suggesting she do this.

She turned her backside to the mirror and bent over to take a closer look. Not one stitch of hair anywhere. *Too bad it has to hurt like a mo fo,* she thought, *or I'd do this more often.*

This was her little surprise for Travis. For the past couple of years he'd been telling her to shave it *all* off. "Bic it," to be exact. She'd *tried* to appease him. Every now and then, she'd shave her parts clean as a whistle, and yeah, he enjoyed that. That guy could spend *hours* between her thighs. *Munchy muncha lunch*, they called it, all in good fun. Well. At least, it was more fun for *him*. Simone could not understand the obsession.

"I could never be a lesbian," she'd tell him.

Nope. She just didn't get the male appetite *at all* or what guys saw in girls, *period*.

But Travis did. *His* sexual appetite only *grew* over the years they'd been married. It seemed the older they got, the more he wanted sex. Simone, on the other hand, could take it or leave it, and ever since getting promoted to senior project manager several years ago, she more often than not could leave it.

"I'm exhausted!" she'd tell her sex-starved husband whenever she crawled into bed late at night. And that's when she was *polite*. Most of the time she felt offended he would even suggest the idea.

He just didn't understand. *His* job was easy compared to hers. He taught classes at the community college down the street. That was the reason they'd chosen this house years ago. Travis could literally ride his bike to work, which oftentimes he did.

But Travis sure enjoyed being a professor of literature. He loved the prestige and even his title: Dr. Sanders. Although recently, one night while he was fixing dinner he laughingly reported how a student of his always called him *The Colonel*. Simone had just pushed the side of his face and said, "Cause you're a nut! *Kernal*. Get it?" But instead of enjoying the joke, he simply lost his smile and went back to chopping the onions.

Anyway. This Brazilian wax of hers was Simone's good faith gesture towards Travis. "In a couple of days, we'll have all the sex you want, my boy," she said to the picture of herself and Travis on the dresser. She kissed her hand and put it on the image of his face. He was *still* so damn good-looking! *She* may have aged a tiny bit over the years, but not

Travis. He had that firm jaw of his and perfectly chiseled bone structure, unblemished skin and same dark eyeglasses he'd had when she met him their senior year in high school. He even kept the same hairstyle with his blonde bangs hanging low and the sides of his hair shaved. *So* 80's. He was fit and trim again, too. They'd both started to put on a *little* weight when their metabolisms slowed down mid-40's, even Simone, who'd always vowed she'd never look like her mother! Which was one of the reasons she'd never had kids. That and the fact she didn't *like* kids. So when Travis had up and started his own workout regimen, complete with gym pass, she'd joined him. Not at the gym but on her treadmill in the basement. The last few stubborn pounds she'd taken off with some crazy starvation diet she'd discovered online.

She put her hands on her hips and looked at the wall of pictures she and Travis had taken of themselves. She smiled, remembering all the locations they'd traveled throughout the years: Italy, France, Sweden, Mexico....

Now they were off to Hawaii in a couple of days. Simone had scored reservations at the place where they got married almost 27 years ago. What better way to celebrate Simone's 50th birthday? Travis had offered to throw her a party, but she didn't want that. "Who wants to announce how old they are?" she'd asked him. "You might not find me attractive anymore if fifty is too old for you!" She'd only meant it as a joke, so it almost started a fight when he hadn't responded. *Besides*, she'd argued. She really wouldn't have anyone to invite. Outside of Travis, Simone really didn't *have* any friends. Which even *she* found odd because she'd been so dang popular back in high school. She'd had all *kinds* of friends.

Oh well. I guess that's just how it goes, she always told herself. So what if no one appreciated her? Simone was very driven and had a low tolerance for human error, which was all around her, apparently. Behind her desk at work was a plaque that said: If you want a job done well, do it yourself! "So true! So true!" she'd told her coworkers when they'd presented it to her. She'd tried to act like she was only kidding, but everyone knew she wasn't. So she just thanked them for the plaque and their *usual* gift to her: a gift card to Stone Cold Creamery. "I guess they think I like ice cream," she'd tell Travis; unless, of course, he'd beat her to the punch and say, "Let me guess. They got you a certificate to Stone Cold."

"Well, there's no bitches in Hawaii, my love," she told Travis' image inside the picture frame. "Just you and me, the way it's always been. The way it *should* be."

She sighed a happy sigh. She took off her bathing suit top and tossed it toward her open suitcase on the floor by the closet. She'd been packing for days. Next, she put on some clothes. Just sweats today, *ah*. She could kiss her high heeled shoes goodbye if only for a week. Comfort was key because she still had a couple more errands to run before Travis got home from work. She had only worked a half day today for just this purpose: errands, including the Brazilian wax. Tomorrow she'd shop for a few more outfits—shoes, too.

Spring break couldn't have come sooner for Simone. Travis would have the whole *week* off, and lucky her, his school vacation happened to coincide with her birthday this year. Perfect!

She looked around her room. Yes. *Everything* was perfect in her life. Simone could not believe how contented she was. *I may be turning 50, but I'm happy.* She laughed. *What is wrong with me?*

She smiled at herself in the mirror as she brushed her shoulder-length, brown hair. That is, it *would* be brown were it not for the blonde highlights. She'd started high-lighting her hair the previous summer, and it actually made her look better, she thought. It camouflaged the "stray grays" and offset some of her wrinkles.

"Damn, you're sexy!" she told her reflection.

Her phone rang, so Simone grabbed it and ran down the stairs. She figured she'd take it to the kitchen so she could peruse the fridge (a.k.a. multitask while talking) because she still needed to donate all the perishables to her neighbor before the trip.

"Hello, Simone."

She'd recognize that cracked voice anywhere.

"Hey, Mom," she said, flatly. "What's up?"

"Oh, nothing," said her mother. "We're just sitting here, getting ready for our shows."

She knew "we" meant her brother and his wife and one of their two grown kids. They'd moved in with her mother ten years ago when Simone's father had passed away "to help mom out," was the ruse. *Yeah. As if!* "You mean to help *you* guys out!" Simone had bluntly said to her brother. *Such a freeloader.*

After all these years, she still felt angry about the whole Ron situation. Ron was two years older than her. He'd been a super star when they were in high school—destined for greatness. Instead, he got his girlfriend, Leesa, pregnant the year after they graduated. Instead of going back to Texas A&M to play baseball, he got a full time job as a stock boy at Food Warehouse. *That's when they probably SHOULD have moved in with Mom*, she thought, *so Ron could go to school.* As it was, her mom took care of their baby during all that would-be college time—Simone's nephew, Brady. And then Ron and Leesa had Bret a year later. Like a couple of idiots. *Did they not give you a lecture on birth control in your health class?* She'd actually asked them this question. *Idiots.*

And who had to suffer because of her brother's stupidity? *She* did! *Good grief!* she'd whine to her mother every time Leesa dropped those kids off at the house. Her father would only shake his head and smile, his way of agreeing with her. At the time, *he* was the roadblock to Ron and Leesa moving in with them, and if *he* were still around, they'd be out of luck on their whole "free rent and board" gig. Heck, Ron was lucky their father even spoke to him after he'd knocked-up Leesa. He hadn't even acknowledged baby Brady the first six months of his life!

But that was her dad for you. Barry Sylvester had always been Simone's idol. They were cut from the same high energy, fiercely driven, choleric mold. Unfortunately, her dad had been forced to take an early retirement for health reasons. That's why they'd purchased the house in Long Beach years before this when Simone was only ten, so he could be near the ocean. Simone the California girl would have probably never left the area, but two good reasons had propelled her to seek her fortune elsewhere. One was her desire to get away from her noisy environment. Brady and Bret were always over, and she just couldn't stand it. The other was to be near Travis, the love of her life.

"I'm real busy, Mom," she said, putting the phone on speaker and setting it on the counter.

"Yeah, I kind of thought so," said her mom. "What time is your flight on Friday?"

Simone sighed. Didn't she already go over this with her? Maybe her mom was getting senile. Maybe her mom really *did* need her son to look after her. She was pushing 80, after all.

"I told you. We fly out of Cleveland at 8:00 in the morning. We'll arrive in Honolulu at around 4:00 p.m. Ohio time, which is really 1:00 Hawaii time." Simone had planned it that way. She wanted herself and Travis to get settled in and relaxed before enjoying the night life. She'd even made reservations for them at the restaurant where they'd had their little wedding reception—just to kick the week off right.

"Oh, okay. Then I won't keep you," said her mother. They really never had much to say, anyway. Everyone knew *she* wasn't her mother's favorite. Ron was a true Mama's boy. But that never bothered Simone because *she'd* always been a Daddy's girl, beloved by her father. Her mother ended the conversation by wishing her a nice trip.

"I'll put your birthday card in the mail—it'll probably be waiting for you when you get home."

"Thanks, Mom."

She no sooner ended the call when her phone rang again. *Grrr!*

"What!" she said, thinking it was her mom. But it was Travis, calling to check on her progress, she assumed.

"Wow," he said. "Is that how you greet your husband?"

"I thought you were my mom," she said. "You coming home soon?"

"Yeah, after our meeting," he said. He sounded tired. "Just trying to wrap things up before Friday."

"Are you so excited or what?" She smiled as she took out the eggs and milk and other items from the fridge and set them on the counter next to the phone. She couldn't just sit and *chat*. She had to be productive.

"Yup." He sighed, but she chalked up his lackluster joy to fatigue. He *had* been working hard, lately, preparing for finals and whatever it was he did this time of year. Grade projects maybe?

"I have a surprise for you when you get here," she said, stretching her sweat pants away from her body so she could take a peek at herself.

"Oh yeah? *You* cooking for a change?"

"Ha *ha*! You're a funny boy, aren't you!" She shut the fridge door and stooped down to grab two paper bags out of the cabinet. She shook them open and started placing the items on the counter inside of them.

"What are you doing?" he asked.

"Just getting ready to take some food and crap over to Josephine. You know her, she'll take *anything*."

Josephine the Ancient lived her life in a Mumu and slippers next door to Simone and Travis. She'd been in the 'hood since time began and knew everything about everyone. She was known to camp out by her living room or bedroom window.

Whichever room she was in, it seemed she was always looking outside. Simone always said *this street doesn't need a neighborhood watch with Josephine around!*

"Then after I do that, I'm going to run to the store for stuff we'll need for the trip, like sunscreen."

Here in Ohio, there wasn't as great a need for sun protection as there was back in California—something Simone had to adjust to all those years ago when she'd first moved here. So she only bought one bottle a year. She figured they'd probably go through one bottle a *day* in Hawaii! Her plan was to soak up the rays, big time. For a *fact*, she'd be planting her butt on the sand every day. She'd already reserved "sun time" on her phone.

"You know I don't want to go to all the tourist traps, right? I mean…you can only visit the Polynesian Center so many times, and Pearl Harbor we've already seen, remember?"

"Mmm." That was Travis' response to most everything she said. Over the years she'd gotten used to it. *But that's how we roll*, she'd tell the neighbors at the annual clam bake. "I'm the loud one, he's the quiet one."

Then again, she knew Travis got into all that educational stuff. He was such a thinker! So as a nice gesture she added, "But I mean, if *you* really want to, I'll suck it up and go."

"No, it doesn't matter," he said. "Whatever you want, Simone."

"I want *you*!" She needed to wrap up this conversation. "So come home and I'll give you your surprise, 'kay?"

"Okay. I'll be home in a little bit."

She kissed the air and told him *I love you* like she always did. Then she grabbed her paper bags and headed out the front door.

"Keep an eye out on my house," she told Josephine. They were on her neighbor's front porch. This was where they conducted *all* their conversations. The one time Simone had broken with tradition and gone inside, she'd regretted it. Josephine just had too many pictures on her walls and trinkets she wanted to talk about, and she'd held Simone hostage for days, it felt like. *I'm not doing THAT again,* she'd told Travis when she was released from her jail sentence.

"Will do," said Josephine, taking the paper bags from Simone's hands. "Ooh, these are heavy!" she said, setting them on the porch bench to the right of the door. "How long will you be gone again?"

"Just for a week. Travis has to get back to school."

"Oh yeah, that's right," said Josephine. "He's got minds to mold!"

Simone smiled. "Okay, well, you have my cell number if anything comes up." Although, saying this was only a formality. Nothing *ever* came up in the quiet little town of North Olmsted. Compared to beach living in L.A., life was relatively safe over here.

"Alright, I will," said Josephine. "And happy birthday early! What day *is* your birthday, anyway?"

"It's next Saturday, our last night there," she said. "But what's a day? This year I get an entire birthday *week*."

"Well, you deserve it," said Josephine. "I see how late you get home from work, sometimes."

Yes, it was true. Simone always worked late, and sometimes entire weekends.

"When you're an event planner for major corporations, you have to oversee that everything goes smoothly," she'd often told Travis. And Simone was the best of the best. She had a reputation to maintain. Some of the most prestigious clients in the county requested her because she always delivered. To a tee. No one was better. One client had tried to nab her away from her job, once, but she'd respectfully declined because she had no desire to work as a wedding coordinator. Then she'd have to deal with kids on occasion, and she wanted to work with adults only.

"Yeah, Josephine. I plan to *relax*. Even I have to get some R&R sometimes."

They laughed, and Simone took this as her cue to get on with her business. She gave Josephine a quick hug *in case I don't see you before Friday!* Then off she skedaddled to errand number two. The store.

"Trav?" She set her purse on the kitchen desk when she walked in through the garage door. She hung her keys on the key rack where they belonged. *Everything* "had a home" in Simone's house. It was immaculate. *Can you imagine if we had kids?* she'd ask Travis. *Nothing would ever look nice. It would look like Bren's house!*

Brenda was a former friend of Simone's from high school. Former because after she'd had her third child, Simone was done. *I don't want to talk to her anymore* she'd said to everybody after Brenda informed her *fifteen years* after her *second* child was born that she was "unexpectedly" pregnant. *As if!* And if Brenda hadn't sounded so happy, she would've told her to *get your fucking tubes tied, already!* That's what Simone had done, soon after she and Travis got married—*just in case* he had a change of heart about having kids down the road. Nope. She had to eliminate the possibility altogether. But her conversation with Brenda had occurred nine years ago, right after Travis and Simone had gone to California for her father's funeral.

Against her better judgment, they'd stayed at Brenda's house with her husband and (then) two kids. Since Bren's "kids" were teenagers at the time, Simone was willing to give it a try. *She* was a teenager, once. She was a *cool* teenager, once. She and Brenda *both* were. Simone Sylvester and Brenda Bartlett were cheerleaders. *All* the boys liked them. But they'd made a pact to be "picky choosy" and Simone wouldn't give *any* guy the thrill of dating her. That is, until Travis came to town. The second she spotted him she tap-tapped him for herself.

"He's not *from* here," she'd tell her circle of friends while staring at him from across the hall. His style of dress was a dead giveaway, beginning with his feet. He wore shoes with no socks. That had been a preppy fad a few years prior, but at the time *he* arrived on the scene, the trend was more of a New Wave look. But she didn't care. He was blond, and everyone knew Simone liked blond-haired boys.

She'd tell her friends, "I'm going to be his first girlfriend in California." And she was. She was his *only* girlfriend in California. She'd made sure of it.

"Travis?" she walked up the stairs, shopping bags in hand. Once inside their room, she tossed the bags onto the bed. They landed next to Travis' phone, and that's when she realized it was on speaker. He was a few feet away in the bathroom. One glance at the foggy mirror through the open door told her he'd taken a shower. He was probably right around the corner, grooming for their trip. She'd complained the night before that he was stabbing her with his toenails in bed.

"I'm going to miss you so bad."

A female voice was on the other end of the call. Simone stopped in her tracks.

"I'll miss you, too." Travis' voice sounded from the bathroom.

Simone picked up the phone. The contact at the top said JN. But she already knew it wasn't one of Travis' sisters. *Their* voices were loud, just like hers. This voice was soft and a little wimpy.

Quick as a flash, she looked up JN in his contacts and sent the information to her own phone. She sat down on the edge of the bed, waiting to hear more from this JN person.

"Will you think of me every day you're there?" the voice asked.

"Every minute," he answered.

Simone pressed the screen to see his texts. She typed in JN and scrolled up. She stopped when she got to a picture. Her heart stopped, too. *All* her bodily functions stopped. She was suspended in time. For what she saw right there on the screen was worse than the pictures she'd discovered last summer.

Last summer, she'd found pictures Travis had saved to his phone. At first, she'd smiled because it wasn't like they were from *Playboy* or anything. And there were only four or five of them altogether...just random girls in bikinis. One was lying back on a rock, spread eagle. She could understand Travis' attraction to *that* one because she knew his favorite part of the female body was that little ligament joining the upper thigh to the torso. That tiny little bone turned him on like nothing else.

It wasn't the fact that these girls were all young that bothered her. *They look like they're 15*, she'd told him. Or maybe at her age, everyone looked younger now! And it wasn't the fact they were all bone skinny, borderline anorexic. *That* she could kind of handle because *she* was never overweight or anything.

What bothered her the most was they looked nothing at all *like* her. For one thing, they all had blonde hair. It had given Simone such a complex, she'd immediately had her hair lightened at her next appointment. *If he wants a blonde, I'll give him a blonde*, she'd told herself.

Further search on his Instagram account had revealed *more* blonde-haired beauties. Let's see, there was Daily GG and also Candice from *Victoria's Secret*. Again, no naked pictures or anything, so why she felt so bad about it even *she* couldn't understand. Other than the fact that her husband was lusting after other women.

"I know you're not looking at them because they're pretty! Or because you want to get to know them better, like explore their minds or anything," she'd told him. "What do you imagine when you look at them, Travis? Huh? Can you tell me?"

And when he'd only stared back at her, she knew it was true. He was wishing he could *do* them. Or at least, do things *to* them.

But the picture she was staring at right now was far worse than any of the Instagram shots. This one hurt most of all. Because *this* one was a real, live girl. Not some model from a magazine. Not someone famous. Just a girl. A young, skinny girl. And she had blonde hair. And she was on her husband's phone. *In a text.* She started to cry. *They know each other.*

A little boy who looked to be about five years-old was sitting on her lap in the picture. *Is she a mother?* Well, that would figure because she'd suspected all these years that Travis had always wanted *her* to be a mother. Well. Not always. Not at first. But he'd always been on the fence about fatherhood. Simone thought she had talked him out of it. Thought she had made him see the light. She'd always programmed him to think *who signs UP for that?*

She scrolled through a few of the messages. A couple of *I love you's* from the girl popped out at her as did a few *I love you, too's* from Travis. She'd have kept on scrolling, but Travis, towel wrapped around his waist, walked into the room. He stopped when he saw Simone.

She looked up at him and raised the phone to her mouth. Not taking her eyes off of him she said, "This is Simone. Travis' *wife*. Who is *this*?"

There was silence. Then the call ended.

Simone's lips started to tremble. Travis knelt down in front of her and put his hands on her knees.

"Simone, I'm *sorry*," he said.

"*Who* are you going to think of every minute we're in Hawaii?" she asked.

He tried to take his phone out of her hand but she put it behind her back.

"Tell me, Travis!"

Maybe there was a logical explanation. Maybe it wasn't too late. Maybe she'd caught him *just* in time, right before he'd have a chance to do anything major with this person. Maybe she was nipping something in the bud.

"I didn't want to tell you until after your birthday," he said. He looked sad. Like he felt bad he was breaking her heart. She *knew* he felt bad.

"You were going to wait until I turned fifty?" *Is that my expiration date?* she thought.

He lowered his head and mumbled, "I know how much you were looking forward to your birthday."

"Oh, so you thought after I opened all my presents and ate my cake, *then* you'd tell me?"

He looked into her eyes. "No, Simone. When we came back, I was going to tell you *everything*."

She backed away from him so he could no longer keep his hands on her knees.

"Tell me everything right *now*, Travis!" She crossed her legs and folded her arms. In a strange way, this helped her to control her tears.

He put his elbows on the mattress, which made it kind of look like Travis the agnostic was praying, the way he had his hands joined together underneath his chin.

When he didn't speak, she said, "You can begin with who *is* she. What's her name?"

"Her name is Jen."

"Well, that explains the J. Where did you meet her?"

She knew he'd be truthful. Travis wasn't

capable of telling a lie. At least, she knew him so well, she could tell if he was lying. And he always owned up to things.

"She was a student in my class last year."

"Last *year*?" Simone shrieked. "This has been going on for a whole *year*?"

He shook his head. "No. Not a whole year. We were just friends until recently."

"*How* recently?"

"About six months ago, our relationship took a turn."

She wasn't sure if it was six months of adulterated pleasure that bothered her more, or his use of the word "our" in conjunction with "relationship." *Our relationship*. She knew then and there that those two words with *his* voice behind them would be forever etched in her mind.

Now she was crying hard. "How could you do this to me, Travis?" Whenever she cried, her voice squeaked, just like her mother's *natural* voice. She wasn't used to crying. She prided herself on not being a crier like other people she knew. Like April.

"It wasn't *about* you, Simone," he said. "I never meant to hurt you."

"Travis, how could you risk everything we *have* together like this? You *know* I don't get over these things." If she was still bringing up the Instagram incident, she'd *never* get over *this*! "How could you risk throwing away everything we have? Everything we are? Everything we *mean* to each other?"

Theirs was a match made in heaven. She'd only loved Travis, and he'd only loved her. Everybody knew that! They had so much history together. They were crowned prom king and queen, for goodness' sake!

"I didn't think that we *had* anything together, Simone."

Before he could explain, she jumped off the bed and stuffed Travis' phone in the waist of her sweats. She grabbed their wedding picture off the wall and yelled, "We don't *have* anything together? What do you call *this*?" She clutched the picture to her chest with one arm and pointed to some of their other pictures. "What do you call *those*?"

He raised himself up off the floor and sat on the bed. "I call those Simone writing her own story."

For a second, she had nothing to say. She stared at him, astonished. Not by what he'd said but by his apparent lack of feeling about everything. *He doesn't care. He doesn't care, anymore.* Travis had *never* spoken like this before. They were *always* on the same page together. They had *always* agreed with each other on *everything*. So how on earth could *her* feeling *so happy* with their relationship mean something so completely different to him?

Then something inside of her exploded. Travis *never* got the better of her. *Never*! If this was how he wanted to play, she'd play it even harder.

She raised the picture frame above her head with two hands and brought it down on the dresser. The glass cracked and a piece flew to the carpet. She stomped over to the closet and threw a couple items of clothing onto her already packed bag on the floor.

"Simone."

But she was beyond listening. No one could reason with her right now, not even a skilled diplomat.

Through her tears and gaspy breathing, she threw a pair of shoes onto her clothes, knelt down and tried to zip things up. All the while, Travis remained where he was, perched on the edge of the bed.

"And you don't even *care*, Travis," she said, putting her knee on the front flap of her suitcase. She tugged the final few inches of the zipper into place.

"Yes, I do care," he said, standing up.

She rolled the suitcase right on past him and leaned it up against the doorway to the bathroom. She reached into the medicine cabinet and drawers and threw whatever products she could find into a little duffle bag from the bottom drawer. Travis watched from the doorway as she forced the duffle bag into the side flap of her suitcase. She wheeled it to the bed to loop the store bags over the handle then pushed Travis aside to walk by, toting her worldly goods behind her.

"Don't try to *stop* me!" She said it sarcastically because obviously, he wasn't moving much or saying much. At *all*.

"Where are you going, Simone?"

"None of your fucking business," she said.

When she reached the bedroom doorway she let go of her suitcase and turned around. She grabbed his phone from out of her elastic waist and pulled her sweats down low, taking her underwear with them.

"Here's your surprise, by the way! I got you a Brazilian bikini wax!" She couldn't tell if the look on his face was regret or excitement. She pulled her pants back up. "Is *she* the one who calls you The Colonel?"

He just looked at her, and this infuriated her.

"Whatever, Travis! I don't want to talk to you right now. But you better bet your ass we're going to talk *tomorrow*!"

She held up his phone and said, "I'm taking *this* with me!"

"Please don't," he said. But there wasn't much he could do, standing there wearing nothing but a towel.

She stuck the phone back into the waist of her sweats, grabbed the handle of her suitcase, and walked out on the love of her life.

Chapter Three

She rested the side of her head on the window of the plane and looked out at the landscape below. It was flat. Just like she felt. She was home, now.

That is, she would be at April's home, now. She thought about how April had discovered her at the office the morning after her world had shattered. She had spent most of that gut-wrenching night at her desk, swiveling in her chair, reviewing Travis' texts.

> **Are you conducting office hours again tomorrow, Colonel?**
>
> **Yes. Wear the white panties with the lace. I'll give you an A. I mean, an O.**

And on and on it went. Simone was not impressed. In the early years of their marriage, she'd sometimes pay Travis a little visit at the college wearing *no* underwear. One time she wore a camo trench coat with nothing underneath. So. Whatever. Apparently, he was resurrecting nothing but an old trend.

From what she'd gleaned in her study of the text messages, it appeared that her husband's *girlfriend,* Jen, had gotten pregnant right out of high school. Didn't sound like she and the boy who'd knocked her up had ever married. It *did* sound like Jen and her 5 year-old son, Robby, currently lived at her parents' house.

Travis made constant reference to Jen's son in his texts. How Robby needed a good dad. How he'd love to raise Robby. How they could be a happy family together.

She hadn't slept at all that night. She was too emotionally drained. The first time she'd drifted off on the black leather couch in the break room, she was awakened soon after by the fax machine around 3:00 a.m. *Who the hell sends a fax at this time?* Then she remembered they had clients in other time zones.

When she couldn't fall back asleep, she grabbed Travis' phone and sent a text to Jen.

> Did you not realize he's married? I hate you. Thank you for ruining my birthday, you bitch.

Minutes later she got a reply.

> I don't know what to say. I can't even tell you how sorry I am.

Wow. Way to fight for Travis, she thought. Was this girl going to give up that easily? She was *so* not Travis' type! Travis liked his women to have a backbone. He needed a *strong* woman, like Simone. She decided to poke at her.

> When my husband comes to his senses, he's boarding a plane with me, and he will forget you even exist. You are nothing to him. You will not break us up.

This time Jen didn't reply. *See? I knew it,* thought Simone. *No spine whatsoever.*

The *second* time she'd almost fallen asleep she was awakened by April; or rather, the coffee machine April was starting, which sounded so damn loud whenever the room was quiet.

April had worked at Com Corp for years, even longer than Simone. Simone had almost felt bad when she'd received the promotion of senior project manager over her. But that feeling had only lasted a second. Simone deserved the promotion. April did not.

April was weak. She was way too nice and not just for show. She was frustratingly nice all the damn time—drove Simone crazy. But as a result of this, April didn't have quite the business savvy Simone had. That and the fact she was also a little flaky. She took a lot of time off, it seemed. And she was constantly on her phone, talking to her mother or her son. *Sooo inappropriate for the work place*, in Simone's opinion. She didn't even dress right. April wasn't that much older than Simone, but she looked ancient. No make-up, frizzy hair, and frumpy sweaters. She never wore heels. Ever. Her butt was a little on the large side, but April said that was from sitting at a desk all day, making calls. Simone thought *yeah. Cut out the personal calls and you'd LOSE five pounds!*

But April was always pleasant, even to Simone. And now she was here at the office super early on a Thursday morning, making coffee.

"Oh, I'm sorry! I didn't mean to wake you up!" April held up an empty cup. "Would you like some coffee?"

"Yeah. Sure," said Simone, sitting up. Her eyes

felt heavier than normal because she hadn't removed her eye make-up from the day before. Some of her lashes were sticking together.

"Did you just get here?" asked April. She walked over and handed Simone a hot cup of coffee—black—just the way she liked it. And April would know. "I wasn't expecting to see you today!"

"No, I got here last night," she answered. "I needed a place to stay and didn't know where else to go."

April gasped. "Is everything okay?"

"No, April. Everything is *not* okay." She didn't mean to snap at her, but *have a clue!*

She felt bad when April remained silent. That was just her way. April was always sensitive to her "boss," Simone. *You can always read me so well,* Simone would tell her on occasion. So she decided to confide in her.

"Do you have a minute?"

April looked at the clock on the wall. "I have *two* minutes," she said, jokingly. "We don't open for two hours. I'm just here, early, to get a head start." Simone knew she was referring to all the extra work she'd have to handle in her absence, beginning today. Simone had taken the day off specifically to shop for her trip. But she knew April had to be home at a certain time every day because she was her mother's main caretaker—another reason April's performance at the office was less than stellar. She couldn't be counted on to work overtime. This behavior would never be tolerated with the newer employees. But the owner, Meredith, was so loyal she'd *never* give April the ax. Not in a million years.

So Simone sipped her coffee and told her all that had happened the previous night with Travis. All the while, April had her hand over her mouth and was shaking her head. Simone thought it was a bit much when April's eyes filled with tears. *It's not like we're close*, she thought. *She doesn't know me THAT well.*

"Oh, Simone, I'm so sorry," she said. "I know *exactly* how you feel. This happened to me with *my* ex four years ago, remember?"

Yes, I do. You missed a whole week of work! And it was the busiest time of year.

But she just said, "Yeah, I remember."

April hesitated as if she were debating whether or not to ask Simone her next question.

"Are you still going to Hawaii?"

Simone shook her head and sipped her coffee. "I don't know at this point. I just really. Don't. Know." She sat back with her head against the couch, sighed, and looked at the ceiling. "*Why* is this happening to me?" She might have cried, but April was watching.

April sat down next to her and put her hand on top of hers, a gesture that had always made Simone feel uncomfortable. Out of pure reaction, she withdrew her hand, so April awkwardly clasped her own two hands together.

"Are you going to stay *here* for a while?"

Again, Simone shook her head. "I don't really want to face anyone right now." *Not even you.* "You won't tell them anything, will you, April?"

"No, of *course* not! It's just between you and me." April almost smiled, and Simone knew why. *She thinks we're bonding.* For years, April had tried her darndest to crack Simone's tough shell and be friends with her. But Simone had no time for people like April. She *never* let her in. And after today's momentary display of weakness, she never *would* let her in *again*.

"I need to talk to Travis. But I'm going to wait till he gets home, later. He has classes today." Travis would never let something as earth-shattering as the potential of losing his wife keep him from his responsibilities. Simone was like that, too, so this was actually something she admired about him. They were both far too practical to put personal business ahead of *real* business. "I'll go home after he leaves for work."

"Would you like to hang out at *my* house for a bit?" April asked. "You could follow me over there real quick. It's still early—I'd be back here in plenty of time."

Actually, it sounded like a plan.

"Isn't your mom there?" she asked, trying to be polite.

"Yeah. MeeMaw's always there. Bradley's there, too. He watches her for me, now."

Bradley was April's wayward son. At least, she assumed he was a problem. He'd dropped out of high school earlier in the year due to social issues, April had told everyone. She'd also said he was going to complete his GED, but Simone had her doubts. *Loser!*

She wanted to say *well, that's the least he can do is watch his grandma!* But instead she said, "Oh, okay. If they don't mind, that would be great."

April didn't live too far from the office. After her divorce, she and her son had moved in with her mother in the two-story house April grew up in. Her ex had moved out of state to shack up with his so-called wife, and according to April, he rarely came around to see Bradley.

Simone had read somewhere that divorce was hardest on boys of a certain age. Was it 13? That was Bradley's age when the divorce happened, *which is probably why at 17 he's such a fuckup*. Simone wished she didn't know so much about April and her problems, but April constantly gave everyone her life story whether they wanted to hear it or not.

When they arrived at April's, it was evident there wasn't a "man of the house," based on all the things Simone spotted right off the bat that needed repairing. Not that Travis was ever any good in this department. But at least they always hired someone who was. No doubt April couldn't afford a handyman because obviously, she could no longer afford a caretaker for her mother—not if *Bradley* was caring for her, now. After a hip replacement surgery gone sour, April's mother was pretty much confined to a bed. This April had also told everyone two years ago.

But for an older house, this one had a pretty nice design. It was spacious. And surprisingly clean. Simone commented on this.

"Let me introduce you to MeeMaw real quick so she doesn't get nervous if she hears you walking around the house."

April knocked on a bedroom door off the foyer and said, "MeeMaw?" She opened the door and walked to her left where a white-haired, frail little woman was sitting up in her bed on the adjacent wall. When she saw her daughter, her face lit up.

"I thought you left already," she smiled. Her face turned up to receive the kiss April was planting on her lips.

"I did," said April. She sat down on the chair next to her mother's bed. "I just came back to let my friend in." She gestured toward Simone, who stood in the doorway.

"MeeMaw, this is Simone Sanders, my boss."

Simone walked over and extended her hand to MeeMaw. "Nice to meet you," she said, marveling at how tiny and bony MeeMaw's hand felt in hers.

MeeMaw smiled brightly. "Oh, pleasure to meet you! I've heard so much about you."

I'm sure you have! And you're a captive audience, too. Simone felt sorry for this poor woman, thinking *April must talk her EAR off.*

"You can call me Grace, if you like," she said. "Or just call me MeeMaw, like everyone else does." She laughed.

"Has Bradley checked in on you, yet?" asked April.

"No, not yet, Sweetheart."

"Bradley!" yelled April, looking up at the ceiling.

"Oh, no, don't wake him up!" said MeeMaw with a frown. "Let him sleep. He's tired."

"I'd *told* him not to stay up all night," said April. She looked at Simone. "He's always playing those games of his."

"Honey, I'm *fine,*" said MeeMaw. She pointed to the tray next to her bed. "I'm still snacking on the nice breakfast you made for me." She gestured toward the other wall. "And I'm watching my morning shows. I'm fine! Leave him be."

"Well." April stood up. "You call me if you need anything, okay?" MeeMaw smiled and nodded.

"And you have Bradley's number, so call *him*, too! Don't be so *nice* to him."

MeeMaw chuckled. "Okay, okay," she said.

Simone spoke up. "I can help, too," she said to MeeMaw. "April has kindly offered for me to hang out for a while so I can sort through some personal business. If that's okay with you, that is."

MeeMaw nodded vigorously and said, "Of course! Of course! Make yourself right at home."

April said, "I'll have Simone put her things in the spare room upstairs. She might want to take a nap!"

Simone and April both grabbed the handle of her suitcase and carried it up the carpeted stairs at the top of which was a big bonus room to the left.

"This is Bradley's boy cave," said April. Simone could tell! It wasn't very tidy. It had a big, brown leather sectional with an ottoman, in front of which was a flat screen TV and every electronic game known to man. The room was dark with the blinds still closed. There were game controllers galore and books and even a fish tank on the wooden shelving unit, spanning the length of one whole wall.

"And this is Bradley's room," she said, pointing toward a closed door as they walked down the hallway to the right. She knocked on it and said, "Make sure you take care of MeeMaw, Bradley!"

She opened his door a crack. This room, too, was dark, even though it had a big window facing the front of the house. Simone saw a big lump, sleeping underneath a charcoal gray comforter. April said, "My friend, Simone, will be here today. So be nice!" The lump groaned, and she shut the door.

April pointed to the end of the hall straight

ahead and said, "That's the bathroom. And this," she opened a door on the left, "Is *your* room." She smiled.

Simone could almost hear the angels singing a refrain of, "Laaaaaa!" because compared to the other two rooms, this one was bright and cheerful. It looked too girly to belong up here with its white furniture, yellow walls, and bedspread with white, pink, and yellow flowers. *This must've been April's room when she was a kid.*

"Just make yourself at home," said April. "There's food downstairs in the refrigerator if you're hungry. The towels are in the hall closet if you want to use the shower."

"April, thank you so much," said Simone. She was so touched by her care and concern. "I promise I won't stay too long. Just a couple hours."

"Stay as long as you like!" said April. "I mean it." And Simone took this to mean that she could stay indefinitely if she chose. But she knew it wouldn't be necessary. She'd straighten Travis out but good, later.

"You know, I probably *will* take a little nap," said Simone. "But please call me if you need me to look in on MeeMaw." She already liked April's mother.

"I'm sure that won't be necessary," said April. "You get some rest."

And that's exactly what Simone did. She hadn't realized how very tired she was. This was so not like her. *I guess extra-marital affairs take their toll on a body,* she told herself when she woke up. She must've fallen asleep as soon as her head had hit the pillow on the flowery bed. One look at Travis' phone told her it was—*shit!*

"Three o'clock?" she said out loud.

Travis taught four classes on Thursdays, beginning at 9:00 and ending at 4:30. Tuesdays and Thursdays were his "heavy" days, he called them, because he didn't have a formal lunch hour. Just office hours from 4:30 to 5:30. *Hmph. Yeah.* As of last night, "office hours" had taken on a whole new meaning!

At least she'd have some time to get ready before heading over to the house. She poked her head into the hallway and was relieved to see that Bradley's bedroom door was open. This must mean he was awake and looking after MeeMaw. She could hear the TV from the bonus room and assumed he was in there. So when she gathered up her shower "supplies" and robe, she quickly grabbed a towel out of the hall closet and dashed to the bathroom.

It felt good to let the warm water fall on her body in the shower. For the first time that day, she allowed herself to cry a little. *How could he do this to me?* It was such a betrayal. *Do our wedding vows mean nothing to him? Do I mean nothing to him?* No. That wasn't true. *She* was the love of her husband's life, not some ho-bag hoochie mom he let himself have a mid-life crisis with!

And though she didn't really have the heart for it, Simone applied her make-up in front of the bathroom mirror. Hair still wet, wearing her white terry robe, she grabbed her things and attempted to exit the bathroom. Except she nearly crashed into Bradley, who was attempting to come *in* to the bathroom.

"Oh! Sorry!" he said, backing up so she could walk by.

"No. My bad," she said. "I'm just leaving."

He gave her one last look—that same look all teenaged boys give anything that's female when it's standing right in front of them wearing nothing but a robe—before the bathroom door closed behind him.

He's surprisingly cute, thought Simone. *Tall. Messy brown hair. Red t-shirt and jeans.* But these were the only snapshot observations she had time to make. She quickly got dressed once inside "her room," then she lugged her suitcase down the stairs.

As a second thought, she propped up her bag in the foyer and rapped a few times on MeeMaw's door. MeeMaw's sweet, soft voice said, "Come in."

Simone opened the door and asked, "Are you okay, MeeMaw? Is there anything I can get for you before I go?"

"Oh, are you leaving?" MeeMaw frowned.

.   "Yeah. I have to meet my husband," she said. "We need to talk."

"Oh. I *see*," said MeeMaw with a little wink. "Well, God bless you, Honey. I'll be praying for you. And don't worry about me. I've got Bradley, and he's a good boy." She smiled.

Yeah. You poor, sweet thing. She smiled and closed MeeMaw's door.

She noticed that Travis had cleaned up the shattered glass from the picture frame. The bedroom wall looked a little bare without it. He'd also made the bed, but then, didn't he always? *Travis is my bitch*, she'd jokingly tell people. He did *all* the house work, mainly because he was the one who was home—at least, home more than Simone was. Simone was the one who was always out, earning the bacon. Travis certainly didn't make that much. Simone always joked that he got paid with colorful beads. Not that her salary was significantly higher, but without her commissions and annual bonus, they could never live in this big, beautiful house of theirs. She'd had it professionally decorated and everything. It was white, ornate, and perfect. Or as Travis called it, sterile.

"Simone?"

It was Travis' voice, coming from the first floor. He must've just walked through the garage door.

She walked down the stairs and into the kitchen. They looked each other in the eye, but neither one of them spoke. Simone grabbed a bottle of wine out of the wine fridge, but Travis grabbed the corkscrew and took it from her.

"Here. Let me."

While he worked on the cork, Simone grabbed two wine glasses.

"None for me," he said. She put one glass back.

He poured her some pinot. She said *thanks* and took a sip.

"Let's sit down," she said. "We need to talk."

He nodded and followed her past the front door, down the hall and into the formal living room. They sat on the same couch together but at opposite ends. Simone kicked off her shoes and tucked her legs underneath her. She took a long sip of her wine.

"How could you do this to me, Travis?"

He looked down. *Yeah, you NEED to feel bad*, she thought. She'd have lots and lots of work ahead of her, several *months'* worth of making him feel bad!

"I texted your *girlfriend*," she said.

"Yeah, I know," he said.

This infuriated her that he didn't deny that "Jen" was his girlfriend.

"And?"

"And she feels really bad," he said. "She never wants to hurt anyone."

"No! She's a *kind*-hearted marriage wrecker." Simone shook her head and took a sip of wine. "Fucking bitch."

"Simone—stop."

"Stop? Really? You mean I don't have a right to be mad?"

"You have *every* right to be mad. But Jen's a good person. She doesn't deserve that. It's not her fault." He paused a second then said, "Take it out on me, not on her."

"I love how you're defending her, Travis!" she said. "Sweet, innocent Jen!"

"She didn't know I was married until recently."

"Oh, *really*! Is that supposed to make me feel better?" Now she was really getting angry. Gut-punching angry. Good thing he was out of her reach!

"I was drawn to her, Simone. I can't explain it." He twisted his body to face her better. "And we have a mutual respect for one another."

Well, *this* was hitting below the belt. Travis always told her she was disrespectful. *I'm just playing with you*, she'd tell him, defending herself. It was the way she'd always treated him. He certainly hadn't minded it much when they were teenagers.

"So you respect her so much you thought you'd lie to her about being married."

"It's not *like* that," he said.

"Then tell me how it *is*, Travis. I'd love to

know. Of *course* she'd respect *you*. You were her professor! The respect was built *in*. But what could *you* have possibly found so admirable about a slutty little college girl who has a baby out of wedlock?"

"Well, that's just it," he said. "She'd made a mistake, but she owned up to it. Her boyfriend skipped town when she got pregnant." He paused. "But she had the baby, *anyway*."

Now she was hurt. Her eyes filled with tears.

"You said you would never bring that up." She started to cry. "In thirty-two years, you've kept quiet about it. Why now, Travis? Why now?"

Travis acted like he wanted to move closer to comfort her but must've thought better of it and remained where he was.

"I'm not bringing it up, Simone," he said.

"Then what do you call it?" she wiped her nose with the back of her hand.

"I just meant to say that for the past five years, she's raised her son at her parents' house, and then a year ago she went back to school to fulfill her dream of becoming a nurse."

"Did that dream include fucking her English professor?"

He shook his head, almost in a cringe. "I'm not going to talk to you if you keep doing that."

"Stop defending her!"

Before her anger could get the better of her, she set her wine glass on the coffee table and stood up.

"Where are you going?" he asked.

"I can't stay here. It's just too much, Travis. I gotta go." She slipped her feet into her shoes.

She reached into her back pocket. "Here." She

handed him his phone. "Call me when you've cut off *all* ties with her. And do it soon!"

"Simone—" he started to say, but she didn't want to hear *any* of it. Not right now.

"Travis, I'm going to give you—" she looked at her watch—"twelve hours to make things right and fix this. If you are not at the airport in time for our flight, we are through!"

Maybe they could sort through all this crap in Hawaii. Maybe *that's* why this trip was planned at such a monumental milestone in her life, for hashing-*out* purposes. And here she'd thought it was only to celebrate her birthday. *Silly me!*

She knew he wouldn't follow her as she left the room, so she didn't expect him to. Travis had a policy never to indulge her little temper tantrums. And being a thinker, she knew he needed to think. He needed to process. It was probably best if she left him alone to do this.

She was glad she'd left her suitcase in the trunk of her car out in the garage—glad she hadn't lugged it all the way up to their room as she'd originally hoped to do. *I must have good instincts*, she told herself.

"See you tomorrow, Travis!" she yelled from the kitchen. She would go back to April's for the night.

As the plane advanced to Cleveland Hopkins International Airport in the distance, Simone ran the entire history of her life with Travis through her mind, beginning with the first day she'd ever laid eyes on him. One look and all she could think was *Baby!* She knew she was done for because she'd never felt so deeply attracted to anyone before this.

She thought about the first time she'd ever talked to him in their biology class. Of course, he'd been too shy to talk to *her*. She'd had to approach *him*, the "new boy" from Ohio, whose dad had been forced to transfer to California for his sales job. Travis had almost looked scared when she'd invited him to hang out with her at lunch that day. But the moment he joined her "group," he'd gained instant popularity at school. Because as of that moment, he belonged to Simone. So he was "in."

Her friends *loved* him. They thought he was so cute. He was different than the jocks they were used to hanging out with. Travis was so smart and so quiet, yet "such a babe!" That first day when he ate lunch with them, he just listened and laughed as they all prattled on as usual about *this* cute guy and *that* cute guy and *can you believe what she's wearing?* Then all he said to Simone afterward was, "Why do your friends call you Rambo?"

So she laughed and told him how on the first day of school her freshman year, her history teacher had called roll with last names first, so when he got to Simone's name, of course he'd said, "Sylvester, Simone." And some derelict kid had said, "Sylvester Stallone's in this class?" So ever since, Brenda (and everyone close to her) had always called her "Rambo."

"But they're the only ones who can call me that," she was quick to add. Then with a smile and tilt of her head she said, "*You* can call me Rambo, too." And he often did. He said it suited her because she was such a fighter.

Simone and Travis soon became the "it" couple on campus. They were plastered all over the yearbook that year, first as the Sweetheart Couple for Valentine's Day, then they were voted "Couple Most Likely to Stay Together," and of course, they were prom king and queen.

Everyone knew Travis and Simone were head over heels *into* each other. They went everywhere together—did everything together, including each other. Simone always insisted Travis wear a condom. But on prom night, they were just so in the moment. They'd scored a hotel room and everything, telling their parents they were (respectively) staying the night at a friend's house. It was just *so* romantic! And Travis for the first time had been able to get his hands on some champagne. Just the cheap stuff, but still.

Then six weeks later, Simone discovered she was pregnant. She'd taken a pregnancy test on graduation day. She'd only told Travis about it—not any of her friends. No *way* could she tell her parents. Her dad would flip! She'd *seen* his reaction to her brother's *girlfriend* getting pregnant. So she'd sworn Travis to secrecy. She'd never been so scared.

And without telling Travis, a week later she'd gotten an abortion. He was so heartbroken when she'd told him, he'd cried for days. Even his *mom* had called her and asked why her son was so sad! So Simone made something up about how they'd broken up.

"But don't worry," she'd said. "We'll get back together, I know it." And his mother had bought it.

Sure enough, they were "together" again not long after Travis' sadness subsided. That's about when his family moved back to Ohio, again for his dad's job. Simone couldn't bear the thought of life without Travis and begged her father to let her attend Ohio State where Travis was, to be near him.

She lived in a dorm throughout her four years as a Buckeye, and during that time she saw Travis every single weekend. They were so happy together. They screwed like rabbits and got married the second they graduated. They took up permanent residence in Ohio so Travis could be close to his family, which was fine by her. Outside of her dad, Simone hadn't really had an attachment to *her* family.

Simone had secured a job right away as a marketing rep for a major catering company, which paid her handsomely. She hadn't particularly enjoyed working there, but with her nice salary, she was able to pay most of her student loans plus put Travis through graduate school. He diligently pursued his M.Ed. degree and later his PhD degree should he ever wish to advance to a four-year college or university. Turned out he got hired at the local community college and never left. He said he'd found his niche.

Not Simone. Soon as she was able, she landed her dream job at Com Corp and advanced up the ranks—*naturally*—and had worked there ever since.

Travis flip-flopped on the "having kids" idea a few years into their marriage, but Simone convinced herself (and Travis, too) during episodes of extreme guilt that even if she *were* the mothering "type" (*somewhere* deep down inside of her) they didn't *deserve* children. Eventually, she'd up and had her tubes tied, just to eliminate confusion down the road. And it had. Or so she'd thought.

They'd had a fabulous time, traveling the world together. Travis had seemed satisfied with that lifestyle—at first, anyway. But after they'd been married about ten years, she noticed how he'd smile at children or take a second look at pregnant women. But she'd never read too much into it. She'd lived their whole married life under the delusion that he was every bit as happy as she was.

And then there were the pictures of the young girls on his phone.

And now Jen.

"Ladies and gentlemen, we will be descending shortly into Cleveland. Please fasten your seatbelts and prepare for landing," said the flight attendant's pleasant, sing-song voice over the speaker system. Simone almost didn't fasten hers. But on second thought, she did. She only complied so as not to cause a problem. So as not to draw attention to herself.

But Simone didn't care about anything anymore. Not even crashing in a plane. *Nothing* really mattered now because Simone knew she was about to go home and kill herself.

Chapter Four

"Please tell me why you feel that you and I don't have anything." Simone smoothed the white sand with her free hand around and around in circles, first one direction then another. *Even the sand is beautiful here*, she thought, looking up for a moment at the clear ocean water in the distance. This was her second day in Hawaii.

Travis had not shown up at the airport Friday morning. Disappointed but not too surprised, she had boarded the plane without him. When she'd arrived in Honolulu and was all settled in to her hotel room—*their* hotel room—she was the one who'd had to call.

"Why aren't you here with me, Trav?" she'd asked him, slurring her words a little. She'd been on her second bottle of wine by then. He'd told her he didn't think it would be productive.

"Not worth fighting for?" she'd asked. "I'm not worth fighting for?" And then she'd hung up. She'd canceled their dinner reservation and gone to bed.

Today she was sober. Today they would talk.

"I've just felt dead for a long time, Simone," he said.

"Why? Was it something I did?" she asked. Whatever it was, she would stop doing it. His not coming here, the fact he was not flying out *right now* on the very next plane, scared her. And for the first time in their marriage, she felt as though she had lost control.

"I don't blame you for anything," he said. "You were just being you all these years."

"But somewhere along the way, you stopped liking me," she said. "When, Travis?" When he didn't respond right away she said, "Why?"

"I think I'm just a different person, now," he said. "We met when we were so young. I never had a chance to figure out who I was or what I wanted in life."

"But that's the beauty of our relationship, Travis," she said. "We figure life out *together*."

"Simone, *you* do all the figuring out. I'm just your sidekick."

"How can you say that?" She switched ears on her cell phone and leaned on her other elbow.

"You always tell me what to think. What to feel. How to act. How to believe."

"But you always agree with me," she said.

"Yeah!" he said. "Or else."

"Or else what?"

"Or else there's a problem."

On and on this conversation continued. They talked for at least an hour, mostly Travis with his list of grievances against her, but the last fifteen minutes or so were about Simone pledging to do better from now on. Promising to change.

"We can get through this, Travis. When I come home, things will be different. I promise."

"Simone—"

"We'll start all over, Travis. We can even get a new house if you want. A smaller house, just like you've always wanted." She laughed a little through her tears. "One with a little dog."

"Simone, there's nothing that really ties us together. There's really nothing to fix. It's not like kids are involved. It's just two people who probably should have explored their options before committing to marriage."

Wow, this hurt *bad*. But she loved Travis *so* much! And she was now *desperate* to do whatever it would take to salvage this mess. She was even willing to let him date his "girlfriend" for a while if only to see how completely *wrong* Jen was for him.

"We can separate for a bit," she said. "We'll live apart for a few months, and you can have your freedom. And then we'll get back together when you're done with her."

She heard him sigh.

"It's too late, Simone. I can't go back."

She was almost too afraid to ask her next question, so she waited a few moments.

"What do you mean you can't go back? You can't, Travis?" And with a voice softer than what she'd ever used before, she asked, "Or you won't?"

His answer sent a dagger through her heart.

"I don't *want* to go back."

She cried. "Why? Tell me *why*, Travis…."

He sighed again. Then he blurted out the two words no wife ever wants to hear. "Jen's pregnant."

There was a long pause.

Finally, Simone pressed end. *Hmm. How symbolic!* She took it a step further. She removed her wedding ring and put it in her beach bag.

Simone remained right where she was—on the sand—for the next three hours, until sunset. No doubt she'd burned herself to a crisp that day, but she didn't care. It didn't matter. Nothing mattered.

When she finally dragged herself up to her hotel room, she had a decision to make. Would she take her life here? Or wait till she got home?

She decided to think on it a few days. What was the rush? The important part was to make an impact on Travis. To mar the rest of his life.

When they didn't talk again the rest of the week—when he didn't so much as call her—this was confirmation to her soul that he really, truly didn't care about her. That's when she decided she wouldn't end her life here where nobody knew her. She would do it back at home.

But today it was her birthday. Her last night in Hawaii. And Simone would have one last night of fun.

She asked the concierge where the happening bars were. If this was her last birthday ever, she was going to party the night away. And if Travis didn't care to be here and see her in the sexy "Rambo" outfit she'd bought special just for him, then someone else *would*.

"You're so tan!"

Lovely. As usual, April was way too cheerful. Simone had tried to make a run for the yellow guest room upstairs, but April had flagged her down mid foyer. She'd been sitting with MeeMaw in her room and had spotted her house guest through the open door.

She'd already informed April that Travis hadn't bothered to follow her to Hawaii...that he'd impregnated his "college student girlfriend." She'd sent April a text back at the airport in the hopes of avoiding an encounter such as this. Although, it was probably the *least* she could do to show her gratitude and say hello real quick to April and her mother.

So she feigned a smile and walked into MeeMaw's room. It took every ounce of fakeness in her, but she greeted them both with a small hug.

"How was your trip?"

"As good as could be expected, April."

She wished she didn't have to pretend to be polite, but April's mother was so sweet, sitting there smiling at the two of them. "I'll have to tell you all about it tomorrow. I'm so tired from all that flying."

"I can imagine!" said MeeMaw. "April, help Simone get settled into her room so she can rest. Are you hungry, Dear?"

April started to stand up but Simone put her hand out to stop her.

"Oh, I'm fine!" she said. She lied and told them she'd stopped for dinner on the way home from the airport. Truth was she hadn't had anything but a cup of coffee all day. She was too upset to eat. Too distraught to nourish her flesh. "I think I'm just going to go to bed early tonight."

"Are you planning to come to work tomorrow?" asked April.

"Actually, no, I don't think so," she said. April's face fell. "I think I need a day to recover."

"You need a vacation from your vacation!" smiled MeeMaw.

"Yes, MeeMaw, you said it." Simone smiled back at her. But in reality, Simone wouldn't be returning to work at *all*. Ever. By this time tomorrow, she'd be dead.

"How about Tuesday?" asked April.

"Why do you ask?" said Simone. She started to inch her way backward out of the room.

"You know that one grocery chain that's taking over Grover's?"

Yes, she knew full well. Grover's Green Grocers had been bought-out by a California company called *Sunset Supermarkets*. It was plastered all over the internet. "A Sunset Supermarket is coming to a community near you."

When Simone nodded, April said, "We got the contract to do their grand opening! It's going to be *huge*, Simone. Huge. We *need* you."

She wanted to ease April's anxiety if only momentarily. "Okay, I'll be in on Tuesday." She tried to act excited. "That's a great account!"

April heaved a sigh of relief. But her smile quickly turned to concern as she walked over and touched the red marks on Simone's chest.

"What are *those* from?" she asked.

Simone looked down. "Oh. Candle wax."

The look on April's face was priceless.

Bradley barely looked up from his TV game when Simone dragged her suitcase to "her room." *Yeah, hello to you, too,* she thought. She knew for a fact that if *she'd* ever had any kids, she certainly wouldn't let them plant their ass on a couch all day.

She thought about taking a shower, but…why? And there was no need to unpack. So she just flopped onto the bed and took her letter out of her designer purse. She'd spent the majority of the plane ride, working on this thing. These would be her final words to Travis, so it had to be perfect. It had to make the ultimate, lasting impression on him. She read it again, one last time.

Dear Travis,

When you read this letter, I will be gone from your life forever. You will be free to live your life with the person you think you love more than you love me. Or did you ever love me, Travis? I always thought you did. What a sick, cruel joke the "universe" as you call it has played on me. I spent the majority of my life, convinced you loved me as much as I love you. How could I be so wrong about something I thought was so right? Or maybe you did love me in the beginning, when we were young. Did I get too old for you, Travis? Was I no longer able to satisfy your needs? Did you feel the need to look elsewhere? Do you have no regard for our wedding vows? What happened to "for better or for worse, till death do us part?" You're not even willing to TRY with me, Travis. The thing that hurts me the most is that you don't even care. Which means NO one cares about me. I don't want anyone else but you. I've always wanted you, Travis. You were the one person in this world I could count on. I loved our life together. I used to be so happy. But now you've taken my happiness away. I have no reason to live. If YOU won't love me, who will? You and Jen (and your baby) can have all the happiness now. Think of it, Travis. I'm doing you a favor. I'm eliminating the need for divorce attorneys. This way you can have it all. The only mess you'll have to clean is my blood. I love you, Travis. Think of me every day and remember that I always loved you. You were the love of my life. And now you are the love of my death. I love you, Travis.

> *Your wife,*
> *Your former life,*
> *Simone Sanders*

She had it all planned out. Tomorrow, while Travis was at work, she'd go to their house. She'd find her wedding gown from the basement and put it on. She'd go to their bedroom upstairs and lie down on the bed. She might even bring a bouquet of flowers for dramatic effect. Not that she'd need them. With the train of her dress splayed out all around her and her veil strategically covering her face, she would make a lasting impression on him. The best part would be all the blood, staining the white on her gown, spilling down all over the white bedspread, dripping down to the white carpet below.

Simone was going to slit her wrists (both of them) with Travis' razor. She sent him a text.

Not that you care, but I made it

safely home from Hawaii. I have
a place to stay (not that you care)
but I'll be at the house tomorrow
when you get done with classes.

He had the nerve to only respond with: K

By the time she woke up the next morning, it was after 9:00. April had left for the office hours ago, no doubt. And Travis was at work, no doubt.

Bradley was asleep in his room. At least, she assumed he was. His door was closed. *Damn him!* She trudged down the stairs.

"MeeMaw? You okay?" she asked, slowly opening MeeMaw's door.

She was where she always was, sitting up in her bed, watching her shows. As usual, April had left a tray of breakfast next to her although Simone couldn't imagine that MeeMaw ever ate anything substantial. She was so tiny.

"Good morning, Dear!" MeeMaw's smile filled the room with sunshine. "Did you sleep well?"

Simone ran her hand through her messy hair and said, "A little *too* well, can you tell?"

"Well, you're still beautiful," said MeeMaw.

"I'll be around for a little bit longer if you need anything," said Simone, glancing at the TV. Some preacher lady was yapping away.

"Oh, I'm fine, Dear," said MeeMaw. "I've got my shows on, and I'm just fine. April brought me breakfast."

She looked at MeeMaw's tray and saw a remnant piece of chocolate cake on her plate. MeeMaw looked at it, too, and said, "We should have waited till *you* got back to eat cake. April's birthday was Friday. But it was *your* birthday, Saturday."

That's right. She'd completely forgotten that her and April's birthdays were just a day apart. But how could she? April always told everyone she was named April on account of she was born in April. "And my middle name is Iris because I was born on tax day, and Iris sounds like IRS." She'd heard that story a million times. Yet another reason Simone shouldn't have forgotten!

"Oh my gosh, I didn't get her anything," said Simone.

MeeMaw laughed. "Well, don't feel bad, Dear. I don't think she got *you* anything, either."

"I've just had so much on my mind," said Simone, looking at the floor.

"Yes, you have," said MeeMaw. "I hope you don't mind, but April gave me the *scoop.*"

I'm sure she did! But Simone didn't care. April had been so generous, offering her a place to stay during her time of need that this didn't bother her.

"Okay, then I'll just let Bradley know when I'm leaving," she said.

"Okay, Dear."

The last thing she saw as she closed the door was MeeMaw's sweet, smiling face.

Since Bradley was still sleeping, she figured she could take all the time she wanted in the bathroom. So after showering and drying her hair, she styled it with her curling iron. She made up her face as though she were going out for a night on the town. Her mindset today was to make herself look as pretty as humanly possible. She even painted her fingernails. Her toenails still looked good after her pre-trip pedicure.

She wore her best perfume and the earrings she'd worn on her wedding day. She'd intended to wear them her first night in Hawaii to impress Travis. *But THAT didn't work out!*

Just for fun, she decided to wear a sexy bra and underwear to give a kick to whomever undressed her once she was dead. Maybe it would be a male EMT or some new guy at the morgue or mortuary. She had no idea where all they'd take her body. It really didn't matter, though. Did it?

Over her sexy undergarments she just wore sweats. She'd be changing into her wedding gown once she got home, so whatever she wore right now was irrelevant. *Hmm. Just like me.*

I'll leave my suitcase here, she thought. That way if April popped by at lunchtime it wouldn't arouse suspicion. She certainly didn't want April poking her nose into her plan and spoiling everything. *Travis* had to be the one to discover her. Not some cop.

She fished her wedding ring from out of her beach bag and put it on her finger. She would place her letter to Travis on the bedroom dresser next to a picture of the two of them and use her ring as a paperweight. *Just another dramatic touch*, she thought. She grabbed the note from underneath a candle on the nightstand by the bed, right where she'd left it, and stuck it in her purse.

She tapped softly on Bradley's bedroom door and when she heard a faint *mmm*, she opened it just a crack. He was sitting on the edge of his bed, rubbing his eyes, which opened wide when he saw her.

"Where are *you* going?" he asked.

This let her know her efforts on her appearance had paid off.

"I'm going to run errands," she said. "Tell your mom when she gets home I won't be back till late."

"Okay," he said. "Do you need me to give you a house key or anything?"

Well, isn't THAT sweet of him.

"No, your mom gave me one before my trip," she said. "Are you going to look after MeeMaw today?"

He nodded. "Yep. I'm getting ready right now." She noticed he was just wearing his boxer briefs.

"Okay," said Simone. "Then I guess I'll go."

"See ya," he said.

"See ya." She closed his door.

When she reached the bottom of the staircase, she walked into the bedroom next to MeeMaw's, which she supposed was April's room. It was. It was the master bedroom, and it had the scent of April's cheap perfume.

Simone dug out whatever cash was in her wallet—looked to be about $200—and placed it near April's pillow. It was the least she could do to repay April for her kindness.

When she parked in her driveway, out of the corner of her eye she saw Josephine's curtain move. If she didn't know better, she'd say Josephine had a look of concern on her face. But Simone didn't want to chat with her. *That would be disrespectful*, she thought, *acting like everything was fine and then going off and ending my life.* Besides, Josephine was too sharp. It would be hard to bluff her way by *her.* At least *this* way, Josephine could tell people *yeah, Simone didn't look right when I saw her, earlier. Something was wrong.* So she told herself she was doing a kindness by simply waving at Josephine who reluctantly waved back.

When she walked into the house through the front door, a female voice said, "Travis?" It was coming from the washroom off of the kitchen.

Simone walked toward the doorway to see the girl she assumed was Jen. *Yep.* Same frame, same hair from the picture she'd seen. Her back to Simone, she was bending down and scooping clothes out of the dryer. *Wow. My body's not even cold, yet, and he's already moved his mistress into MY house!*

Jen picked up the laundry basket full of clothes, and when she turned around, she gasped.

The two women proceeded to stare at one another. Simone more or less was studying her replacement. Maybe it was her mood to blame or the fact that life would soon be over, who knew, but Simone almost felt relief. This Jen person wasn't that pretty. *Maybe if she fixed her nose….*

Simone smiled wickedly. Even more wickedly, she said, "Hi."

"Hi," said Jen. She looked worried. "I hope you don't mind. Travis said I could wash clothes here this morning while my son is at school. He goes to Pendleton this year." Pendleton was the little elementary school down the street from the house.

Simone didn't say anything. *We'll just give her an uncomfortable silence. Let her squirm a little.*

But Jen was obviously a talker.

"I meant to be gone before Travis—before *you* got home," she said. "I just had one more load, but I can leave now if you want."

Simone thought about this a second. *Hmm.* It might work in her favor if Jen was here to discover her body *with* Travis. She could hear the poor girl, now, screaming bloody murder. *Hmm,* she could have a little bit of fun with this.

"No, that's okay," said Simone, walking toward the washing machine. She pointed at another basket of clothes on the floor. "Are these yours?"

Jen nodded.

"Here, let me." Simone began to throw them into the front-load washer.

"You don't have to do that," said Jen.

"No, I don't mind," said Simone. She pulled out the tiny drawer and filled it with detergent and fabric softener. She set the dial to warm and turned on the machine.

"Thank you," said Jen.

"No problem." She smiled wickedly again.

Jen walked her basket of clean clothes over to the table by the kitchen window and started folding them. Simone opened the freezer and grabbed a bottle of Fireball.

"Want a shot?" she asked.

Jen turned to see what she was talking about. "I'd love to, but…." She looked down and put her hand on her stomach.

"When are you due?" asked Simone.

"November."

"Are you going to find out what you're

having?"

She couldn't believe she was having this conversation. Here. In *her* kitchen. With the woman who was essentially the reason Simone was about to kill herself. *Hmm. Maybe that's why I'm still talking to her*, she thought. *Because soon it will all be over. May as well get some answers.*

And either Jen was extremely stupid and dense to be standing there, talking to her boyfriend's *wife*, or she was just a super friendly person. Simone couldn't decide. She downed a shot of Fireball.

"I'm hoping it's a little sister for Robby. But Travis wants to be surprised."

"Oh, he *does*," she said. Like they were talking about something totally normal, not the baby her husband was having with some other woman.

Simone downed another shot of Fireball. She sat down on the end chair, the one with the armrests, next to Jen and all the clothes. She set her bottle of Fireball and shot glass next to the basket. Already she was feeling the effects of the red beverage. She'd had nothing to eat yesterday, and nothing today, either.

"I'm really sorry about how everything happened," said Jen, placing a folded shirt on top of another folded shirt. "You probably think I'm a horrible person. In a way, I guess I am."

This was too good to pass up.

"Why do you think that, Jen?" she asked.

"Well, I mean…Travis was my teacher, and he was just so *nice*." She looked at Simone. "No one's ever been that nice to me before." She went back to her folding. "I never meant to break up a marriage."

"He said you didn't *know* he was married."

Simone downed a third shot of Fireball.

"No, I didn't," she said. "And I was really super mad when he told me. We got in a *fight* about it."

Simone raised her eyebrows, pretending interest. *She acts like SHE'S the one with the major history with Travis. Like SHE'S known him for 32 plus years. She hasn't even been alive that long!*

"How *old* are, Jen?" She set down her shot glass.

"Twenty-three."

Before her Hawaii adventure, this would have floored her. But she supposed Finn had desensitized her to the concept of age. *Ha, Travis! MY fling is two years younger than yours. At least...I hope!*

Now she was feeling borderline silly. So much so, that she started folding some of Jen's clothes. They were all little clothes. Little shirts, little jeans, little socks. *These must be Robby's.*

"So how did you and Travis get together? Who approached whom?"

"He gave me a failing grade! So I went in to talk to him about it. I figured it must've been a mistake because I'd scored high on the final exam."

"Hmm. A mistake, huh?"

So he lured her to his lair.

"So when I went in to talk to him in December, one thing led to another, and—" she put down the pajama bottoms she was folding. "Simone, I'm so sorry. You don't want to hear any of this."

Hmm. Travis said they got serious six months ago, but it was more like four.

"It was just a progression from there. I promise you, if I even thought he was married, I wouldn't have done any of that! I'm not like that."

How do you know WHAT you're like? thought Simone. *You're 23.*

The more Jen talked, the more Simone could see that Travis was right. She should direct her disappointment at *him*, not at Jen. But she had to ask.

"So when you *did* find out he was married, why didn't you break up with him?"

Jen's face looked sad. Then her eyes welled up with tears.

"He didn't tell me he was married until I told him I was pregnant. That was April 1st. I totally thought it was an April Fool's joke."

"Yeah, I guess I'm a joke, alright!" said Simone, shaking her head. *Wow. Travis, you are such an ass. Lying to me, lying to her! So much for your integrity.* To think she thought she knew Travis so well.

Now Jen was crying. "I don't know what to do! My *parents* don't even know about this. And I was just starting to get my life together. Travis says he'll take care of me, but I'm like destroying your marriage! I am such a bad person!"

Out of sheer, knee-jerk reaction, Simone stood up and gave Jen a hug. This girl could technically be her and Travis' daughter! And while Simone didn't possess a maternal bone in her body, she all of a sudden felt compassion for this poor, fellow female and her sad, sorry plight. She rubbed her shoulder a little, hoping to stop all the crying.

"You didn't know," she whispered.

Jen pulled away slowly and wiped her tears with her hands. Simone sat back down on her chair.

"And you're *so* nice," Jen said. "And so pretty. What did Travis ever see in *me*?" She walked to the counter and yanked a paper towel off the roll and blew her nose.

Simone once again examined Jen's face. She certainly wasn't *ugly*. A little plain, maybe.

"He saw *something*, Jen." *Like a young, new body!* "Obviously, he wants *you* more than he wants *me*. Don't be so hard on yourself."

Was she really saying this? Was this really happening? *I must be buzzed!*

It did seem to make Jen feel a little better because she smiled. But then when she glanced at the clock on the oven she said, "Shoot! I have to get Robby! School's out in ten minutes. He's on the early bird schedule."

Simone nodded as Jen grabbed a manila envelope on the counter by the espresso machine. *But wait a minute*, she thought.

"Are you coming back here?" she asked.

Jen nodded. "Just to finish this," she said, pointing at the laundry. "Then we'll go, I promise. I know Travis said he was meeting with you later, and I know you guys need to talk."

"So you're bringing *Robby* back here?"

Jen nodded.

Shit.

"But I can take him to my parents' house if you don't want him here. Travis left me his car because I had to sell mine last semester to pay for tuition." *He must've ridden his bike to work,* thought Simone. Her anger returned when she thought *hmm, I'll bet he let Jen and Robby stay here at MY house the whole week*

I was in Hawaii. They probably slept in OUR bed!

Her suspicions were confirmed when Jen handed Simone the envelope. "This came in the mail for you a few days ago. Travis was planning to give it to you, later." Simone glanced at the return address. *Hmm.* It was the promised birthday card from her mother.

Before Simone could process a response, Jen said a quick goodbye and left through the front door. Simone looked out the window and watched her walk at a quick clip down the street.

Well, this would never do! She couldn't let little *Robby* be here when Travis and Jen discovered her dead body! Simone might be selfish, but she would never scar a child for life like that.

She put away the Fireball. And after she finished folding the few remaining pieces of clothing in the laundry basket, she grabbed her purse and the envelope and left the house.

She would have to come up with a Plan B, later.

Chapter Five

She exited her house the same as she'd come in—through the front door. The morning glare was so bright, she dug her sunglasses out of the glove box. She sat in her car for a bit, ignition off, feeling a little too dizzy at the moment to drive. True, she wanted to end her life and end it quickly, but she didn't want to take anyone else *with* her. She wasn't like that. Otherwise, Travis would be at the top of her list. But no. It was better for him to live. *Live and suffer, Travis. Spend the rest of your life, living with the knowledge that you're responsible for the death of your wife.*

Simone closed her eyes and allowed herself to drift off into a pleasant little cat nap. Maybe it was the alcohol or the warmth of the morning sun, pouring through the windshield—whatever was drugging her at the moment, it felt good for the short time it lasted.

When the gardener started up his mower, Simone gasped herself awake, flailing her hand and knocking the birthday card off her lap. She leaned down to pick it up off the floorboard where it had landed, underneath the gas pedal. Her mother's writing on the front of the large, manila envelope jumped out at her. She sighed and tore it open.

Enclosed were two smaller envelopes. She opened the yellow one, first, and read the card inside. *Why can't she be a normal person and just buy me a funny card?* But Simone's mother never bought her a humorous card. It was like she searched high and low for the card with the most sappy writing possible, both on the front flap and on the inside. And while she knew it was her mom's intention to cram into one annual birthday greeting all the words she never spoke aloud to her daughter, the only effect all those empty, pre-printed words ever produced was to make Simone feel even more distant in their relationship. So much so that it was hard for Simone to drum up a time when she'd *ever* felt close to her mom.

Her mom wasn't a *bad* person. By most standards, she was actually quite likeable. She was soft spoken, pleasant, *agreeable to a fault!* But to Simone, these were negative traits. They made her mother spineless. Boring. She was such a "yes" woman. Her dad, for example, had *always* gotten his way with her.

All Simone ever heard, growing up, was her mother saying, "Yes, Honey. Whatever you want, Dear." So Simone learned at an early age that if you allowed people to walk all over you, they would! *Thank goodness I'm more like my dad*, she always told herself. He was more like a sergeant, and so was she. *No* one told Simone what was what. Especially not at work. Simone was Queen, and everyone knew it.

Simone sighed and ripped open the other envelope, the white one. *Two plane tickets? What the F, Mom?*

The handwritten note inside said:

> *Dear Simone,*
>
> *Happy Birthday, Sweetheart!*
> *I never know what to get "the girl*
> *who has everything," so I thought*
> *I'd be a little selfish this year. As you*
> *know, I'll be celebrating 80 years*

*of life on the planet this May, and I
was hoping you and Travis would
come to California for a little visit.
Ron and Leesa are throwing me
a party, and it would mean so much
to me, Simone, if you would be here
with all of us. We haven't seen you
in so long—over 10 years! I hope you
don't mind, but I took the liberty of
purchasing plane tickets for the two
of you. I know it's short notice, but if
you could find a little bit of time to
come see me, you'd be making an
"old lady" very happy. I hope you
and Travis had a wonderful vacation
in Hawaii. Call me when you get the
chance and tell me all about it. Miss
you!*

*Love,
Mom*

*Way to go, Mom! Thanks for the heads up!
AND the fucking guilt trip!* Now she was pissed.

Ron and Leesa? Throwing a party? *You mean
YOU are throwing a party and saying it's from them.
THEY couldn't afford to throw you a party!*

She shook her head and tossed her birthday
"gift" onto the passenger seat. *I guess I dodged THAT
bullet,* she told herself. And then for the first time, it

occurred to her that her suicide would probably have a bad impact on her family. Once again, Simone had been living in Simone World, as Travis called it, never giving one thought to her family of origin. And what with her *own* birthday preparations, it had completely escaped her attention that an 80th birthday was a huge deal. Not that she *ever* gave much thought to her mother's birthday. The past couple of years, she'd assigned her mom's gift package to Jodi at the office.

And that's probably what she'd do this year, too. She sighed. *One last good deed before I die.* Although, even Simone had to admit to herself that her death would definitely put a damper on her mother's birthday celebration. *They'll probably cancel the party.* And for a split second, she entertained the possibility of going. But only for a split second. *No.* She shook her head. *Not happening.*

She was startled by two raps on her window. It was Josephine. Simone opened her car door and stepped onto the driveway.

"Josephine!"

Not knowing what was coming over her, she grabbed onto her neighbor in a big bear hug. They stayed that way for quite some time. Then Josephine put her hands on Simone's shoulders and pushed her back at arm's length to study her eyes and face.

"You look like hell," said Josephine with a frown.

"I've *been* through hell," she responded.

Josephine nodded and tried to pull Simone closer for another hug. But Simone didn't want to hug anymore. She wanted to get out of Dodge.

"How could he do this to you?" her neighbor

asked her.

Simone shook her head. Under normal circumstances, she'd probably cry. But Simone didn't feel like crying anymore. Simone felt numb.

Josephine's eyes looked moist, and they started to turn a bit red. "Simone, I wanted to call you in the worst way, but I just couldn't bring myself to do it. I didn't know what to say—"

"It's alright, Josephine," she said. Then to make her feel better she added, "I wouldn't have picked up, anyway. I was too—(she almost said depressed)—emotionally drained to talk to anyone."

Now Josephine's eyes took on an angry demeanor. "Are you going to let them do this to you, Simone? Are you going to let some other woman move in on your territory? She's been here the *whole* time you were gone. Has she no respect? Or morals? And then she brings her *kid* here! They just walked right past you into the house—didn't you see them?"

She shook her head. "No, Josephine, I didn't. I was sleeping."

"Is there anything I can do? Anything I can say on your behalf? Ooh, I just want to *strangle* that man!"

If she wasn't so out of it, she'd have laughed at Josephine's face. No doubt Josephine *would* strangle Travis if Simone had the inclination to sic her on him. She was touched by her elderly neighbor's moral indignation—and loyalty.

"It doesn't matter, Josephine," she said, weakly.

"What do you *mean* it doesn't matter?"

Oh no. Simone didn't want to give herself away. The tone in Josephine's voice frightened her just a little. So instead of coming off as though "life" didn't matter, she decided to change her approach.

"Josephine, you can't make somebody love you," she said. "I have no control over my husband's feelings." It sounded strange even to *her* ears. Never in a million years would Simone have imagined uttering these words...admitting her lack of control over Travis. But she did it for Josephine's sake. Why should her neighbor feel burdened with all this junk, especially when it would all end soon? "If *that's* what he wants," she said, pointing to her house where her husband's mistress and son were, "then what can I do?"

"You can fight!" said Josephine. "You can march right on in there and kick her out. This is *your* house, Simone. *You* worked for it, she didn't."

Simone hadn't even thought of it that way. She'd more or less had the attitude of *ruining* the house so that *no* one would live in it. *But hey, if they want to live here after I'm gone...after they clean up all the blood...w*ould she really care?

She did appreciate Josephine being on her side like this. But she was *so* tired. *So* exhausted, and now the after-effects of the Fireball were making her just want to curl up into a fetal position and fall asleep. Forever. She had to get out of here.

"Josephine, we will talk. I promise," she said even though it was a blatant lie. She put one foot back inside her car. "But right now, I just need to get away from here and think for a while."

"Do you need a place to stay, Simone? You are always welcome at my house."

Good grief, no! thought Simone.

"Oh, that's so kind of you, Josephine, but I'm staying with April—she works with me at Com Corp. Besides, I don't want to be too close to all *that*." She tilted her head in the direction of the house.

"No, I guess you wouldn't," said Josephine, shaking her head in apparent disgust. "Well. You know I'm here for you."

Simone sat down on the driver's seat. "Yes. I know. Please don't worry about *me*, Josephine." And for the first time that day, Simone manufactured a smile if only to calm her neighbor down.

She figured she'd go right up to "her room" and sleep awhile. The morning's events had completely worn her out. She tossed her purse and keys onto the little credenza in the foyer and tromped upstairs.

Bradley was sleeping, or she *assumed* he was because his bedroom door was closed. She sighed. Did she not see him wake up earlier? *Loser went back to bed!* Now it was lunchtime. MeeMaw was probably hungry. So instead of flopping down onto the flowery bed as planned, she tiptoed back downstairs.

"What can I get for you, MeeMaw?" she asked, opening the bedroom door just a crack.

"Oh, hello, Simone!" MeeMaw smiled enthusiastically as though Simone were a celebrity or something, gracing her with her presence. *The poor woman's probably starving.*

"I don't suppose Bradley's come in, yet, has he?" she asked.

MeeMaw chuckled as though her grandson were still a tiny, little infant, or like he was a toddler who was too young to do anything a grown-up might do, like care for an aging family member.

"That grandson of mine sure needs his beauty rest!" MeeMaw shook her head and continued to chuckle.

Simone marveled at this woman's positive attitude about everything. She was sure if she could bottle and sell it, she could become a billionaire.

"Can I fix you some lunch?" she asked.

"Oh, Honey, no, that's okay," said MeeMaw. "I don't want you to go to any trouble."

Simone took this as a hint. MeeMaw really *was* hungry. So she lied.

"It's no trouble at all, MeeMaw. I was just going to fix myself a sandwich. I can just as easily fix two as I can one." She smiled.

"Oh! Well okay, then," said MeeMaw. "Sure, I would love a sandwich." She smiled that bright sunshine smile of hers.

So it was settled. Simone made her way to the kitchen, hoping she'd find all the right ingredients. Instead, what she found was an almost empty carton of milk in the sparsely filled refrigerator and a bunch of way brown bananas, resting on the counter. *Ew*. She was just about to toss them into the nearby trashcan when a shirtless, barefoot Bradley padded in.

"Don't throw those out. MeeMaw likes banana bread. When they're brown like that, we bake bread."

Simone turned to face him. "Who's we?"

He yawned and ran his hand over the top of his bedhead hair. "Sometimes my mom. Sometimes me," he said.

"Oh." She set the bananas back on the counter. "Well, don't let *me* stop you. I was just going to fix

MeeMaw a sandwich, but you guys don't have any food!"

Bradley opened the refrigerator door, grabbed the carton of milk, shook it, and then poured the remainder of its contents into his mouth. He laughed and nearly spit the milk back out when he looked over at the shocked expression on Simone's horrified face.

"Don't worry," he said, after gulping it down. "I only do that when it's almost gone."

Yeah, sure you do, she thought. Now she was getting irritated with this lazyass adolescent, towering before her.

"Are you going to make the bread or what?" she asked with a bit of a snap to her tone.

"Can't," he said. "Not till later. My mom does the grocery shopping on Monday nights, and I need butter. And eggs."

"Why don't *you* just do the shopping *for* her?"

"I used to," he said. "But the guy who bought Grover's fired us and never hired me back."

"You used to work there?"

"Yup. Got a discount and everything."

"Well, why doesn't your mom just leave you some cash so you can still shop for her?"

"Can't. I don't have a car."

Bradley crushed the empty milk carton with both hands and said, "Kobe!" as he tossed it into the trash can by the pantry, perfect follow-through and all.

"Let me guess. You used to play basketball in school." Simone was set on getting some answers to her questions about this screwed up son of April's.

He leaned back on the counter with both hands gripping the rounded edge.

"Yeah. Actually, I played a few sports my freshman and sophomore years—"

"Why did you quit?" she asked. Now *she* was leaning on the counter directly across from him.

"My mom couldn't afford it anymore," he said.

"I mean school." Simone folded her arms across her chest. "Why did you quit school?"

He looked down at the ground. "School sucks," he said.

Yeah. Lots of things suck, she thought. *What does that have to do with anything? My whole life sucks! So no.* This was not an acceptable answer.

"School is a means to an end," she said. "If you want to go places in life, you need an education. Are you at least getting your GED?"

He shook his head, still looking at his feet.

Wow.

Before she could comment, he turned and mumbled something about checking on MeeMaw. Simone followed him down the hall and into her room.

"Hi, Bradley!" MeeMaw's eyes lit up when she saw him.

"Hi, MeeMaw," he said, bending over to give her a kiss—or rather, allowing her to kiss him on the cheek. "Sorry I slept late."

"Oh, it's alright, Bradley. Simone's looking after me. She's going to fix me a sandwich."

"Actually, I can't," said Simone. "Apparently, we're out of food at the moment." Then she had an idea. "But Bradley and I were just about to do a little grocery run. Can I make you some tea in the meantime?" She could give her crackers, too. She'd seen a box of crackers on top of the refrigerator.

"No, I'm fine, Honey," she said. "I was just drifting off to sleep, so maybe I'll take a little nap."

Simone began to back out of the room. She pointed at the TV and asked, "Want me to turn this off?" She almost said want me to turn this *crap* off because that one preacher lady was on again. *What, does she have a 24-hour show or something?*

"Oh no, that's okay, Dear," said MeeMaw. "I kind of like falling asleep to a good message." Now she was whispering. "Don't tell anyone, but I do it every Sunday at church." She covered her mouth with one hand to hide her laughter.

Oh, MeeMaw, are you just the cutest thing or what? Too bad you got stuck with a grandson like Bradley!

Bradley followed Simone out of the room, closing MeeMaw's door behind him.

"Are you really going to go shopping?" he asked.

"*We* are going shopping," she said. "Go put a shirt on and meet me back, here."

She waited for him to disappear at the top of the stairs, then she dashed into April's room, grabbed the money she'd left by April's pillow, and said out loud, "Sorry, April. It's for a good cause."

She beat Bradley back to the foyer. When he came back down, he looked like a different person. He was still wearing his jeans, but he'd combed his hair and put on a Polo shirt. And shoes. With no socks.

"Nice car!" he said when they were out on the driveway. He stepped into Simone's white Lexus.

Yes. It was. She was about to tell him it was a "gift" from Travis last birthday (because she always bought her own gift then informed Travis that it was from him) but Bradley interrupted her.

"Tell me we're not going to Grover's," he said. "I hate that place."

"Why didn't they hire you back?" she asked, pulling out of the driveway. *She'd* worked at a grocery store when *she* was a teenager. She knew it was a common practice—at least, a long *time* ago, anyway—for new ownership to eliminate the current employees and take back only the best ones. Based on all she'd observed thus far, it wouldn't surprise her if Bradley hadn't been one of the best ones.

"I don't know," he said. "The new manager said he checked my records, and I was missing too many days—said I was late to work a lot, too. Not *my* fault my mom doesn't get me a car."

Clearly, Bradley enjoyed playing the blame game, another pet peeve of Simone's. She could totally see why the new management had overlooked him.

"You don't drive?" she asked.

"I got my license, but I'm not on the insurance," he said. "I was saving to buy a car, and then I lost my job."

"Why didn't you just go somewhere else?" Simone asked. *How ridiculous*, she thought, *although pathetic is more the word.*

He sighed loud and long. "I don't know. It all just sucks. It pisses me off, too. They hired back all the people they *should* have fired, only no, they fire *me*."

"Oh yeah?" she asked. "Like who?" Simone had certainly done her fair share of hiring and firing in her day, so she was curious what would prompt a manager of a grocery store to fire or hire someone.

"Well, like the bakery bitch. What a troll," he said. "She's so fucking rude. And then there's this one cashier I'm convinced steals from everyone."

Simone wasn't buying *that*. Not with all the surveillance cameras these days. Obviously, Bradley just had a big chip on his shoulder. Obviously, he didn't understand the concept of unions.

She pulled into the parking lot at Grover's and almost laughed when he yelled, "No! *Why*?" But the corners of his mouth were turned up, just a little.

So she said, "Let's just check it out. We'll hold our heads up high and show those fuckers you just don't care."

This made Bradley smile. For real, now.

Then *Simone* had to smile when they were getting garlic bread at the bakery because the woman behind the counter really *was* a troll. Bradley was smiling right back at her as if to say *see?* And if Simone had cared about making a new friend, she'd say the two of them bonded a little just then.

When they eventually made it to the checkout line, Simone was in such a flurry, throwing their cart's items onto the rolling counter (*how DID Travis stand this? She* just wanted to get it over with and get *out* of there!) that she didn't notice the tall, African-American man standing right behind her in line. Until she backed into him, that is. He was so firm and solid that she practically bounced right off of him. She spun around, quickly, her first reaction that of placing her hands on his forearms, which were loaded with grocery items. Her hands felt miniscule on his smooth, dark skin.

"I'm so sorry!" she said. She wasn't sure what it was that caused her to take special notice of this man.

She'd never given a perfect stranger a second look before. But Simone Sanders was mesmerized. Was it his eyes? They were green as green could be, almost outlined with two dark circles. As stunning as the color was, it was more than that. They were almost...holy. So warm, so loving and yet so cutting. So sharp.

Maybe it was his mouth that captivated her. His lips were sculpted to perfection. No plastic surgeon could *ever* hope to replicate *those*. When he smiled, one side rose a little higher than the other, revealing a row of straight, white teeth. Maybe it was the two, sharp canines on the sides that were of special interest to Simone. *Character teeth.* They gave his smile a touch of personality.

Or maybe it wasn't his physical looks at *all*. Maybe it was his spirit, his aura. His attitude. He was strength. He was calm. He was the embodiment of pure peace. This guy had it all under control.

Rarely did anyone ever make such a powerful impression on her, so she wasn't sure what it was that caused her to think so many thoughts about him, all at once. But it wasn't as if the thoughts had actual words, forming in her mind. Not at all. This was more of a spirit thing—something that couldn't be put into words. Or if it could, perhaps just *one* word: *damn!* That about summed up her primal evaluation of the tall, dark customer at Grover's.

After their grocery line collision, he just smiled at her and took a step back to give her some space. The corners of his eyes crinkled a bit—she guessed he was in his 40's. She chalked him up as a typical male who only got better-looking with age. He had no moustache, which probably contributed to his youthful looks. She felt awkward all of a sudden, and it was such a foreign feeling for her. Simone *never* felt awkward.

In her nervousness, she asked him if he'd like to go ahead of her.

Still smiling (if she didn't know better, she'd say he was smiling *at* her, like she was a five-year-old acting cute) he said *no, I'm good. But thank you.* Even his voice was calm and peaceful. Not quiet. But smooth. And intentional.

Simone was relieved to get to turn her attention to the checkout girl, who greeted Bradley with a *hey hey, Bradley, what's up?* She obviously had a crush on him, but why wouldn't she? Bradley was cute. The girl asked him if he'd be coming back to work, and he told her no, unfortunately he wouldn't.

"Can you believe that?" asked Simone, interrupting their brief conversation. The girl said *no,* looked passed Simone then quickly went back to scanning the remaining items in silence. While Bradley bagged everything (skillfully at that—Simone was impressed) she couldn't help but sense the tall, dark man's presence near her. He wasn't standing particularly close—he certainly wasn't invading her personal space or anything—but it was as if his body was surrounded by an energy field that only *her* energy field could pick up on. She wanted to close her eyes and lean into him—or not *him*, per se, but the *idea* of him.

She couldn't help but look back at him one last time before she and Bradley walked off with their fully loaded grocery cart. She only saw the man's profile this time. But it was a smiling profile, the same smile as before, as though he were smiling at a five-year-old old acting cute.

"Oh wow, what is that smell?"

It was April, home from work, walking all the way from the front door to the kitchen at the back of the house.

"What is *this* I see? Bradley? Cooking dinner?"

Simone rolled her eyes. Maybe she was tired and *that* was why she felt grumpy. *But have a clue, April! Why chide your kid for doing something nice? YOU might think it's all in good fun, but give me a break!* April was so not cool.

Once she and Bradley had returned home from Grover's, the pace had been non-stop. First, they had to bring all the groceries into the house. Putting them away had been another nightmare. It had almost made Simone appreciate Travis for always doing all the grocery crap their entire marriage.

Then they had made sandwiches—one for MeeMaw, of course, and they'd made themselves a couple as well. As an afterthought, Simone had even prepared and tucked away an extra one for MeeMaw for the following day in the event Bradley felt too lazy to fix her anything. That is, if he even got out of bed!

Then after they'd eaten lunch, Bradley told Simone he'd show her how to make banana bread. He mashed the brown bananas in a mixing bowl and added who knows what. Butter? Baking powder? She really hadn't cared to pay attention let alone take notes. It wasn't like she'd ever use this skill in the future. But she'd appeased him by pulling up a barstool and displaying artificial interest.

After he'd popped the loaf into the oven and they'd cleaned up the mess, Bradley suggested they start dinner so his mother wouldn't have to after a long day of work. If Simone didn't know any better, she'd say that Bradley was stalling. *Hmm. He must enjoy my company or something. Either that or the kid's just plain lonely,* she'd told herself, marveling that such a good-looking boy his age had nothing better to do than to spend an afternoon with such a has-been like *her.*

So *this* time, she made herself useful, chopping onions and browning the sausage and ground beef for the lasagna. Bradley did everything else.

"When did you become such a great cook?" she asked, impressed with his know-how.

But he didn't seem to want to talk about it. In fact, for the next several minutes, his smile disappeared, like he was too immersed in his present task to cook *and* talk at the same time. *Oh well.* She'd ask April about it, later.

And now it was later. She grabbed April by the arm and ushered her out of the room.

"Why are you making such a big deal out of your son cooking dinner?" she said softly, so Bradley wouldn't hear. "Leave him alone. Just be glad he's not in bed, sleeping!"

Simone certainly intended her comments to cast judgment. A normal person probably would have taken offense to this reprimand. But not so April. She just did a silent *oh!* then retreated to her bedroom. Simone followed right behind her but stopped in the doorway. She watched as April set her purse on her nightstand—watched as she sat on the edge of her bed, taking off her shoes. April moaned.

"Oh, my feet are *killing* me."

Killing you? HOW? Simone wondered because April's shoes were boring and flat. Just like April. And it wasn't like April was on her feet all day.

She looked up at Simone. "Did you talk to Travis at all?" she asked.

But Simone really didn't want to get into it. Why? And besides, April would probably think she was a fool for folding Jen's laundry the way she had. Who *does* that? Although, now it made her want to laugh a little. *Wait till Jen tells Travis that I folded Robby's clothes.*

She just shook her head no by way of answer and changed the subject. "How did Bradley get to be such a good cook?" she asked.

April rubbed the heel of one foot, then the other.

"Pure necessity," she said. "When his dad left us, I had to work full time—"

"Yeah, I know," she interjected so April wouldn't sidetrack and go into every last detail of *that* whole train wreck.

"And Bradley was only thirteen at the time."

That all-important age, thought Simone.

"So he was pretty young, and I guess it was fun for him at the time to surprise me with dinner. He got really good at it. I wish he'd cook more often! But nowadays, he doesn't really get into it too much."

No, thought Simone. *He doesn't really get into anything, much.*

April's eyes filled with tears although she smiled super big.

"Thank you, Simone," she said. "I haven't seen

him this happy in a long time."

This was happy?

"I really didn't do anything," she said. Because she hadn't. What did she do except get him off his ass to help MeeMaw?

April started to get up. But before she could get any crazy idea in her head about walking over and getting all mushy and huggy, Simone said, "I think dinner's ready," and walked out of the room.

Dinner was delicious. Or at least, the three or four bites she'd eaten were delicious. April had set the table and they'd even wheeled MeeMaw out, special. The conversation was pleasant—mostly April talking about the Sunset Supermarket account and then Bradley telling her how they'd gone to Grover's that day to buy food. "It still has the Grover's sign," he'd told her.

"Simone, I'll give you some money to reimburse you for all the groceries," said April.

"No, that's not necessary," said Simone. "It's my treat."

"No, I can't let you do that!" said April, starting to get up from the table.

"April." Now her voice was stern. April sat back down. "I mean it. It's the least I can do."

Once April was okay with Simone's grocery offering, she switched gears and went on and on about how glad she was that Simone would be returning to work the next day and how badly everyone needed her help for the Sunset Supermarket grand opening event, "Which is scheduled Memorial Day weekend!" Simone could only roll her eyes and check her phone.

She had a text from Travis.

Thought you were coming by tonight.

Crap. She had honestly forgotten all *about* that after all the day's distractions, plus it had never been her real intent to *talk* to Travis. He was only supposed to discover her body…it had completely slipped her mind.

He'd sent the text a couple hours before. She noticed it was now after 7:00. She thought a moment, then feeling in complete control, she texted:

Woops. Maybe tomorrow? Will Jen still be there?

Maybe she could do the deed tomorrow if the coast was clear. Or maybe not.

I won't be around tomorrow. How about Thursday?

And little did the unsuspecting Travis realize it, but *that* served as the inspiration for Simone's Plan B. She smiled, wickedly, and with slow, calculated deliberation texted:

Sure. I'll meet you in your office at 4:30 during office hours. See you Thursday.

Chapter Six

Her suicide was reading like a novel.

The house was quiet. Bradley was asleep, what else was new? MeeMaw was napping in her room. April was at work.

Simone felt all alone. All alone in the big, two story house that wasn't even hers. She hadn't even realized what a pain in the ass it was to live out of a suitcase, so disturbed was she. It was all so confusing.

How does a person go from sheer happiness to utter despair in just a matter of moments? Before she'd walked into her bedroom that one fateful night, only to discover that Travis was having an affair, she'd had such a spring to her step. Her cup had literally spilled over, so abundantly filled was it with joy. She and her lover boy were off to Hawaii to celebrate her 50th year, how exciting! Life was good.

But just like Travis had killed all her hopes and dreams for a lifetime of happiness by screwing one of his students, by turning himself into a soon-to-be father to somebody else's child, by abandoning Simone on such a milestone birthday, he had also killed her physically. Of course, he didn't know this. Yet. But he'd soon find out.

For Simone was carefully preparing to give Travis the biggest surprise of his life, and no, it was not a Brazilian wax this time. All the same, she wanted to look perfect. So she showered and washed and dried her hair. She didn't curl it. Just left it straight. Travis always liked the messy look on her. Said it made her look as though she had FFH, which was their little code for *Freshly Fucked Hair*, like she'd just enjoyed a romp in bed.

"He'll get the message," she told her reflection in the bathroom mirror.

She went a little heavy on the make-up. This was for the papers. Should anyone photograph her, post mortem, she would look good. Even in death.

She put on her wedding earrings. And that's about all she put on. The only garment she intended to wear beneath her trench coat was a pair of white lace panties. These, too, would send a message: Office Hours. He would get the subtle meaning.

Satisfied that she couldn't make herself look any more appealing—*such a shame all this beauty must go to waste*—she dug a pair of high heeled shoes out of the bathroom drawer. She didn't know why they were here in the drawer, but why not? They may as well be. Nothing was organized in her life anymore.

I hope I can find my camo trench coat, she thought. She searched for it in the bedroom closet. *Aha, here it is!*

Her mind was in such a haze—all her confused thoughts. She couldn't even remember driving to the college campus where Travis worked. Nor did she have any recollection of where she'd parked her Lexus. She'd left a note on the windshield: *Give this to Bradley. He needs a car.*

The next thing she knew, she was in Travis' office. Except it looked different, now. How long had it been since she'd last paid him a visit? *Hmm. Well.* This would be the end-all of *all* visits. Literally.

He wasn't here, yet. She knew she had to hurry because time was running out. So she took her letter out of her coat pocket and tried to read it, but she couldn't see one word. It was all a blur. She set it on his desk and weighted it down with her wedding ring, which she'd also dug out of her coat pocket.

She glanced around the room. *Should I lie on top of his desk,* she wondered? *Or across the floor by the door?* That way he'd trip over her on his way in. His office wasn't too spacious.

No. She'd lie on his desk. She cleared herself a space, and amidst some books and papers and pencils and pens and Travis' phone, she carved out a little nook for herself.

Here goes. Her heart was pounding now. *This is it. This is the end,* she thought. *I'll just close my eyes* (she closed her eyes) *and die!*

She had no idea how *good* it felt to die! It was the deepest most relaxing sleep she'd ever had—a sleep from which she never cared to return. She just wanted to drift *deeper* and *deeper* into her state of nothingness. Into her state of nothing but darkness.

She didn't even feel scared when Travis' desk turned into an 18th century, wooden coffin. She never once felt afraid when she heard them nailing the lid shut. Tap tap tap. Nope. Simone was in a deep, deep sleep…she didn't care to wake up.

"Wake up." Tap tap tap.

It was April, softly knocking on the bedroom door. She had opened it just a crack. "Simone," she whispered loudly. "Wake up! I need you to come to work today. *Please* get up."

Simone opened one eye. The room was dark, but she could see April's shadowy form, standing in the doorway.

Simone wiped the drool off the side of her cheek and closed her mouth. She shifted position to lie on her back and crisscrossed her wrists over the bridge of her nose.

"What time is it?" she asked, but it came out almost in a whisper, her throat was so dry.

"It's almost 6:00. I didn't know how long it would take you to get ready, so I thought I'd give you an early wake-up call."

Simone groaned and rolled on her other side, facing away from the lady of the house.

"April, no," she said, weakly. "I don't think I can go in today."

April almost gasped. "But you *have* to! Simone, it's an important day. We're putting together the poster before the big meeting."

The "poster" was Simone's term for Concept Board. Anytime Com Corp planned an event of major proportions, they put one together—"they" meaning Simone, of course. But not this time. In her absence, the poster had logically defaulted to April.

"April, you don't need me. You'll do fine!"

Now April's voice sounded like pure panic. "No, I can't do it, Simone. Not like you! And rumor has it the owner of Sunset Supermarkets is an *asshole*—very hard to please. And we're meeting with him in just two days! This account is *huge*! Meredith is freaking *out*. Do you know how many stores are in California—how many are eventually starting up in Ohio?"

Simone shook her head no. She really didn't care, either.

"A *lot*! If we do a good job, there will be plenty

more grand openings. Meredith says we can all retire on *this* account alone. And if I mess things up, Simone—" April couldn't finish her thought because now she was crying. Full on *crying*.

Simone sat up. "Good *grief*, April!"

And it was at that moment Simone had to weigh her options: go to work? Or sit here and listen to April cry? She hated it when April cried!

She chose to go to work. Besides, her fateful meeting with Travis would not occur for another couple of days. At least this would keep her busy. Give her something to do rather than mope around and cry herself a river all day. Then she'd be no better than April!

So she comforted her by telling her *okay, okay, I'll come to work*. She told her to go on ahead of her. She didn't want to ride to work *with* April lest it arouse suspicion.

"Just tell me you haven't told anyone about me and Travis," she said.

April shook her head no.

"You didn't tell anyone I'm staying at your house."

Again, April shook her head.

So when Simone walked through the front door of Com Corp a couple hours later and Heidi smiled and mumbled a *hello* and Jodi made a sad face and said *hi, Simone* and when Meredith acted like everything was calm—like they had nothing at all to do, like they *weren't* in accelerated stress mode—Simone stopped in her tracks. She looked over at April, and if eyes could talk, hers would have said *really?* April just mouthed out *I'm sorry!*

"Welcome back, Simone," said Meredith. "I'm sure you don't care to talk about anything that's been going on with you, recently. But please know that we're all here for you. We all support you."

Now. In her usual frame of mind, Simone would have said something very sarcastic. Or something like *yeah, Meredith, you're right. I DON'T want to talk to any of you about anything.* And then she'd look around at everybody and say *what the hell are you all just standing there for? Get your asses in gear and let's get this account DONE. Today!*

But now, Simone was like a balloon that had run out of helium, hovering a little above the floor. She was too tired, too drained to expend that kind of energy on one of her biggest pet peeves, which was allowing anyone to feel sorry for her.

So she just looked around the room and said, "Thank you, Meredith. Yeah. It's really hard to talk about it right now, so I'd prefer not to. But I do appreciate your concern, everyone." And this seemed to suffice. It apparently also inspired unusual gratuities by her coworkers.

Jodi brought her a coffee. Heidi volunteered to answer her calls that morning. April updated Simone on the poster. And Meredith shut herself up in her office. Thus began her work day.

"April, I'm really impressed by the great job you did on the poster." April beamed like she was a kindergartener whose teacher had just told her she was Helper of the Day. She even sat up a little straighter, not in her usual slumping posture. "I'm particularly impressed with the check list."

"Heidi helped me with that," said April. *Of course, leave it to April to give credit where credit was due.* Never would Simone have allowed someone working under her to get any credit, the rationale being *they only did what I told them to do.*

And never would Simone do what she did just now. She turned her attention to Heidi and said, "I couldn't have done it better myself."

It wasn't *entirely* true. Simone was a stickler for details, and *no* one could ever do it *better*! But it looked to her like Heidi had thought of everything, from the contact list to the fire permits to the volunteer and security kits. Every T was crossed.

"In fact, Heidi, I would like to put you in charge the day of the grand opening."

Now it was Heidi's turn to look like a little kid on Christmas morning. But for Heidi, this was better than a pony. This was Heidi's *dream.* Over the past two years that she'd been with the company, she'd always begged Simone to give her more responsibility. But Simone had a policy of either doing everything herself or assigning the major tasks to other, more experienced employees from different teams. She never felt that *her* team with novices Heidi and Jodi and flaky April was trustworthy enough, insofar as obsessive compulsive expectations were concerned.

Com Corp had 20 employees, managing an average of 10 major events a month, along with a few minor. They were mainly corporate events. As senior project manager, Simone delegated accounts to teams of four. She along with April, Heidi, and Jodi were a team together. Meredith, the owner, oversaw *all* the teams, lending support wherever she was needed.

Simone sometimes envied Meredith because *her* job was easy! She really didn't need to do any thinking or planning. Meredith's main talent was marketing and sales, and she really knew how to lure the clients in. *She* never had to "get dirty in the trenches." She couldn't! Everyone always said that stress and Meredith didn't mix. So it was *Simone* who had to talk clients off the ledge. It was *Simone* who had to solve the unforeseen problems that inevitably cropped up all the time.

But that's what Simone did best. And that's why they were all looking at her right now with shocked expressions. Not that Simone paid much attention.

She broke the silence by asking, "So when do we meet with the asshole owner?"

Meredith couldn't help but let out a brief laugh, then she looked at the notebook on her lap. "Thursday."

"Okay, I want Jodi to handle all the visuals and handouts. And I want Heidi to present. April, you sit and take detailed notes of the client's requests. I don't even know his name. What's his name?"

"Desmond Reynolds," said Meredith. "As you may know, Simone, Sunset Supermarkets is a privately owned, California chain of about 112 stores. But just to fill you in, our client's son is taking over the new Ohio branch, and he's communicated to us that he chose Com Corp based on our good reputation—he knows we're a *small* company, but he's intimated that he'll continue to use us if he's satisfied with the service we provide. So we've *got* to get this right."

Meredith looked at Simone over her black

reading glasses. They seemed so dark against her milky white complexion and blonde hair. Meredith was 10 years older than Simone but *she* didn't have any wrinkles. Then again, her face had more surface area. Perhaps this gave the skin more room to stretch. She was a larger woman than Simone. Tall. Whatever pounds she'd accumulated over the years were born of motherhood to three grown children, all on their own now and dispersed across the U.S. and Canada. Her more recent pounds were the afterbirth of nightly, liquid medication from "the divorce" dating way back to when her last child graduated high school. Meredith sure loved her collection of fine wines.

"Why is he coming to Ohio?" It was a good question, wasn't it? Why set up shop in Ohio?

"He has family here."

Meredith went on to give Simone the details for the meeting although she didn't need to. Simone knew the drill. As usual, they'd meet the client for happy hour at The Fajita Grill, preferably at 4:00. Meredith was so cheap. Despite this client potentially bringing in big business, if she could get away with $3 cocktails and chips and salsa, by golly she would!

Simone said, "Sounds good. I'm sure my team will do great."

There was a pause, then April said, "You're coming *with* us. Right, Simone?"

Simone shook her head.

Meredith cleared her throat and said something to the effect of *no, let's not pressure Simone into a meeting right now. She's got enough on her plate.*

This was typical Meredith. At least where Simone was concerned. Simone was the one employee

Meredith had a healthy fear of. Their relationship was like that of a Rottweiler to a feisty cat, Simone being the cat. The Rottweiler might have more muscle and power and could devour the cat if it chose to do so, but the cat always maintained the psychological edge. Meredith could never be too sure if Simone would purr and rub against her leg or scratch her eyes out. And Simone was *far* too valuable to Meredith, so like an intimidated dog avoiding eye contact with its nemesis, she always looked the other way to keep Simone happy.

Simone could tell that April wished to protest. She opened then shut her mouth. But unlike Simone, April would never have the balls to go up against the big boss. And before anyone could say anything more, Simone concluded the meeting. Besides, it was lunchtime.

Her team shocked her by inviting her to lunch with them. Her coworkers *never* socialized with her. Not that it was their choice. It was Simone's preference to ride solo in her career. So if anyone was shutting anyone out, clearly it was Simone. She had everyone trained to just leave her the hell alone.

All the same, she smiled and thanked them for the offer, "but I think I'll have to decline," she said. "I think I'm going to call it a day." This inspired a room full of "sad face looks," but it was hard to tell if these were bred from genuine concern for a coworker enduring hardship or from fear that Mama Bird was leaving her babies to fend for themselves in the nest.

In any case, it made no difference to Simone, who felt compelled to check in on MeeMaw. What on earth was getting into her? She chalked up her feelings as hormones gone haywire because if anyone had told her a year ago that she'd ever care about someone's aging mother, she wouldn't have believed it. She didn't even care about her *own* aging mother. Which reminded her.

"Jodi? I need you to do something for me."

"I know." Jodi smiled. "Your mom's birthday is coming up."

"Damn, you're good!" said Simone, dishing out her second compliment of the year.

Jodi smiled to kingdom come.

It was a good thing Simone had gone to April's when she had. MeeMaw had just awakened from a snooze and needed a bathroom break. Simone had *wondered* how this was accomplished, and now she knew. With Simone's assistance, getting her to her bathroom via the walker, MeeMaw was able to lower herself down to the toilet by holding onto the custom railings. Right before she did this, all Simone had to do was reach up underneath MeeMaw's nightgown and gently pull down her "granny panties." Normally, it was Bradley who was graced with this task, so Simone was relieved to realize he didn't get to see "anything important," as MeeMaw jokingly put it. Once that was accomplished, MeeMaw could do the rest. When she was finished, her sweet voice called from the other side of the bathroom door.

Now it was Wednesday, and Simone's other question about MeeMaw was answered. *How on earth does she shower or bathe?*

She was delighted to learn that every

Wednesday and Saturday without fail, three ladies from MeeMaw's church came over and drove MeeMaw to a facility that basically took care of all her grooming needs. Of course, Simone would have required this to be a daily service were *she* in MeeMaw's predicament, but she supposed the older generation had different views about cleanliness. Simone's World War II era parents were once-a-weekers as far as hair washing was concerned. When she'd asked them about it during her teen years (when for *her*, daily showers were a must), they'd just told her *when you grow up with cold water, you wash your hair once a week!*

April was at work. Bradley was in his room. MeeMaw was with "her girls." So Simone figured this was as good an opportunity as any to make one last, final phone call to her mother.

She plopped herself down on the leather couch in Bradley's boy cave, sighed, and dialed her mom's number.

"Hi, Simone!"

Oh great. She was sounding way too optimistic and hopeful. Simone decided to let her down quickly.

"How was Hawaii? Did you get my birthday card?"

"Yeah, Mom. Um. I'm afraid I have some bad news."

She could picture her mom's smile morphing into a frown.

"What's the matter, Honey? Are you okay?"

"No, Mom, not really," she said.

This was so weird. Simone wasn't used to doing what she was about to do, which was spill her soul to her mother. Well. Not about *everything*, of course. Just the part about Travis. Normally, it wouldn't occur to Simone to sell him out. She'd always been his staunchest defender and protector, especially to her own family—she'd always painted a picture that Travis was the best thing since sliced bread, and they never argued with her. But now she wanted *someone* out there (before her impending demise) to know what a scoundrel he was.

So she told her mother everything. She left no detail uncovered, from her first step into the bedroom, to her conversations with him from her cell phone on the beach in Oahu. She told her about her encounter with Jen. She left emotion out of the equation, basically stating the facts.

Her mother listened without a word. She just let Simone go on and on. And because of this, Simone felt like a little bit of pressure from her chest was let out in however long it took to tell her sad story which was what, twenty minutes?

When she wrapped things up, her mom let out a big sigh. "Simone. I am so sorry. I don't know what to say. I can only imagine how you feel."

What? This sounded odd. "Mom, what do you mean you can only *imagine* how I feel? How did you feel when you lost *your* husband?"

"Well, that was different," she said. "He didn't walk out on me. He died."

"So how is that different? Loss is loss! Weren't you devastated?"

Not that Simone would have any recollection. When her father had died, she was miles away, living her life in Ohio with Travis. Her mother's emotional state had never made a blip on Simone's radar.

And then her mom rocked Simone's world. Rocked its very foundation. Her mother, whom she thought was the total devoted wife, accommodating to a tee, had lived a phony life.

"Simone…I didn't love your father."

What on earth was she talking about? *How could she not love Dad?* Her mom was always by her dad's side as far back as she could remember. They never argued. They never fought.

"How can you say that, Mom? If you didn't love him, how could stay together with him for forty-five years?"

"Simone, the way I was brought up, you didn't leave your spouse. You stuck together no matter what."

"Don't give me that, Mom. Two of your siblings divorced their spouses! Why did *you* have to be the exception?"

"It's complicated, Simone. I didn't *hate* your father. He was good to me—in his own way, I suppose. As long as I played along with him, everything was fine. Sure, I shed a few tears when he passed away, but I've never really missed him." She paused. "Maybe I shouldn't be telling you all this—"

"No, Mom, I'm glad you are," said Simone. And if only for those few brief moments, she felt the tiniest connection to her mother. Not by shared experience—she'd always been gaga for Travis—but through *communicating.* Woman to woman. *Finally.* Being real with her mom was such a welcome first! But unfortunately, she had to get on with things.

"Mom, I hope you'll understand, but I won't be able to come out for your birthday."

She knew how much it would mean for her mom to have her daughter *be* there for her on her special day. Simone knew she was letting her down big time, so she braced herself for the worst. She expected tears. She expected a major guilt trip. What she got was a total surprise.

She got understanding.

"No, Honey, I wouldn't expect you to come out. Not now! Good heavens, you have a lot to sort out. If anything, I should come out to see *you*."

And while it would be the last thing Simone would ever want—a visit from her mother, pointless as that would be—she was touched by the thought all the same.

"Oh, Mom, it's okay," she said. "You know me. I've got a handle on this. I've got everything under control."

Her mom laughed a little although it wasn't a happy laugh. "Yes, Honey, I know. You're a trooper."

"I'll get you a refund on the plane tickets," she said.

"Oh, don't worry about that," said her mother. "I'll take care of it."

"Mom. No. Please let *me* take care of it." *It's the least I can do,* she thought. *My last good deed for you.*

Her mom protested a little more till Simone got that tone to her voice—then her mom crumbled. She always crumbled. Her voice trembled a little when she told her daughter goodbye, and this caused Simone to choke up. A *lot*. She felt stupid, too, because when she hung up, she noticed Bradley was standing there.

She quickly swiped her cheek. "Hey," she said.

"Hey."

He sat sort of next to her on the couch and put his bare feet up on the ottoman. And this made her *really* want to cry.

Because in the best way this young, teenaged boy knew how to do, he was comforting her. With silence. By his presence. The close proximity of his body next to hers was all she needed in that moment. He must've heard every word of her conversation. And now he knew. Now he knew why she was invading his home.

Simone had no idea exactly how long they sat there together.

Chapter Seven

"I promise not to stay here much longer."

April looked up from the huge mess she was making on the dining room table, which had completely transformed from a few hours before. A few hours before, it had served as a gathering place for four tea-sipping old ladies. When MeeMaw's friends brought her home from her grooming appointment (and lunch), they had all gathered around the table for their Wednesday afternoon Bible study. Although, it sounded more like a bunch of adolescents at a sleepover. When Simone had tried to slip by the room to grab herself a slice of banana bread from the kitchen, they had reeled her in to their little world for a few animated moments.

"You guys are having way too much fun," said Simone, and this caused a wave of laughter.

"We're just plotting," said MeeMaw.

"Plotting and planning," said a blue-haired woman on the other side of the table.

When Simone raised her eyebrow, MeeMaw said, "Don't tell April, but we're setting her up on a date!"

This caused Simone to smile. *April? On a date? Really?* She didn't mean to be rude, but she said, "With *who*?"

Who would go out with April? She felt bad for thinking this, but honestly. The woman had zero game. April couldn't pull a tooth let alone a man!

"With someone she's had *googly* eyes on," said another of MeeMaw's cronies. A second wave of laughter filled the room.

"Oh, so you're a bunch of meddling little matchmakers!" said Simone to a table full of smiles. *How cute ARE they? They're like the Old Lady Club!*

So now, sitting across from April at the messy, messy table, she couldn't help but want to tease April about it. She just didn't know how to bring it up, which was why she thought she'd begin with, "I promise not to stay here much longer."

"Simone, you can stay here as long as you like!" said April. She set down her scissors next to a pile of colorful papers. April was scrapping, as she called it. Apparently, working in her scrapbooks was April's way of "unwinding" whenever she felt overwhelmed by life. Which baffled Simone. Just the sight of all this crap (all over the table) *gave* her stress. She'd even asked April *HOW do you possibly find this relaxing?*

But April had explained to her it was a hobby of hers. She said it was her goal to put together a compilation of Bradley's life. "Not that *Bradley* cares to have a record like this," she'd told her. "But his future wife might like it. So I do this with *her* in mind." It was as if by saying it out loud, it would come to pass, and April's face immediately reflected the comfort this happy thought undoubtedly brought her.

"You've been so nice, April, but I just want you to know I don't plan to keep on taking advantage of your hospitality and kindness."

Now April's face completely lost its smile. "Simone, I don't see it that way at all. I know what's happening to you is awful. It's horrible what you're going through. But you are a *godsend*, Simone."

???

Simone had no response. A godsend? *How does she figure?* April filled in the silence.

"You have brought *joy* to our home, Simone."
Joy?

"April, are you feeling okay?" She leaned over and put her hand on April's forehead for dramatic effect.

"No, I mean it," said April, crying now.

"Oh good grief, April, *stop* it," said Simone.

But April continued to cry. And cry. She was beside herself. Simone walked to the kitchen counter, ripped a paper towel off the roll, and thrust it at April so she could blow her nose with it.

When April calmed down a bit, she said, "You know, I look at these pictures of Bradley when he was a little boy, and...." her voice became a squeak. "It breaks my heart."

There were *tons* of photos of Bradley. And it came as no surprise to Simone when April had told her she was only on album number eight, which meant Bradley's eighth year of life. But she could already see why this was such a major project—the books were so elaborate! Simone picked up a picture of Bradley, decked out in his baseball uniform. His little boy smile knew no limits. He radiated happiness...energy...life. *Potential.*

"Is this your ex?" asked Simone, referring to the man on one knee next to Bradley.

"Yes. He always coached Bradley's teams when he was in Little League. This was one of our best seasons—or so I thought."

Simone's eyes popped. *Damn, April!* she

wanted to say. *How did YOU ever get THIS guy?* Not that he was better looking than Travis or anything. He was certainly not anything Simone would give a second glance at. But he was way too cute for April. *Clearly*, he was out of her league. At least, *now* she knew where Bradley got his good looks.

"What happened, April?"

She intended for it to sound ambiguous, like *what happened that season?* But now she really wanted to hear about April's ex. She'd heard the gist of the divorce before but hadn't paid much attention to the details.

"He destroyed our family, Simone. This here season was the beginning of the end for us because he slept with a mom from our team." Here she had to collect herself. "The affair lasted *four years*. And then one day he left us. I felt *so* blindsided. So *stupid*."

Boy, do I know the feeling! thought Simone.

"You must have been devastated," she said.

April nodded. "But not just for me," she said. "For Bradley. He hurt Bradley the most."

"I can imagine," said Simone.

"No. I mean *really* hurt Bradley." She was barely speaking above a whisper now, as if her son were in the kitchen instead of upstairs. "Bradley *worships* his father. But his father can't seem to make any time for him. He's only visited him *three* times in the past *three* years! He just strings him along, Simone. Gives him all these empty promises, telling him he can come live with him and his new family, only it never happens. He doesn't even have Bradley over for a visit. Bradley doesn't even know his half-brothers!"

"April, I'm so sorry." She didn't know what

else to say.

"He doesn't even pay child support half the time. And then Bradley takes his anger out on *me* when I can't afford something for him, like a car. I can't *buy* him a car! And then he kept missing school, and I couldn't deal with *that* anymore, so I let him drop out. And ever since losing his job at Grover's, he just sleeps all the time." She was crying again. "He's just always so depressed. But since *you've* been here, he comes out of his room. You get him to *do* things. I've even seen him smile a few times. And I will always be grateful to you, Simone."

Wow. She'd had no clue! All this time, she'd just chalked Bradley up as a lazyass. *But he really isn't a bad kid.*

"He's not a bad kid, April," she said.

"No," said April, blowing her nose into the paper towel again. "No. He's not. He's a good boy. It's just that he needs so much more than I can give him. I'd give him the *world* if I could, Simone. If I could wipe all his sadness away, I'd do it."

For a long time after that, neither one of them spoke. Simone, not quite knowing what she was doing, picked up some scraps and started making a colorful border around a blank page. April slid three pictures in Simone's direction across the table. Their eyes met, and April smiled. Simone arranged the pictures inside the center of her nice, new frame. Then she added other embellishments for decoration. *Hmm. Maybe this IS therapeutic.* It *did* take her mind off things. Until....

"Simone?"

"No."

"You don't even know what I was going to ask

you."

"Yes, I do. No."

She looked over at April. April stuck out her bottom lip. Simone narrowed her eyes to the size of a slit.

April stuck her bottom lip out a little farther. Simone rolled her eyes and picked up her phone, which had been resting *somewhere* among the debris on the table. After she sent the text, she showed it to April.

> **Sorry, Travis. I can't meet you tomorrow, after all. I have an important business meeting.**

April smiled and hummed a little tune as she and Simone went back to scrapping. Simone didn't even have the heart to tease her about the Old Lady Club, scheming to set her up on a date. She would wait to bring that up some other time. *If* she was still around.

April, Heidi, and Jodi carpooled to The Fajita Grill together. Simone rode with Meredith in the company Mercedes.

She could see that like her, Meredith had also dressed to perfection for the big event: the presentation to Desmond Reynolds. Not that they hadn't looked nice in the office earlier that day. But it was obvious they'd all refreshed their make-up and changed into something that screamed *we are professionals—we know what we're doing!*

Even April was wearing heels. Back at the house, Simone had insisted. But April hadn't complained. *Much.* She figured at this point, April would go topless if that's what was asked of her. They both knew Simone was doing her a huge favor, attending this meeting.

Simone wasn't nervous like the rest of her team. On the contrary, she felt powerful. She was walking into the restaurant with the knowledge that this would be her last business meeting ever. She couldn't care less if they got the account. She couldn't care less if the client didn't like her. Although, this was not possible. She would wow his socks off, and she would do this in as few words as possible. Simone knew that an attitude of not caring was precisely the key to success that night.

Evidently, Meredith was not sharing this same feeling. Her red, manicured fingernails tapped on the steering wheel at every red light. She'd sighed at least three times since they'd stepped into the car. Why she would be anxious, Simone couldn't understand. Well. Maybe she could. If Sunset Supermarkets set up as many stores as they had in California, this really *would* be Com Corp's biggest account ever. On the flipside, did Meredith really *need* this? Meredith was set for life. She could live to be a hundred and never experience one, tiny little financial worry.

Simone decided to distract her. "How are the kids, Meredith?"

Meredith always enjoyed talking about her children. Instantly, a smile replaced her frown as she went on and on about Courtney's new baby. "I wish I could see her more often, but they're in Canada, now." She mentioned Landon and his wife and their new business endeavor. "They're so busy all the time."

"Like mother like son," said Simone.

Meredith laughed. "Yes. Oh my, I taught them my bad habits, didn't I!"

Her youngest son, Chase, was "chasing his dream," as she put it, in New York as an editor for a major business magazine.

"Your kids are so accomplished. What's your secret, Meredith?" If Simone could lend a few tips to April, she would!

"I just instilled in them a strong work ethic," she said, looking at Simone, briefly. Simone could tell by her smile that Meredith felt very proud of herself. It even made Simone wonder, if only for a moment, how *her* life would be right now had she and Travis had any children. *Maybe we'd still be together*, she thought. *Maybe a few kids would have provided just enough of a distraction to keep us on the straight and narrow.* Then she shook her head and looked out the passenger window. *Maybe he'd have a conscience about screwing something the same age as a daughter!*

They pulled into the parking lot right behind the others. No one was talking, now. The only sounds were car doors and trunks opening and shutting and heels clacking on the asphalt. It was time to perform.

Simone had already pre-determined to take a backseat tonight. She was really only here to lend moral support, so she would play a wallpaper role and step in only when necessary. She didn't even help set up, much. She wanted to see what Heidi and Jodi were made of, and much to her surprise, they were extremely efficient. Of course, they'd all arrived long before the client was due. It would just be the owner today. *Easy peasy.*

They had requested a table in the back corner

of the room—their usual spot. They always sat the client in the corner, and with their own backs toward the other restaurant patrons, the ladies of Com Corp minimized distractions. It worked like a charm.

Once everything was all set up and perfect, as if on cue, in walked Desmond Reynolds. Simone's heart skipped a beat. Not because she recognized him. Not because he was dressed to perfection in a designer suit. It wouldn't surprise her in the slightest if it were a Brioni. But it wasn't because of this, nor was it because of his perfectly shaped sideburns and his exquisitely shaped eyebrows, emphasizing the green eyes she'd seen at Grover's a couple days before in the checkout line. No. Once again, it was his aura. His presence. She'd never experienced anything like it. If he were a rock star, she'd undoubtedly rip off her underwear and throw it at him.

They were all lined up as he walked in, although swagged in might be a better term. Desmond Reynolds exuded extreme confidence and class, and Simone could see that everyone knew it. Even April stood a little taller.

Simone was the last one in the line-up. *Her* hand he shook a little differently than everyone else's. When he looked into her eyes, or rather peered into the very depths of her soul, he got that same smile on his face that he'd had at the grocery store. She wouldn't say he shook her hand firmly, strongly, like two men would shake hands. But the way he grabbed her hand caused a feeling of utter safety to travel up her arm and into her whole body, like he had her. Like he was her own, personal bulwark. That one handshake made her feel as though as long as *he* was around, she could move freely about the country, safe and snug and secure with no worries whatsoever.

This completely caught her off guard. So much so she didn't even utter a greeting. She just stood there, mouth open. Gaping.

"I know you," he said.

She meant to agree with him and say *yes*. She meant to say *we bumped into each other at Grover's. Literally!* But all that came out was, "Grover's."

"Won't you sit down, Mr. Reynolds?" asked Meredith, gesturing toward the corner. But Desmond Reynolds said *after you* and waited politely for Simone and her team to be seated.

"And call me Des," he said, choosing the seat by the wall, across from Simone. Obviously, he didn't need Meredith dictating where he should sit.

Dez, she thought, liking the sound of it. Even his name was mysterious. *Although he probably spells it D-E-S.* She was right because of course, Jodi had to ask! In the past, Simone would have reprimanded her in the ladies' room for "being such an airhead." But at least *someone* was breaking the ice. As for Simone, she was completely useless. She didn't say *anything*. Anything whatsoever. She was mute.

Throughout the first part of the meeting, it didn't help that every time she looked up from her margarita, he was staring back at her with those eyes of his. *He's gotta be married*, she told herself. *He shouldn't be looking at me like this if he's married!*

But Des wasn't married. Come to find out, he'd been divorced for many years. He was the oldest of six in his family, and he had three grown children of his own. His eldest son, Dante, had fallen in love with

Ohio on a family visit one summer when he was a kid and had always determined to raise his own family here someday.

"I don't blame him," said Des. "I grew up here, so I know what I'm talking about."

He went on to explain that he was at a place in his life where it was time to pass the torch on to his kids. "My younger two want to manage the California stores with their mother. I'm just here to help Dante set up shop in Ohio. But he won't be coming out just yet. His wife is on bed rest till their baby is born in June, so he has to stay in California a couple more days until his mother-in-law can get out there and take over."

They oohed and aahed, even Simone who couldn't really relate to stories of babies, but she pretended to comprehend that this was a big event for Dante Reynolds.

"After the baby's born, my son and his family will be moving here," said Des, taking a sip of his water.

"So Dad got suckered in to getting things all set up!" said Meredith. Good thing *she'd* said that! If anyone else had said it, it might have come off wrong. But Meredith had a way of schmoozing with people. So Des just laughed, and this granted silent permission for everyone else at the table to laugh along with him.

"I guess you could say that," he said.

"Well, I think it's commendable of you to help him out like this," said Meredith. "Don't you agree, Simone?"

She'd caught Simone (who'd hoped that a little alcohol would calm her nerves) mid-sip of her margarita. Simone nodded and set her drink down. Or at least, she *meant* to set it down gracefully. Instead, her glass toppled over and *horror* of *horrors*, a liquid stream of tequila and ice headed straight for Des' lap! He tried to react by pushing his chair away from the table, but he couldn't go very far as his large stature was pinned against the wall. Unfortunately, his beautiful suit was splashed with Simone's former drink.

If *ever* she wanted to die, it was now. *Why did I come here?*

Simone knew Meredith felt horrified but didn't break with character. Not for one second. In typical Meredith stride, she calmly asked their server for more napkins.

"I'm so sorry," said Simone, putting a hand over her mouth.

Des just laughed and thanked the waiter for the napkins. "No harm, no foul," he said, wiping his pant leg. "It's just a dot, no worries."

And as if he could read Simone's embarrassed, very troubled mind, he went right back to talking about Sunset Supermarkets and what he envisioned for a grand opening on Memorial Day weekend. As if nothing had happened.

"I thought we could incorporate our men and women in uniform. Maybe do a military theme with camouflage colors."

Simone's internal temperature shot sky high. Hopefully, her cheeks weren't turning beet red. Hopefully, he couldn't see on her face how embarrassed she felt. She wished she had never in her entire life ever been called Rambo before.

Simone didn't remember much about the rest

of the three hour meeting. Meredith, of course, had to break out the company card, eventually, and order dinner. Simone just picked at hers. She was sure Heidi did a phenomenal job of presenting all the ideas they'd come up with. Even April had remembered to record all of Des' requests. And Jodi's handouts were fabulous. Their client seemed quite impressed and said as much when it was time to depart.

When he shook Simone's hand goodbye, he put his other hand on her shoulder blade. If she were a man, he might have given her a nice, firm pat. But no. The warmth of his touch permeated all the way to her bone marrow. She did manage to once again apologize for the spillage incident. He just smiled at her the way he'd smiled at her in line at Grover's. Then just as smoothly as he'd come in, Desmond Reynolds walked out the door.

Minutes later on their way to the car, Meredith said by way of nudge, "What do you know? He's not an asshole at all." Simone just nodded in agreement.

No. Just the opposite, she thought.

He was wonderful.

He was beautiful.

He was *Des*.

And for the first time in several melancholy days, if only for a little while, Simone Sanders forgot to think about dying.

Chapter Eight

Bright and early the next morning, it felt strange to walk up the winding, brick pathway to the front door of her own house. It felt like it was somebody else's house. Like she'd never lived here.

Simone flipped through her keys to find the one for the door but stopped when she heard crying. She assumed it was Robby, and he was *not* happy.

She sighed. *Why are they always here?* She paused a moment before knocking. But Jen must've seen her walk up and was already opening the front door. Her pale face looked troubled and pained.

"You look like hell," said Simone.

She did. Jen was wearing a robe and slippers. Her hair was a mess. Not a trace of make-up could be found on her gray, unsmiling face.

Unlike his mother, little Robby was dressed for the day. Even his hair was gel-ed into dark, spiky peaks on top. As if willing her out the front door, he was tugging on his mother's robe, leaning his head back in a big wail. Crocodile tears rolled down his puffy marshmallow cheeks. Jen braced herself with one hand on the doorjamb, saying *Robby, please stop.*

But he didn't stop. He continued to block the doorway, or rather, Simone's purpose for gaining entry, which was to pick up a few more clothes and the pile of mail Travis had left for her on the dining room table. When she'd canceled their meeting the night before, his only response to her text was: *you might want to pick up your mail. It's piling up on the table.*

She'd taken this as a green light to come over.

She figured she'd stop by the house, first, then get a refund for her mom's airline tickets. Maybe she'd pop by the office for a couple of hours—grace them with her presence. If Meredith was being lenient with her, why not take advantage of it? Plus, Meredith had thanked her and thanked her the entire car ride home last night just *for being there at the meeting.*

But she certainly hadn't anticipated *this.* She hadn't expected to encounter *Jen* again. And she especially hadn't thought she'd ever meet Jen's son.

"He's upset because he wants to go to school. It's the Spring Sing today, and he has a special part. But I'm too sick to take him. Oh my gosh, I can't do it!" And with that, Jen wrenched her robe out of Robby's clenched, little fingers and ran down the hall to the nearest bathroom. Robby ran after her, and Simone stepped into the foyer, only to hear the lovely sounds of Jen, retching into the toilet.

When she came out, she was blowing her nose and wiping her eyes with a big piece of toilet paper. Then she burst into tears. Simone couldn't decide who was crying harder. Mother? Or son?

"I have terrible morning sickness," she said. "Worse than the last time."

"Mommy, I want to *go...*!" wailed Robby. "You're making us *lay-hay-hate*!"

He had a super thick lisp.

Jen looked at Simone in sheer desperation. "Travis couldn't miss work today," she said, "or else he'd take him. I can't ask my mom because my parents aren't speaking to me ever since I told them I'm pregnant." She put her hand on her stomach. It was hard to hear her over Robby's cries.

Jen raised her eyebrows. "Simone? Do you think *you* could walk him down to the school real quick for me?"

What?

Robby's crying stopped. He looked up at Simone with his big, brown eyes, chock full of tears. His fate was in her hands. Even a five year-old could perceive this.

"Um…" She looked down at Robby. She looked at Jen. Then she looked back at Robby. "Okay. I guess so."

Robby's frown instantly turned upside down. Jen reached into her robe pocket for what Simone hoped was a fresh piece of tissue because she crouched beside Robby and wiped his cheeks with it. She told him to blow his nose, and he obediently complied. She dabbed his upper lip with the crumpled up tissue ball and stood upright. Robby grabbed the backpack that was on the floor, and she helped him put it on. It was as if he hadn't been crying at all. He was happy as could be. Simone thought *wow. If only it were that simple. Wait till you reach adulthood, Kid.*

Jen attempted a smile. "Simone, *thank* you. You don't know how much I appreciate this. Robby, what do you say to Simone?"

"Thank you, Simone," he said, looking up at her like she was Santa Claus in the flesh. Except he said her name "Thimone," and this made her laugh a little.

"Robby, take Simone to your classroom." Now she looked at Simone. "He knows where to go. Just tell Miss Harper to send him to Child Care after school. I'll have Travis pick him up later, after work."

Simone could only nod and stare at Jen, blankly. She waited as once again Jen crouched low to the ground so that Robby could give her a proper hug and kiss goodbye. Jen stood in the doorway as Simone and Robby walked down the brick walkway. Robby kept turning back around to wave. "Bye, Mommy!" he'd say each time. Jen waved back and blew kisses. She didn't close the door until they could no longer see each other.

Simone slowed down her pace when she realized Robby's little legs and feet were taking four steps to her two. The poor kid was practically running to keep up with her. But she just wanted to get there and leave and get on with her business.

"I have a *big* part!" he told her. "Miss Harper says it's the most important."

Simone nodded, looking at the school in the distance. They were obviously running late because there weren't many people around—just a few remnant cars were pulling out of the school parking lot. The crossing guard was still manning her station but from a sitting position, now, on a neon yellow fold-up chair.

Out of nowhere, Simone felt little fingers, grabbing onto her hand. It was the strangest, most unexpected sensation. Surprised, she looked down. Robby was smiling up at her. But as uncomfortable as she felt, she couldn't bring herself to let go of his little hand. *He* obviously thought nothing of it. He just acted as though this was standard operating procedure on how to walk to school. You held someone's hand. Even if it was the hand of a complete stranger who'd just shown up on your doorstep.

He chattered *on* and *on* the whole way there

about *this* and about *that*, from his favorite superhero to what he'd had for breakfast that morning. Apparently, he wasn't a fan of cold cereal, but "Mommy was too sick to make pancakes," he told her.

Robby led her up to the door of his classroom, inside of which was a flurry of excitement. A few late comers were still taking papers and snacks out of their backpacks and placing things in cubbies by the door. Some were hanging their now-empty backpacks on coat racks, lining the wall to their left.

There were three adults, chatting together in the carpeted center of the room. Simone assumed that two of them were moms and that the one who looked younger than fuck was the teacher. She was right.

"Oh, thank goodness you're here, Robby!" Miss Harper marched over to give him a hug. "We need you!"

Robby smiled and looked up at Simone as if to say *see?*

"Hi, I'm Simone," she said, shaking the teacher's hand. She started to introduce herself but stopped. What would she say? *I'm Robby's mom's boyfriend's wife?*

Instead she said, "Jen couldn't bring him in today." She said this just to be clear she hadn't abducted someone's child or anything.

"Oh, no!" said Miss Harper. "She's in charge of the cue cards."

"I can do it," said one of the moms.

"You can't," said the other mom. "Not if I'm doing the music." Miss Harper explained to Simone that they needed at least one adult behind the risers at all times for safety reasons.

"Well, Jen's sicker than a dog," she said, not knowing if she should mention the morning sickness. Some people were funny about keeping their pregnancies a secret. Perhaps Jen was one of them.

But Robby blurted, "The baby in her tummy makes her throw up!" Then he darted to the carpet where his little friends were sitting with their legs "criss cross apple sauce," as Miss Harper gently reminded them to do just then.

She turned to face Simone, and acting as though they were old friends from way back when, she grabbed onto Simone's forearms and said, "Do you think *you* could do the cue cards for us?"

And before she could respond either yes or no (and it would have been a *hell* no!) Miss Harper was forced to direct her attention once again to the squirming mass of bodies on the color-coded carpet. In fact, she walked over, swishing her long cotton skirt as she stepped over this child and that child, till she finally reached the big, wooden rocking chair. She sat, facing her miniature-sized pupils. She put a finger to her lips. She folded her hands in her lap. And just like that, every child followed suit. The room was perfectly silent.

"Boys and girls." Miss Harper was practically whispering now. "I know you're excited. This is a very special day. But we have a lot to do before our program, so I need you to listen carefully."

Simone didn't know what to do. Should she make a dash for the door? It was still open. She could run right on out if she wanted to. But for some strange reason, she remained with her feet glued to the tiles.

"We have a special guest this morning. Can

everyone say hi to Miss Simone?"

Now every little eye was on her. Twelve smiling faces looked her way. Little hands waved at her. And a chorus of little voices said *hi, Miss Simone!*

"*She* came with *me*!" Robby said, proudly. "I brung her."

"Yes, you brought her, Robby," said Miss Harper. "Miss Simone, would you like to help us with our program this morning?"

Wow. This was unreal. What a low blow. Asking for favors in front of a bunch of little kids. *Miss Harper, you are a piece of work.* How could she possibly say no to all those faces looking expectantly over at her?

Now she knew how George Berger from the musical *Hair* felt in the last scene of the movie. Just like George Berger, Simone made a faint grunting sound, and Miss Harper took this as a yes. And without one second of boot camp training, Simone the Despiser of Children was whisked into an army of little soldiers, all happy as clams to just plain *be* with her. *She* didn't need any credentials or experience—they couldn't care *less* about any of that. They just wanted *her*.

So Simone put on her best Rambo bravado and got down into the trenches. First, Miss Harper had her at the phonics center, then at the writing center, and then on the floor with the learning games.

"Look!" A little blonde haired girl walked over to Simone and put her finger on the gap between her teeth.

"You lost a tooth?" said Simone.

The little girl nodded her head.

A little boy came up to her and extended his

foot in her direction. She took this to mean he wanted her to tie his shoe, so she got on one knee and did so. While she was finishing the bow, a little girl walked up from behind her and threw her arms around Simone's neck in a big hug. It nearly choked her, and she almost had to *pry* the little girl *off* of her.

And just when Simone didn't think life could get any crazier or that time couldn't pass any faster, the "late birds" came in. Now the room was literally swarming with excited, little varmints. She had no idea how on earth Miss Harper was going to control all of them all at once, but she soon discovered that Miss Harper was *magical*. When she shouted, "Flat tire!" They all went *shhhhh*.... And when she told them to tip toe over to the rug, quiet as mice, that's exactly what they did.

Before she knew it, they were all walking in a quiet line to the multi-purpose room for the Spring Sing. The room was filled wall to wall with parents, all sporting phones and cameras and taking pictures of their carrots like they were the end all and be all of creation.

Once the business of lining up three classrooms of kindergarteners on the risers was accomplished, Simone was handed a stack of tag board cards. Her job was to sit on the floor in the front row, facing the kids, holding up the picture cards during each song so that the kiddos would know what came next in the lyrics. One little girl in the front row assured Simone that it would be "easy peasy lemon squeezy."

Simone had to admit, the program was pretty cute. Even more amusing than the five year-olds were the kindergarten teachers, sitting on the floor beside her, making all the right hand gestures and singing the songs along *with* them. She thought *you've got to be a special breed to teach school.*

She even thought to snap a few pictures on her phone in-between songs, just so Jen would at least get to see her son perform. He really did have a special part during the last song: it was his job (along with five thousand other kids) to hold up a triangle, and whenever the kids sang the word "spring," he had to ting the triangle with his metal wand. Simone just shook her head and rolled her eyes, but afterwards when they walked back to class, she told him, "You did great, Robby!"

The way he smiled ear to ear reminded her of Jodi and Heidi just then—pleased as punch to get a compliment from her.

After countless expressions of gratitude from Miss Harper, it was time for the "early birds" to depart. And instead of putting Robby in the Child Care as Jen had suggested, Simone decided she could just as well walk him back to the house where she had to go, anyway, to retrieve her car.

As they approached Josephine's house, she told Robby, "Let's say hi real quick to my friend." She led him by the hand up to Josephine's porch where her neighbor sat in a rocking chair, knitting something— *probably doilies for all her knick knacks!* Josephine set her needles on her lap and raised her eyebrows.

"Yeah, yeah, I know," said Simone. "Don't even say it."

Josephine smiled at Robby and said, "Who have we here?"

"This is Robby," said Simone. "Robby, can

you say hi to Josephine?"

When he said her name in his adorable lisp, Simone could tell Josephine would be forever smitten.

"What are those?" Robby asked, pointing to a collection of tiny, ceramic cat figurines on the little shelf by the porch bench.

"Those are my cats," said Josephine. "Would you like to play with them?"

Robby nodded, enthralled as could be to touch such delicate items. Simone could only imagine what all he'd found amusing to play with at *her* house.

Josephine and Robby had obviously hit it off with each other, so much so that Simone felt invisible as they chatted on and on about the stupid cats.

"Josephine, can you watch him a sec? I'm going to see if his mom is okay to have him home or if she still wants him to go to Child Care."

When Josephine gave her a puzzled look, Simone whispered, "Morning sickness."

"Oh, good Lord!" gasped Josephine. Then she gasped again, as if she'd just put two and two together. "You mean...."

"Yes." That meant: it's Travis' baby.

"Oh, good *Lord*!" said Josephine again.

Simone didn't feel like getting into it, so she hopped down the steps and jogged over to her front door. She let herself in and said, "Jen?"

She heard a faint reply from the living room. She found Jen, reclining on the couch, her feet elevated on a pillow. Simone looked at all the plastic cars and toys and games on the floor and thought *it's a fucking Romper Room in here!*

"Hi, Simone," said Jen, weakly. She still

looked horrible, but at least her face had a little color now.

"Robby's talking to Josephine next door out on the porch," she said. "I brought him home for you. Unless you want him to go to Child Care?"

"Oh no, that's fine. Thank you so much! Were you there this whole *time*?"

Simone nodded. She really didn't want to admit that a kindergarten teacher and her horde of minions had held her at gunpoint all morning, forcing her into a day of hard labor.

"I just stayed to take a few pictures for you," she said. "Here, I'll send them to Travis."

"You can send them to me, if you want," said Jen, sitting up and reaching for her phone.

Simone held out her hand, like don't bother.

"Oh. You have my contact information," she said, lying back down.

Simone responded by sending the pictures. "There."

"That's so nice of you, Simone. Thank you." Jen smiled then smiled even bigger as she oohed and aahed over the performance shots. She laughed and said, "Look at *this* one!" She showed it to Simone, who nodded like *yeah, I was there.*

"Jen?"

It was Travis. Of course he'd be coming home right now. Mondays, Wednesdays, and Fridays his work day ended before noon.

"Over here, Babe," said Jen.

Babe. Wow. Just hearing that brought Simone back to a very dark place. Back to very dark thoughts.

Travis stopped in his tracks when he saw

Simone. Or maybe it was the sight of his wife and his girlfriend in the same room together that gave him the stupefied expression on his face. He looked at Jen.

"Everything okay?"

Before Simone could crack a sarcastic reply, Jen beat her to the punch. "Simone took Robby to school for me," she said. "Look at these pictures!"

"He's next door at Josephine's," he said, no doubt afraid to walk closer to see Jen's phone. Because *Simone* certainly wasn't going to step aside. No way was she going to make life comfortable for him.

"He's okay," said Jen. "I was so sick this morning, and Simone happened by—"

"I just came over to get my mail," she said. "And some clothes." She didn't need permission to go upstairs, did she? Because that's where she headed. Travis followed her. She wanted to say *don't worry, Travis. It's not like I'm going to slit my wrists and let you discover my bloody body on our bed or anything!*

Simone walked over to the closet, trying to ignore the unmade bed. But she couldn't help but notice that all the pictures were gone.

Her back to him, she said, "I see you've removed all evidence of *us*." She slid the hangers in quick, jerky movements, as one item of clothing clinked up against another.

"Simone, what do you want from me?" He said it like *he* was the one who'd been wronged. Like *he* was the one who'd had his whole world ripped right out from under him without so much as a warning.

She turned to look at him. "I just want my mail," she said. "And this." She grabbed a couple of blazers and a blouse. "And these." She grabbed her signature pair of Jimmy Choos. She pointed at the big container of handbags on the shelf and said, "I'll have to get those another day."

"Simone, we need to talk," he said. "We have to come to a few decisions about things."

She spun around, arms full. "Travis, just—whatever!" She walked past him with her bundle of goods. He followed her down the stairs.

"I'm serious, Simone," he said. "I don't want to hurt you. I don't want to cause you any more pain than I already have. That's not my intent. I just don't want to keep kicking a dead horse. We need to move on."

Now she was angry, but this was good. It made her feel alive. In some weird way, it gave her back her power. He was reminding her of her ultimate goal. And just the thought that she could end it all, here and now, was very vindicating indeed. Just the idea that *she* could decide if she would live one more week, one more day, or one more hour brought her tremendous satisfaction. It brought her an immediate sense of control. She held all the cards, and he was merely playing into her hand.

"Just take it all, Travis," she said. "You can have everything. I have a car and a bank account and a job. I have a place to stay. Don't you worry about *me*." She practically hissed the last part. "I'll come back and get my shit out of your way, and you and Jen can live happily ever after together."

"I don't think it works that way," he said. But she was ignoring him, now. She shifted her belongings to one arm, and with her free hand she grabbed the stack of mail on the dining room table.

"All this mine?" she asked. He nodded.

He followed her out the front door. They both looked over at Josephine's house when Robby's little voice yelled, "Daddy!" He had his arms out and was running around Josephine's big yard, making zooming sounds like an airplane.

Travis waved. Simone thrust her handful of mail onto Travis' stomach. He held it for her as she unlocked her car with the clicker. She hung her garments in the back seat and took the mail from Travis and set it on the console.

"Daddy, huh?" she said. She could see that Jen had made her way over to Josephine's, and the two of them looked as though they were engaged in conversation. Josephine was standing on her porch. Jen was looking up at her, shielding her eyes from the sun with one hand. She didn't seem at all out of place, like it was totally normal to stand in a neighbor's yard in the middle of the day wearing a robe and slippers. *Hmm. Just like Josephine.*

Simone slipped into her car and rolled the window down. "Just do what you need to do," she told Travis. "I won't contest anything."

"I'll be fair, I promise," he said.

"Travis—it doesn't matter," she said. She rolled up her window—his cue to step away from the car. She watched him as he walked over to Josephine's yard. Robby ran straight to his arms, and Travis swung him up high in the air, placing him on his shoulders. They walked over to where Jen was standing.

The way Travis gently put his hand on the small of Jen's back to get her attention and the way she looked up at him and Robby made the three of them look like the picture-perfect family.

Simone no longer felt high and mighty and powerful. Now she knew how Jen must have felt earlier that morning.

Simone backed out of the driveway and sped down the street, hoping she could delay herself from hurling until she could reach April's house.

Chapter Nine

She hadn't planned on getting out of bed that morning, but she had to. Of necessity. Her head was pounding to beat the band.

Simone had never made it to the office the previous day. Nor had she possessed the energy to get a refund for the airline tickets her mother had purchased for her. After witnessing the Norman Rockwell scene of Travis, a pregnant Jen, and Robby (with Josephine as the backdrop), all Simone had had the strength to do back at April's was change into her pajamas, pop a couple of sleeping pills, and read and reread her death letter to Travis until sleep kicked in.

Mercifully, she'd slept all the way through the night, and now it was after 10:00 a.m. Simone wasn't much of a pill popper, and she attributed her pounding headache to all that sleeping medication. Now she needed *different* pills to combat the pain. *Such a vicious cycle*, she mumbled, putting on her robe. But she wasn't complaining. She decided that physical pain was better than emotional pain any day of the week. A deep sleep was just what she'd needed to erase the image of her husband with his "new family."

"Morning!" said April. She ended up coughing once she said it. She was on her knees in the living room, dusting then setting on the floor next to her each individual object adorning the coffee table. "Cleaning day," she said, and once again, she coughed.

Simone grimaced in response and made her way to the kitchen where she saw another unusual sight. Bradley had been busy, scrubbing the stove top.

Apparently, he'd removed all the burners and was in the process of putting them back.

One look at Simone told him not to mess with her, so he just pointed to the coffee maker on the counter. Simone poured herself a cup then opened three cabinets until *eureka!* She found something for her headache. Bradley handed her a bottled water.

"Thanks."

He smiled and went back to work.

"What are you doing?" she asked. "I mean, I know what you're doing, obviously. But...*you* help your mom clean the house?"

"No, not usually," said April, walking in to the kitchen. She threw her dust cloth on top of the laundry basket and grabbed a fresh one from out of a bottom drawer. Then she took a can of furniture polish out of a lower kitchen cabinet.

Her voice sounded scratchy, like she'd been coughing all night or something. "I told him I'd need a little help today." Instantly, she got that stuffy-head, itchy nose look on her face and sneezed two times into the crook of her arm.

"You clean your own house, April?"

April looked up and nodded. She grabbed a paper towel and blew her nose.

Wow. And it's always so clean, too!

"I can't afford a house keeper," she said. "Why, do you have one?"

"Yes. Travis!" Simone sipped her coffee. *But obviously his standards are relaxed, now*, she thought, remembering the unmade bed from yesterday. *Maybe Jen doesn't care about the appearance of the house.*

"Bradley, make sure you mop the kitchen floor,

too," said April. "And dry it, or it'll leave streak marks."

"I know, Mom!" But he said it good-naturedly. "I've done this before."

"Well, it's been a long time," said April.

And once again, April, you're dissing your son for doing something good. Will she ever learn? If Simone dared to think it, she'd say Bradley looked chipper. So why would April want to mess with him?

She followed April, coffee mug in hand, to the living room where April kneeled before the coffee table and proceeded to polish its already shiny surface. But her movements were slow and lethargic.

"Why is *he* so happy?" Simone asked quietly, planting herself on the edge of the sofa. Seemed strange to her that a little bit of cleaning would put Bradley in such a good mood.

"His dad's in town, and he's coming to see him tomorrow. Or so he says!" April stopped to sneeze again. "Oh, my! *Excuse* me." She pulled a tissue out of her pocket and blew her nose. "He's taking him out to dinner tomorrow so they can talk about their plans together. Bradley's all excited because he's going on a week-long fishing trip in June with his dad and his two half-brothers."

April set down her dust cloth and proceeded to have a coughing fit. Her eyes watered and she shook her head by way of apology when Simone's face showed her disgust.

"Good grief, April. You need to get to bed!"

April shook her head. "I can't." She kept coughing. "If Tim's coming over tomorrow, I want the house to look good."

It already looks good, Simone wanted to say. But in some small way, she completely understood where April was coming from.

"How about *you* get some rest, and I'll clean *for* you." Her head was already starting to feel better, so why not? Maybe it would keep her mind off things.

April looked like she was going to protest, so as they both stood up, Simone just put her hands on her shoulders and led her—*pushed* her—all the way to her bedroom.

"You go in here and lie down." She helped April get all tucked into her bed. She turned on the TV for her but put the volume low. "I'll bring you whatever you need. You want some tea?"

April shook her head and grabbed a cough drop from her collection on the nightstand. "No, I think you're right, Simone. I'm just going to sleep."

"Okay. You sleep, and don't worry about a thing. I got this."

April smiled and nodded. She started to say something but coughed instead. Simone left the room, closing the door behind her.

She wouldn't say that cleaning the house with Bradley was *all* bad. Yes, it was annoying and time-consuming and she couldn't fathom how April could endure this kind of torture week after week, year after year. But if she were completely honest, she'd have to admit there were a few fun moments, especially when she'd insisted they clean to music. Watching Bradley dance along to some of his favorite songs made Simone laugh a bit. She wished he was still going to school so he could enjoy *real* dances. That was one

memory Simone cherished from her teenage years—
all those high school dances. But at least Bradley was
dancing *now*. April was right. It was great to see him
this way, all happy and optimistic.

Interestingly, Simone decided she *enjoyed* her
conversations with Bradley. He had a unique way of
looking at things. Like when they were talking about
Jodi and Heidi from the office, whom he knew only
from pictures on his mother's phone—Simone told
him how *nice* they'd been to her, lately, which was a
far cry from how they usually acted. But he wasn't
impressed. He said, "They're just jealous." She looked
at him like *of me?* She couldn't imagine why two
young women in their late 20's would ever be jealous
of a 50 year-old. But Bradley had no problem telling
her why.

"Cause you're hot and they're not," he said.
Her smile must've encouraged him because he then
added, "They're just a couple of catty fatties," and this
made her laugh. *Well, THAT certainly puts things in
perspective,* she thought. She reached up and ruffled
Bradley's hair.

"What," he said. He smiled so big he had
dimples.

"Yer funny." To herself she said *Bradley, you
exaggerate!* All the same, his words made her feel
good.

When she told him how everyone always gave
her gift cards to Stone Cold, he said, "I know why."

Now he had her full attention.

"My mom told me everyone calls you Stone
Cold behind your back. That's their nickname for
you."

Oh, really! "And your mom is a part of this?" she asked.

"Maybe at first she was," he said. "But not anymore. My mom likes you. A lot."

Hmm. So all those gift cards only served to feed a mean, inside joke for her coworkers. *Nice.*

"Well, I'll tell you what, Bradley," she said. "I happen to have a few of those cards in my purse, so when we're done with all this cleaning shit, we'll go have an ice cream. On *them*."

And that's exactly what they did. But only *after* Simone called a reputable cleaning service and booked and pre-paid for someone to clean April's house, twice a month, for the rest of the year. *This* was how she would repay April for taking her in. This and also forgiving April for ever calling her Stone Cold behind her back. Out of loyalty to Bradley, Simone would take *that* secret all the way to her grave.

Despite all the rest she got on Saturday, April's condition was even worse come Sunday. She didn't so much as venture out of bed. Simone offered to fix her a nice breakfast, but April didn't have an appetite. So Simone brought her some hot tea with honey.

"Thank you," whispered April, taking a sip.

"How did you catch such a bad cold?" asked Simone, sitting at the foot of her bed.

"I think it's all this stress."

Simone knew she meant the Sunset Supermarket account. She told April, "That's a *good* kind of stress. Just embrace it. *Go* with it."

Man! Simone had *always* enjoyed a work-related challenge. The bigger the challenge, the higher the thrill factor as far as *she* was concerned. She'd always thrived on it.

But not April. She could never handle *any* stress, and since being here, Simone could see why. April had enough issues to contend with.

"I can't go to church today," April whispered. "MeeMaw will be so disappointed."

Yes, she supposed this was true. She thought *when you live life in a bed in front of a TV set, the smallest excursion becomes the biggest excitement.* She'd seen it on MeeMaw's face yesterday afternoon when her friends had picked her up and whisked her off to her Saturday grooming appointment.

"I wish Bradley could drive her," said April.

Without hesitation (she'd do *anything* for MeeMaw) Simone simply said, "I'll take her." She asked April for directions to the church, but a coughing fit prevented an answer. "Never mind. I'll ask MeeMaw!"

MeeMaw looked beautiful that morning in the pale, yellow pantsuit Simone had dressed her in. She'd even put a tiny bit of make-up on her face. MeeMaw had enjoyed the attention, praising her "personal stylist" up and down on a job well done.

"I look like a movie star!"

Simone inquired if she ought to wake Bradley up so he could go, too. But MeeMaw informed her Bradley didn't *go* to church. Just she and April went.

"He says his dad doesn't go to church, so *he* doesn't have to go," explained MeeMaw, shaking her head. And Simone had a feeling this was the closest MeeMaw would ever come to saying one bad thing about anybody.

The drive over wasn't so bad. MeeMaw told her where to turn, where to park. Simone had borrowed the handicap placard from April's car so they could park close to the front door. This was a good thing because The Lamb's Book church was huge! Simone couldn't get over all the smiling, patient people in orange vests, directing traffic out in the parking lot. The circular building was like an amphitheater. It didn't look much like a church; at least, not the handful of churches Simone had ever stepped foot in for weddings or funerals. She wasn't raised in a church kind of family, and being married to Travis, it just wasn't a priority for her. But unlike Travis, with his Darwinian bent, Simone believed in God. She figured it wasn't like she was a *criminal* or anything, so she *must* be on the "straight and narrow."

She helped MeeMaw navigate her walker up to the front door, which took longer than expected because MeeMaw, apparently, was quite popular and had to stop and talk to just about everyone passing by. *I guess when you're old, you talk to everybody,* thought Simone.

She hadn't expected to see elaborate statues or stained glass windows or anything typical in *this* type of a church—maybe she'd see a cross or something— but what she did see completely captivated her.

On the far wall as they walked into the foyer, a larger-than-life art piece caught her eye. "MeeMaw, what's *that* all about?" she asked, inching the two of them over to it.

"That's the Lamb's Book of Life," she said.

Simone tilted her head back as if to say *oh*, as

if to indicate she understood what MeeMaw was saying. But the truth was, she had no idea what that meant. The Lamb's Book of Life? She figured it was décor created to fit in with the church's name. She stepped a little closer to the massive edifice to take another look.

The book spanned the length (and nearly the height) of the wall before her. It was open wide to reveal pages upon pages of names, some of which were blotted out with black ink. *Hmm. Interesting.* She thought *maybe when you become a member here, they write your name on a page, and if you stop attending, they black it out.*

The music started playing and MeeMaw said they'd better go in and get a seat. But where? The place was already filling up.

"Our spot is up yonder," said MeeMaw, and it was then Simone spotted one of the ladies from MeeMaw's Old Lady Club, vigorously waving them over. Of course, they were sitting fifth row from the stage. Simone would have preferred to slink inconspicuously into a back row.

MeeMaw's friends were thrilled to see them. One by one, they each in turn reached out their hands to greet them as Simone situated MeeMaw in her place at the edge of the pew. Simone sat up extra straight and tall, leaning back a ways so that MeeMaw and her friends could conduct their conversation across her personal space. *Everyone* in the building was yapping away. Simone looked to her right and to her left at all the people around her, people of all ages and ethnic backgrounds. And then she spotted him.

Desmond Reynolds was sitting two rows in

front of them. Simone had to do a double take. Yes, it was him! In the flesh. He was sitting next to an elderly woman in a powder blue dress. Her hair was nearly all gray, and just like MeeMaw's, it looked as though it had been freshly styled the day before. On the other side of Des sat a younger version of himself. He could have been Desmond's clone, only 20 years younger. *That must be Dante*, she thought.

"See that man over there?" MeeMaw was leaning closer to Simone, pointing to Desmond's row. At first, she thought she was pointing at Des himself, but upon further inquiry she figured out MeeMaw was pointing to the guy sitting directly in front of Des.

"What about him?" asked Simone, more or less keeping her eyes on Des.

MeeMaw's friend to the right of her said, "That's April's future beau!" And then MeeMaw and her friend proceeded to giggle like little school girls. And wouldn't you know, at the precise moment of these two matchmakers, laughing and pointing, Des just happened to turn around. His eyes locked with Simone's and looked every bit as surprised to see *her* as she had been to see *him*. He smiled. She smiled back. He whispered something into the elderly lady's ear, and she turned around. When she spotted Simone, she smiled really big and nudged Des with her shoulder. The two of them laughed then turned back around as the worship leaders began to sing.

Simone frowned. *He probably told her I'm the one who spilled the margarita on his nice suit!* Simone felt her cheeks grow warm just remembering this.

She found it very difficult to pay attention to any of the lyrics of the song. Her eyes just had too much to drink in. She looked at Des' hair. At his neck. At his broad shoulders.

And then everyone got up on their feet.

Now she looked at his strong back and his trim waist. Today his teal colored dress shirt was tucked into the waist of dark jeans. Her eyes camped out a while on his ass. She hadn't realized how tall he was. He towered over the woman next to him. *Maybe that's his mom? Or his grandma?* Des' son was even taller than Des.

In any case, Simone could not take her eyes off of him. She liked how engaged he became in all the songs he was singing, he and his son both. They swayed, they clapped, they even raised a hand occasionally. But what really impressed her occurred when the music stopped. The pastor said *please be seated, let's pray.* Simone was awed by how Des bowed his head and closed his eyes. He even leaned forward a little bit, resting his elbows on his thighs. Dante followed suit. She didn't know why, but this completely endeared them to her. Here was Des, this strong, intimidating, powerful man assuming a pose of complete humility, bowing before God, in a sense. Without uttering a single word, Des was demonstrating by volumes who *God* was and who *he* was in relation to this God. *Des knows his place*, she thought.

"He's good-looking, isn't he!" whispered MeeMaw. At first this comment scared Simone, thinking she'd been caught, staring at her client. But then she realized MeeMaw was referring to the guy that April allegedly liked. Simone thought *yeah, he's okay*, but she nodded in eager agreement. If MeeMaw was excited about him, then she would be, too. She didn't want to steal MeeMaw's thunder. She also didn't want to mention Des to MeeMaw at all. *Oh heavens no*, she thought. She didn't need to be the next victim in the Old Lady Club Dating Service.

So when Des walked up to her as they were exiting the church—or attempting to in the oversized crowd at the end of the service, she was grateful that MeeMaw was heavily engaged in conversation with someone on the other side of her.

"I didn't know you go here." Des captured her attention by gently touching her elbow.

She looked up into his gorgeous, green eyes. Her heart fluttered, and she felt light-headed.

"I don't," she said. "This is my first time."

Why she said *that*, she had no idea. She knew full well it would be her *last* time.

"Well, I'm glad I saw you," he said. "See that fine young man over there?" He pointed back to where he'd been sitting. She nodded when she saw Dante and the elderly woman, talking to a group of people around them, one of whom was the pastor.

"That's my son. The new owner of the Ohio Sunset Supermarket."

"Yes. Dante," she said, hoping to impress.

"He just flew in yesterday. And I know this is short notice, but I'd like to set up a meeting for him with Com Corp."

She nodded. "Of course. Any time."

"Like tonight."

Tonight? She checked his expression. *No, he's not kidding.* She cleared her throat. "I'm not sure that will work," she said. "I'm afraid our acting project manager is a bit under the weather at the moment." *And he can just think that's April cause no way am I calling Heidi on a Sunday,* she thought. Saturday, perhaps. Sunday, no. Heidi had an 18 month-old and considered Sundays sacred mother-daughter bonding time.

Des said, "What about you?"

She gave him just about every reason she could think of as to why this was not possible. She summed up her excuses by humbly admitting that she wasn't as up to speed as the others on this project, what with all the time off she'd had lately. She told him she didn't feel prepared.

"It's really just a meet and greet," he said. "A dinner. Could you be prepared to eat?" He smiled that warm smile of his. Now her heart was fluttering out of control.

"Besides," he said. "I have it on authority the secretary would like to meet you."

She thought nothing of this comment, so she just nodded as they continued to walk. Clients usually did want to meet Simone Sanders. Her reputation preceded her.

As they reached the front door, MeeMaw still chatting with the friend alongside of her, Simone smiled and said, "You have my contact information from Heidi, so just text me the address and time."

He said, "I'll do better than that. If you'd be so kind to text me *your* address, I'll send a car for you at 6:00."

Hmm. So much for shuffling this off to Meredith. Desmond Reynolds was nothing if not persuasive. What could she say except *that sounds great?* He said *see you later, Simone,* and he walked back to his family.

Before she quite had time to think about what had just transpired, she got suckered in to lunch. With the Old Lady Club. *Just a short lunch*, they promised.

Apparently, every Sunday after the church service, April drove MeeMaw to wherever her friends wished to do lunch or brunch. Simone figured today was a good day to take her. MeeMaw should probably be kept away from April's germs as much as possible.

She called Bradley real quick, now that she had his phone number. April had given it to her in the morning before leaving for church, just in case MeeMaw had a senior moment and forgot how to get to The Lamb's Book.

Thankfully, Bradley was already up. He sounded excited about the day ahead. She sought his opinion about dinnertime. If he was going out to dinner with his dad and if she was going to a meet and greet at 6:00, who would look after MeeMaw and April? Satisfied by assurances from Bradley that his mother was already attempting to put herself together (probably for the benefit of her ex!) and having administered the reciprocal lecture about "fixing your mom lunch, warming her tea, stocking her up with tissues and cough drops, and tidying up any messes around the house so that *she* won't feel compelled to do so," she concluded the call and turned her attention to the ladies sitting all around her in the booth.

Much of the conversation centered on April and how the man in question was completely willing to go on a date with her. So as the pancake stacks grew shorter with each bite, the ladies strategized on how to build a web that would catch the fly.

When Simone about had enough of all their schemings, she changed the subject.

"So tell me about the artwork in the foyer of your church," she said to no one in particular.

"Oh, you mean the Lamb's Book of Life?" asked the lady sitting next to her.

"That represents Revelation 20:15, Dear," said MeeMaw.

Another lady at the table quickly scrambled for her Bible, put on her glasses, and found the verse in question. She read it out loud:

> *"And whosoever was not found written in the book of life was cast into the lake of fire."*

She looked up at Simone and closed her Bible. Nobody said anything for a few moments although it felt like five minutes. Simone looked expectantly at MeeMaw, hoping there was a punch line somewhere.

Finally, she said, "MeeMaw, do you believe that's true?" She knew sweet little MeeMaw couldn't *possibly* believe *that*!

But MeeMaw smiled and said, "Oh yes, Dear. I believe everything in God's word is true."

Now Simone looked around at the other faces at the table. They were innocent faces. Smiling faces. Faces that were agreeing with MeeMaw. You'd have thought they had just told her that the God of the universe was a God of love, not wrath. That he was in the business of *blessing* people, not casting His creation into a burning lake of brimstone!

"Do *you* believe it's true?" MeeMaw asked

Simone with a smile.

It wasn't like she'd ever thought about this before. Today was the first she'd ever heard of it. But *certainly* it wasn't true! No *way* could she ever accept that. She wanted to say *are you serious, ladies?* She might not know that much about God, but she did know that God is love. *And a loving God does not do that!*

"To be honest…" said Simone, already bracing herself for a big debate ahead, "…no. I don't." Then one more time, as if saying it twice validated her position, she said, "No. I don't think I believe that."

Amazingly, no counter arguments ensued. MeeMaw simply wiped her mouth with her napkin and said, "Well okay, Dear. If you're right, then there's nothing to worry about."

No. She *didn't* have anything to worry about. What those ladies were proposing was unfathomable. Unacceptable.

So why was she worried about it?

So distracted was she by thoughts of impending judgment that for the rest of the afternoon, her underlying nervousness about the meet and greet with Desmond was put on the back burner.

She couldn't talk to *April* about burning lakes of fire because…April couldn't *talk*. And Bradley was busy, organizing his room all day. Simone was disappointed she'd miss meeting his father, but he was due to pick up Bradley at around the same time Des would be sending a car for her. How she'd love to give Bradley's dad a piece of her mind! Granted, he was finally doing a *good* thing where Bradley was concerned. And Bradley didn't seem to hold anything against him. *I guess a once-in-a-while dad is better than NO dad*, she thought.

Then she sighed. If Bradley was happy, she would be happy *for* him.

"*You* look pretty!" whispered April when Simone popped her head in to let her know she'd be leaving soon. She could have said the same for April, who was wearing a tiny bit of lipstick!

As for Simone, she wasn't *too* dressed up. She had opted for a more casual look for this evening. But Simone's casual was most people's dressy, and yes, she was *well* put together. She'd chosen an old favorite: a sleeveless, empire waist cream dress with black accents. Her pointy, sling-back pumps looked deceptively uncomfortable, but they weren't, even with no nylons. They were her favorite pair of shoes. She'd pulled her hair back into a bun. This may be a casual affair, but the professional in her would settle for nothing less than her best foot forward. She looked "all business."

At the eleventh hour (or panic time, as she came to label it) she'd called Meredith in the hopes she'd be available and willing to accompany her to the meet and greet. If nothing else, she'd at least wanted to clue Meredith in on what she was doing. But it was a wasted call. Meredith seemed so out of it. She was slurring her words, which Simone found odd because she'd called her at 4:00, which to her seemed a bit early to be *that* buzzed off her wine. *Then again, maybe Meredith has the right idea!* She figured *oh well*. No one expected a business dinner on a Sunday. If she and

Des hadn't run into each other at church, it probably wouldn't even be happening.

"You'll do fine," Meredith assured her. "He requested *you*, not me, so *you* go. Don't worry it— about it. Don't worry about it, Simone."

April barely had the time (and the voice) to brief Simone on the latest developments with Sunset Supermarket's grand opening because before she knew it, the doorbell rang. It was the driver Des had sent for her, and *wow. Seriously? A Rolls Royce?*

As she stepped inside the car, Simone imagined what a celebrity must feel like. Because if she didn't know better, she'd say she was getting the red carpet treatment from her client.

Chapter Ten

Now she was glad she'd dressed up a little. From the back seat of the camel interior of the black Rolls Royce, Simone checked her face in her compact mirror. She really didn't need to, but this she did to combat the butterflies that were awakened by the prospect of being up close and personal to Desmond Reynolds.

As soon as the car pulled away from April's house, Simone made conversation with the driver, which was something she wouldn't normally do because this guy smelled faintly of cigarette smoke. Maybe it was a deep-rooted, generational California thing, who knew, but Simone was somewhat prejudiced against smokers. But now, out of sheer nervousness she asked him, "So where are we headed?" He responded, but she was too jittery to even hear clearly the street he'd named. It sounded like an industrial park, and she sluffed it off as normal, as the logical place Sunset Supermarkets would set up their local headquarters. Com Corp as well was also situated in such an area known as Central Parkway. She'd always liked the sound of that name.

But she could see this was no Central Parkway. The place where the driver was taking her was all residential. When he pulled up to a gray, two-story house with an expansive front yard and enclosed front porch, she thought *hmm*.

"Is this it?" she asked the driver, who was already halfway out the door and dashing to open *her* door.

"Here you go, Ms. Sanders," he said, offering his hand, which she gladly took. Her feet safely on the curb, the driver stood at attention, hands folded in front of him. *Hmm. At least he's professional.* She assumed he would not depart until she was safely received into the house, and she was correct.

She stepped gingerly across the never-ending stone walkway up to the residence, feeling more or less like she was walking down an aisle because it was located smack in the center of the yard. She never understood how a geographical region with so much annual snow boasted such long front yards and driveways. Ironically, in Southern California where the weather was mild year-round and roads did not require shoveling, driveways were short and so were front and back yards. And where *she* came from a front yard was more like a token, especially for homes located closer to the beach.

The porch door opened before she reached the steps. It was Des in all his good-looking glory and behind him, the elderly woman she saw at church that morning. Now she felt self-conscious. If she could make it down the path without tripping, she'd be grateful! Des and the woman looked past her a second and waved at the driver. Simone looked over her shoulder as he got into the car and drove away.

"Welcome!" said Des, extending a hand to assist Simone up the remaining two steps. She could tell he liked what he saw. "Wow, you look fabulous!" he said, putting one hand on her back and gently leading her toward the woman whom he introduced as his grandmother. Pearl was her name. She was still wearing the same, nice dress she'd had on at church.

"Just call me Granny. Everyone else does," she said, giving Simone the warmest, most loving embrace, like the two of them were family. "I hope you don't mind the commotion. We've got the whole crew here tonight!"

Not knowing quite what to say, Simone looked up at Des who quickly averted his gaze to her eyes instead of at her body. It was a subtle movement, barely detectable. She wouldn't have held it against him, anyway, even if he *had* been more obvious about it. He may be someone with whom she might have a "professional relationship," but he was still a man.

"I hope you don't mind," he said. "But I figured the best way to have you meet everyone from Sunset was to bring you here to Granny's."

"We do a family dinner every Sunday," Granny told her, turning to walk into the house. "And we're always so excited when our Desmond is in town, aren't we, Baby." Des put his arm around his granny who leaned into his side as he helped her walk through the front door to the house. He paused and allowed Simone to walk in ahead of him.

The foyer was long and wallpapered in a tiny, floral print from days gone by. She could see that Granny was into antiques, but the décor was very quaint and fit the age of the home. Family photos, including a few black and white ones of older family members, adorned the walls on either side of her. A couple of children were chasing each other across the hall where the foyer wall ended.

Before they'd quite made it down the hallway to the main living area in the back of the house, a train of people intercepted them. One after another, they rounded the corner and greeted Simone as Des introduced her—and not with handshakes—with hugs. Simone felt like a princess, like royalty. She quickly discovered that Sunset Supermarkets was not only a privately owned company but strictly a *family* owned company. It seemed all of Des' family members had a title, which he stated with each new name.

"This is my brother, Donovan—he's our Executive Vice President of Operations and Distribution. And this here is my sister, Danae. She's our Vice President of Marketing. You already met Granny. She's our Secretary of Finance."

"*Former* Secretary of Finance," Granny corrected him. "I'm retired, remember?" She laughed, and her family laughed along with her.

"We still call her Secretary sometimes," said one of Des' other siblings. Simone looked at Des just then, remembering how he'd told her "the secretary" wanted to meet her. He looked back at her as though he were saying *yep. You caught me,* and she smiled.

There were so many names to remember! The ones she caught onto the quickest were Donovan and his wife, Muriel. Danae was the mother of the two kids running around the house—Mikayla and Demitri. Des' youngest brother, Dominic was easy to remember. He and his fiancé kept to themselves once they said hello, too caught up in each other to notice a newcomer much. Simone liked that.

"Don't mind them," smiled Des, looking over at the two lovebirds as they engaged in a kiss.

"That's so sweet," said Simone. She and Travis used to act like that when their relationship was new. But of course, she kept *that* thought to herself.

As they finally reached the kitchen from whence the heavenly aroma of chicken fried steak filled the room, one of the two hired chefs handed Simone a glass of champagne from a tray, which was then dispersed to everybody else. Donovan raised his glass and made a quick cheer to the newest Sunset Supermarket, and this was eagerly received with a "hear hear!" as everyone took a drink then went back to socializing.

When Des told her the rest of his family lived in California, she opened her eyes wide, and this caused him to laugh. "Yes, there are more," he said. "I told you I'm the oldest of six."

"Good grief, do all your names start with a D?"

She'd only intended for Des to hear that, but Simone was never known to have a soft voice. Her question caused a loud roar of laughter throughout the room.

"Don't blame me!" said Granny, pointing toward the entry way. "Blame my daughter!"

With that, everyone's attention was directed toward the couple now entering the room. Another round of hugs and kisses ensued, until finally the Red Sea parted and the two people were able to make their way over to Simone.

"These are my parents, Delilah and David Reynolds," said Des. And Simone was greeted with the warmest hug of all from Des' mother. She was the spitting image of Granny only 20 years younger. Her hair was not completely gray like Granny's, but starting to get there. She had more of a modern, Michelle Obama type cut that gave her a professional-looking edge. Des' father was Caucasian, and he had the same intense, green eyes that Des had. He was a bit thick in the middle, but this was camouflaged nicely by his height and loose-fitting, extra-large-sized t-shirt. When he smiled at her with the same lopsided grin as Des, she liked him instantly. She couldn't get over what a striking resemblance Des had to both parents. It was like God had been having a creative moment the day He'd made Des. *What a unique combination!*

"Where's Dante?" asked Delilah.

"He's running a little late," said Granny. "But he's coming, he's coming." She handed a glass of champagne to her daughter. Her son-in-law was too preoccupied with the appetizer trays laid out on the counter to be interested in a beverage.

Delilah Reynolds went on to tell Granny and Simone that she and Des' father had "enjoyed a nice drive out here a-la the Rolls" and that they'd arrived in North Olmsted earlier that afternoon. They lived a few hours away in Dayton, she explained, and were staying at a hotel nearby for the weekend. She told Simone that it was easier on Des this way for *them* to come *here* whenever he was in town because this way the whole family could be together.

"And we so enjoy Granny's Sunday dinners," she said, giving her mother a hug.

"Except I don't cook anymore!" said Granny, smiling at Des. "My grandson sees to that."

Des looked over and smiled at the mention of his name although it felt to Simone as though he was carefully monitoring every word being said in all corners of the room, despite standing a few feet away. He might be talking to others, but it felt like his full attention was always on Simone.

And as unorthodox and unusual as all of this was, Des springing his entire family on her like this, she felt extremely comfortable. How could she not? They were so lovely, each and every one of them. And when they all sat down to eat in the formal dining room, which felt like it was straight out of a scene from a Victorian play, what with the crystal chandelier and brocaded wallpaper (Granny was obviously big on wallpaper!) she was moved by how they all joined hands to pray before the meal was served.

Des led the family in prayer. He sat next to Simone who sat next to Granny (who sat at the head of the table.) Directly across from Simone was Des' mother, so this seating arrangement made her feel as though she held a position of prominence, as though she were the special guest of honor. And when Granny interrupted Des' prayer to add, "And thank you, *thank you*, Lord, for bringing Simone to us tonight," she could almost feel herself blushing.

Nope. It didn't feel like a business dinner at all. In fact, not much business was discussed, other than Des telling everybody that Simone was the Director of Operations (as he put it, causing her to smile) at Com Corp. Simone was quick to inform all the eyes now looking over at her that she was basically overseeing the grand opening but that her team was very capably handling all the grunt work. Well. She didn't use those words *exactly*. But to hear Simone talk, anyone would think that her team was the greatest thing since sliced bread. This was a technique she always employed with *all* her clients. She called it *instilling confidence in the company*. She'd learned this from Meredith.

As if on cue, Dante arrived just as dinner was

served. An eruption of greetings filled the room as Dante made his way around the table, hugging and kissing all his relatives.

"He's like the cartoon character that drifts through the smoky air, led by his nose to where the food is coming from!" Danae stood up after saying this to give her "favorite nephew" a big hug. Simone remained seated, so Dante extended his hand and told her it was a pleasure to meet her.

"He looks just like you," she said to Des, who still had that proud dad look on his face like the one he'd worn in church that morning.

Dante thanked Granny for asking the chefs to prepare his all-time favorite dinner.

"You'll be having it all the time, now," she told him.

"That's right," he said. "There's nothing like a good, family recipe. You need to pass it on to Kim."

And now Dante's wife, *Kim*, became the new topic of conversation, everyone asking Dante how she was feeling, what the doctor had to say, how the baby was doing—they all squealed to learn the results were in: the baby was a boy. Dante seemed enamored by his wife and to hear him talk about her one might think she was the Queen of Sheba. Simone commented on this to Des, and he said *we raised our boy to respect women and cherish his wife*.

Simone was glad to hear that *some* parents in the world were raising their children right! She was even more glad at the moment that the conversation continued on because now she was able to thoroughly enjoy her meal. She'd had chicken fried steak before, but nothing quite like this! She was borderline embarrassed by how entranced she was by the mashed potatoes alone. They had bits of potato skin with just a trace of bacon. Combined with the creamy, white gravy, it was all she could do not to inhale her entire plate. Granny must've noticed her enthusiasm because she put her hand on Simone's arm and whispered, "We need to fatten you up!"

At this, Simone remembered her manners and forced herself to set her fork down for a little breather and take a sip from her glass. She smiled at Granny, and Granny gave her a little wink.

Looking around the table, it was evident that this family had a lot of love for each other. So much laughter, so much encouragement. She could tell that put downs were not permitted. Heck, Simone and Ron had made an art form of poking fun at one another when *they* were growing up—all in good fun, of course. They hadn't been malicious or anything. But this family was different. They were good. They were wholesome. And they were obviously wise.

It was almost as if they knew not to tread on matters of a personal nature with Simone. When they asked her to tell them a little about herself, they seemed satisfied with her very basic life description: California girl till the age of 18. Com Corp employee for the past 17 years. Currently residing with a coworker due to circumstances beyond her control.

At this, they mercifully switched gears to discuss the grand opening and what her vision was for the big event. Now Simone could shine. She was in her element, painting an animated picture of all the main events.

"I think you chose the right company, Des,"

said his mother from across the table. Des smiled and looked down at his plate.

"It's a shame Cynthia can't be here for the big opening," said Granny. She looked at Simone. "She's Dante's mother."

"My ex-wife," said Des. But yes, Simone had already pieced that one together.

"How's your mom, Dante?" asked Danae.

And now the focus was on Cynthia, with Dante telling everyone how excited his mother was about becoming a grandparent but how she was still as busy as ever.

As they chatted amongst themselves, Des leaned into Simone a bit and said, "My ex-wife is buying me out, and in six months I can retire."

"You look kind of young to retire," she said.

"I'm 49. *"*

"Well. Cynthia sounds very ambitious," said Simone, wishing to hear more about The Woman Who Let Des Go.

"Oh, that she is," said Des. "She's the driving force behind our success."

The way he talked about her, Simone could tell he still loved her. Or at the very least he respected her. True, they were divorced, but they obviously had a good relationship. And never having met her, Simone could tell that Cynthia Reynolds (if that was still her name) was one incredible person. She'd *have* to be to have raised such a fine son as Dante.

"Do your other two children live in California?" she asked. She was sure he'd probably mentioned this at The Fajita Grill that one night. But another of Simone's business tactics was to get clients to talk about their passions, and clearly Des' passion was his family.

Des nodded and finished his bite of steak. "Yes. My daughters," he said, wiping his mouth with his napkin. "Delaney and Daria are a lot like their mother. Now that Dante's relocating here, they'll be manning all the Sunset Supermarkets in California from here on out." Now he laughed and shook his head. "You know, you always think it's your daughters who will settle down and have families. But *my* girls are career women. It's my *son* who wants to start a family."

Granny, who'd obviously been listening to their conversation, added her two cents by saying, "And I'm the lucky one who gets to be around the new baby!"

Now Dante joined in and told Simone that he and Kim were moving in with Granny for a while until they could settle in to a home of their own.

"It'll be so good for everyone," said Danae. "Granny will be in *heaven*, caring for that baby, and there's plenty of room, here. Kim loves this house."

She went on to say how this was the only house Granny had ever lived in since she'd married her dearly departed husband (evidently known to all the grandkids as Gramps.)

"That is so sweet!" said Simone, caught up in the wonder of this incredible family. They were so solid. So strong.

"If you think that's sweet," said Granny, gesturing toward the two chefs walking into the dining room, each brandishing a platter of tasty-looking desserts, "you gotta try my cheesecake!"

Everybody excitedly made their selections

from the assortment of flavored cheesecakes on the platters. Granny suggested they "take dessert to the family room," and one by one, chairs were pushed in and the dining room was vacated.

When Danae mentioned a rousing game of Pinochle, Des groaned and said, "Count me out."

"My brother hates card games," Danae said to Simone.

"Your brother hates *all* games," said Delilah to her daughter with a smile.

"Yeah, and we're not going to torture Simone." Des looked down at her and said, "Why don't you join me on the front porch, Simone?"

"Oh, I think that's a great idea," said Granny, giving Des' back a little pat. "I'll bring you some coffee."

Simone followed Des to the front of the house. When he flipped on the porch light, it was pretty cozy-looking out there. They no sooner sat down—he on one padded wicker rocking chair and she on the one next to it—when Granny came out with a little tray that had two cups of coffee, some sugar, and cream. She set the tray on the little wicker coffee table and said, "I wasn't sure how you like your coffee."

Simone almost said *black* but stopped herself.

Granny walked over to a little bench by the door and grabbed the fleece throw that was resting on it. This she lovingly draped around Simone's shoulders, giving her a little pat.

"She's so *sweet*," she said as Granny quietly left the room. She looked at Des, who was looking at her bare leg, popping out from where the two edges of the throw didn't quite meet. Once again, he repented by immediately looking her in the eye. "She reminds me of MeeMaw. I wonder if they know each other."

"Is she the lady I saw you with this morning?" Des asked her.

Simone nodded, taking a bite of her cheesecake. "Oh my gosh, this is *amazing*," she said, taking one more bite, a big one this time. But that would be *all* she would eat. It was Simone's policy where desserts were concerned to take *two* bites and "set the bitch down," which was what she did now. She reached instead for her nice, hot coffee.

"Is she your grandmother?" he asked.

Simone shook her head. "No, she's April's mother."

"Ah, yes. April," he said, looking longingly over at her dessert plate. "You gonna finish that?" he asked. He had already finished his. Simone picked up her plate and handed it to him, saying *be my guest*. He smiled and took a bite. *Such a sexy bite at that!*

"I'm amazed you don't weigh 500 pounds with all this good food!" she said.

"I know!" He set the now empty plate back down on the wicker table. "Good thing I live on the coast."

Now he loaded up his coffee cup with cream and sugar. Simone must've looked at him funny because he paused then said, "I like a little coffee with my cream and sugar," and they both laughed. When the moment of mirth ended he said, "Is April the coworker you're staying with?"

Simone nodded. Des must've interpreted this as her not wanting to discuss her personal life with him. But she didn't mind. For some unexplainable reason she was feeling so *comfortable* with him. Like he was an old friend. So when he apologized and said *never mind, I don't need to know*, she said *no, that's okay* and proceeded to tell him about all that was going on with her and Travis. And Jen. And the new baby.

Des just frowned and shook his head while he listened. *He probably thinks I'm crazy*, she thought, *going on and on about my personal problems.*

"I'm sorry." Now it was her turn to apologize. "This is all probably too much information. I shouldn't have said all that."

And then he did something that wowed her. He put his hand on top of hers, the one that was resting on the arm of her rocking chair. Except she didn't recoil from his touch as she would from April's. *His* touch was rather comforting. And he had no problem, squeezing her hand a little and letting it linger awhile to the point where Simone thought sure she was going to liquefy and spill right down to the floor. But just as she was thinking how she didn't want him to ever let go, he must've realized the inappropriateness of touching someone else's wife this way, especially during the context of a "business meeting" no less. When they heard a loud albeit muffled-sounding peal of laughter from inside the house where brethren were dwelling together in unity, playing Pinochle, he withdrew his hand.

Neither one of them spoke for some time.

It was Simone who broke the silence. She cleared her throat and said, "Anyway, April is letting me stay in her guest room until I can figure things out."

"What do you want to do?" he asked. "I mean, do you want to get back together or split up?"

Actually? I want to die! she wanted to say. But she couldn't say *that*. So she decided to put herself in the position of a *normal*, jilted wife, if only for Des' sake, hoping perhaps it might inspire *him* to reveal the cause of *his* divorce to Wonder Woman.

"I don't see us getting back together," she told him. "Not now. Not now that he's finally becoming a father." The brief "picture perfect family" scene from Josephine's front lawn came to mind and she frowned. "Plus he loves her. I can see it." She traced the top of her coffee cup with her finger. A bit more softly she added, "And she loves him."

And for the first time, the realization struck her. Jen really did love Travis. In her naïve, young, dumb way…Jen loved Travis. And maybe she loved him in a way that Simone never could. Not that this brought her much comfort. But perhaps it was true.

"I think that's really big of you to say that," said Des, still shaking his head. "You've *got* to be drawing on God's supernatural power within you to have such a good attitude."

Good attitude? Really? She wanted to say that if Jen weren't so sweet she'd probably kill her! And what did he mean God's supernatural power within her?

"It's times like these that make us glad we have a relationship with the Lord," he said.

"Des, what are you talking about?" she asked, then realized *oh. He thinks I'm a devoted Christian like he is.* She figured she'd set him straight, right off the bat, even if it meant he no longer liked her.

"Des, I don't go to church at *all*," she said. "*Ever*. I only went today because April was sick, and I know how important it is to MeeMaw to be there."

Des just smiled again, the way he'd smiled the first time she saw him at the grocery store.

"Yeah? How did you like the service?"

She wanted to say *I had a great view!* Because that's all she could honestly even remember about the service. *Service shmervice*, she thought. *Her* eyes had been on Des! But she couldn't tell him *that*. So she told him a fib.

"Oh, it was great," she said. "I really enjoyed it." She told him how she'd gone to lunch with MeeMaw and her friends afterwards. And this made her laugh.

"What's so funny?" he asked with a smile, eager to hear the inside joke she must be harboring.

"Oh, I was just thinking about the silly conversation I had with the ladies this afternoon," she said, setting her cup on the coffee table. "They were telling me about The Lamb's Book of Life and acting like one day God is actually going to cast people into a big, burning lake of fire." It seemed so ridiculous to her now—all that worrying she'd put herself through all afternoon. Surely, *Des* didn't believe that!

But Des lost his smile. "Hmm. That's not the most pleasant lunchtime topic," he said.

"And you know…they're all so sweet. It's just comical to me how these ladies can be so *nice* and yet they talk about something so awful!"

She stopped rocking and so did he. She thought he was going to reassure her that it was nothing to take seriously, all those idle ramblings of a bunch of old ladies, spinning their stories around the booth of a pancake restaurant. But he didn't. What he did say completely surprised her.

"They *were* being nice," he said.

She leaned back a ways. *What?* Since when was talk about hell fire and condemnation *nice*?

"But wasn't Jesus all about love?" she asked. "Didn't He teach us to be kind to one another?"

"Yes," he said.

"So you mean to tell me that MeeMaw and her friends were demonstrating kindness at the restaurant today?"

Des nodded.

"I don't understand," she said, looking at him.

He looked into her eyes. "Simone, there's nothing more loving than to warn someone of destruction," he said.

It was silent for a while. Then in a quiet voice, Des asked her something no one had ever asked her before.

"Is *your* name written in the Lamb's Book of Life, Simone?"

At first, she thought he meant was her name physically written on one of the pages of the artwork in the foyer of MeeMaw's church. But then she realized he meant the *real* Book of Life. The one allegedly in heaven.

And she didn't know what to say. She couldn't lie and say *yes* because she didn't believe such a book existed! And she couldn't tell the truth (even if such a book did exist) and say *no*, because what if that type of response caused Com Corp to lose the Sunset Supermarket account? Meredith would flip. If she ever thought she'd seen Meredith go postal on occasion for much lesser accounts in the past, this would be the end-all of all such episodes.

But more than that, she *couldn't* say no to Des because his eyes looked so sad. Like he already knew that a person like her would not be included on any kind of acceptance list into heaven. And yet...she knew his eyes were pleading with her to say *yes, yes I'm in the Book. Yes, don't worry, I'm in!*

So Simone employed another one of her tactics she often used with her clients during sticky situations. She made light of it and answered a question *with* a question.

She smiled coyly and said, "What do *you* think, Des?" Then before he could reply she changed the subject—another weapon in her arsenal. "Does your driver always camp out on the curb like that?" she asked, looking out the window at the street. It was dark outside, and the only way she knew he was still out there was because she saw the flame of his lighter when he lit his cigarette.

"He's not my driver," said Des. "I don't have a driver. I just hired him for the day. He drove my parents out, and then he picked you up, so he's just there for when anyone needs to leave."

This gave her the perfect "out." Simone slowly stood up. It was time to quit while she was ahead.

"Let me guess," said Des, looking disappointed. "Are you ready to leave?"

She nodded. She didn't want him to feel bad, like he was chasing her away or anything with his somber words, so she told another fib.

"I have to get up early tomorrow," she said. He looked at his phone and said *yeah, I guess it's getting late for a school night.*

She stopped moving for a second.

He closed his eyes and shook his head. "Open mouth, insert foot. I didn't mean anything by that, Simone." She assumed he was referring to the fact that her husband (the one who was leaving her for a former student) was a college professor. "It's just a phrase we've used with the kids for so many years."

"It's okay," she said with a manufactured smile. She started to carry her cup and dessert plate into the house, but he said *just leave it, I'll take care of that.*

He escorted her into the house all the way back to the living area where Simone spent the next twenty minutes (or so it felt) hugging each person goodbye. *Off so soon?* they asked her. But she just chalked up the pleasantries to a quality family behaving politely toward a guest. She thanked Granny for her hospitality, and Granny handed Simone her purse, which she'd hung on a kitchen stool when she'd first arrived earlier that evening. Delilah put her arm around Simone and walked her to the front door as Desmond trailed behind them.

"It was a pleasure meeting you, Simone," she said, giving her one last hug. "Thank you for all you're doing for my son and grandson."

Simone smiled warmly. No. The pleasure was all hers, she assured her.

Desmond walked her all the way to the car and opened the back door for her. He watched as she slid inside.

"Thank you for coming out tonight, Simone," he said. "You were a big hit with the family. I hope you didn't mind."

"No, not at all," she said.

He hesitated a moment. Then he said, "I guess I'll be seeing you around."

She smiled and nodded her head.

Then he closed her door, and the driver slowly pulled away from the curb. Had she looked out the back window, she'd have seen Des, still standing on the parkway as the car rounded the corner and left the street.

But Simone was too dazzled by all the events of the evening to notice such things. She was still feeling confused as the Rolls Royce pulled up to April's house. So many things were whirling through her mind. Had she really made a good impression? Did Des think less of her now? And if he did, why would she care? Simone usually *never* cared about these kinds of things!

But so *many* questions bounced off the sides of her brain as she exited the Rolls Royce. She didn't even know if she'd thanked the driver and told him goodnight, so caught up was she in her thought life.

That is, until she reached the front door. She heard lots of yelling. At first, she thought it must be coming from the house next door but realized the noise was coming from the second story of *April's* home. The commotion was spilling out into the night air from Bradley's open window on the roof above the porch. Simone quickly searched for her house key and unlocked the front door, anxious to see what was the matter. To see why all hell was breaking loose.

Chapter Eleven

"I don't care, Mom! He's a *fucking* asshole!"

Simone could very clearly hear Bradley as her feet took the steps two at a time, but she couldn't hear April's much softer reply.

She heard a loud crash as something hit the wall in Bradley's room. Once she reached the top of the stairs, she saw April standing in his open doorway. Bradley was inside the room by the far wall near his bed. He'd obviously just swept all his sports trophies off the shelves above his desk, apparently with such violence they'd bounced off the neighboring wall and onto his bed. Some were on the floor. Now he picked one up. It looked like he was trying to break it, like it was alive and he was trying to snuff out whatever life was in it.

His appearance was almost frightening. His hair was a mess. His eyes looked downright rabid. He'd obviously been crying. He was *still* crying.

"Fucking bastard!"

"Bradley, stop!" said April, walking over and attempting to grab him by the arm but to no avail. He hurled the trophy out the open window.

As he stooped down to grab another trophy, April practically sat on him. One of her slippers fell off in the scuffle as they both lost their footing and keeled to their sides onto the floor.

"Get *off* of me, Mom!" Now Bradley was breathing very hard, like a steam pipe ready to blow.

"Not until you calm down!" she screamed or at least tried to scream. What little voice she might have had the past couple of days was completely gone, now.

Simone had to do *something*. She couldn't just stand there and watch them wrestle on the floor like this. Bradley was a big, strong boy and she couldn't bear to see April get hurt.

She flung her purse onto the bed and ran over. She crouched down and grabbed April by the arm, attempting to pull her out of harm's way. It was then that mother and son noticed her for the first time.

She successfully peeled April off of Bradley who immediately jumped to his feet. Perhaps Simone had deluded herself into thinking that once he noticed her presence, he'd feel embarrassed by his behavior and clean up his act. But one look into his crazed eyes told her that *this* boy was *disturbed*. Disturbed with a capital D. He was beyond reason at this point.

"Don't let him get to you, Bradley," April said as Simone walked her backwards toward the door. "You're so much better than him. He's not worth it!"

"No, Mom!" yelled Bradley. "*I'm* not worth it! Why did you even have me?" He was crying hard, now. "You guys shouldn't have fucking *had* me!"

For a split second, he made eye contact with Simone. But even this wasn't enough to calm him down. He turned away and kicked his desk chair so hard it fell over.

Before anyone could utter another word, Simone picked up April's slipper off the floor and said, "Come on, let's leave him alone." It took some degree of effort, but she escorted Bradley's distraught mother out of the room, closing the door behind them.

April's tear-soaked eyes desperately looked into Simone's. She said, "I don't want him to hurt himself!"

Simone continued to walk April around the corner and down the stairs.

"Shh. I'll take care of him," she said, which was half a lie. She had no *clue* how to help a kid like that! Even as they tromped down the stairs, they could still hear objects being hurled against the wall and expletives being shouted from Bradley's cracked, adolescent voice.

"Tell me what happened." Simone took April to her bedroom and made a beeline for her bed. She sat down on the edge next to April.

"About an hour after you left, Bradley's dad picked him up. Of course, he was *late*."

"Did he come inside?"

April shook her head. *Hmm. So much for cleaning the house.* How had she known *that* would be wasted effort?

"No. He said hi to me, but that was about it." April reached for the glass of water on her nightstand and took a drink. "Sorry. I have to whisper."

"It's okay," said Simone.

"They weren't gone very long," she said. "I was just about dozing off when I heard a car driving off and then the front door slammed. Then when I heard Bradley slam his bedroom door, I went upstairs to see what was wrong."

April hung her head and sobbed. Instinctively, Simone put her arm around her, and April leaned on her shoulder. April's body felt so weak. Like she didn't have any strength left in her at *all*.

"Shh, it's okay," Simone whispered, not knowing what else to say.

When April collected herself, she sat up again and said, "He's not taking Bradley fishing this summer."

"What? Why?" Ooh, now Simone was piping mad. How could he do this to Bradley? *He'd better have a life-threatening good reason, or I'll give him one!* she thought.

"He blamed it on his wife. He told Bradley she doesn't want him around her boys. That he's not a part of their *family*."

Now Simone was fit to be tied. How dare he? How dare this man be such an asshole! At the very least, why couldn't he just *lie* to Bradley? Why couldn't he have made something up, like the trip was canceled? But then she supposed he'd told Bradley all *kinds* of lies for the past few years. Maybe for once he was being honest with his son. *Oh, how the truth hurts!*

"I guess Bradley caused a scene at the restaurant, so his dad brought him home—just dumped him off at the curb. And now he's so upset, and Simone, I don't know what to do anymore." She leaned on her again. "I don't know how to help him."

Simone grabbed April's shoulders and held her at arm's length. She furrowed her brow because now it was time to tell *April* the cold, hard truth.

"You enable him, April! You keep him coddled and sheltered up there in his room, and he doesn't have a life!"

"I know," April said. Simone released her grip, and April grabbed a tissue and blew her nose.

"Why don't you make him go back to school? Or get another job at least? No wonder he's always so depressed. He's bored!"

"You're right," she said. "I know. I shouldn't let him lie around all day. But I haven't been completely truthful with you, Simone."

Simone raised her eyebrows. She waited patiently while April blew her nose again. April looked into Simone's face.

"Bradley didn't drop out of school. He was expelled."

"Why? What did he do?" she asked. When April just sat there, she said, "*Tell* me, April! I'm not going to judge."

"He brought a knife to school."

"What for?"

"Some girl who liked Bradley was dating a football player, so this football player and his friends were harassing Bradley every day at school until Bradley couldn't stand it anymore. Then one day when they approached him in the halls, Bradley pulled out a knife and said *you touch me again, I'll kill you.*"

Simone shook her head. "I can imagine there's a no tolerance policy for things like that."

April nodded. "You got *that* right. Bradley was not only expelled, he had to attend mandatory counseling for *months*. That's why he lost his job at Grover's. He didn't want to tell them what had happened at school, but he missed a lot of days due to his counseling appointments."

Simone sighed. *That poor kid.*

"I'd enrolled him in another school, but by then he'd *mentally* dropped out. He was truant a lot. So finally I said fine, stay home. I thought maybe if I paid him to take care of MeeMaw—"

"What?" Simone couldn't believe it. "You *pay*

him to neglect her?" *Oh, good grief, April!*

April looked at her lap. "Yeah. You're right, Simone. Not the best plan. I know he's a little lazy."

"He's not lazy, April." She couldn't believe she was defending him. How far she'd come! "He's isolated. He needs *friends* his age. How come he never has anyone over?"

"After the knife incident, the two boys he hung out with stopped coming around. I think their parents were afraid of Bradley having an episode."

Well. That was understandable, based on what she'd just witnessed upstairs!

And as if they were both thinking the same thought, simultaneously, she and April looked at the ceiling. It was way too quiet up there.

April grabbed her arm. "Simone, would you go check on him for me? Please? He won't mind if *you* go talk to him."

She nodded. "I will, if you promise to check on MeeMaw." *Poor MeeMaw!* She was probably scared to death, hearing all this commotion.

"Oh, MeeMaw's sleeping," said April.

"April, she can't possibly have slept through all of that—you check on her!"

April shrugged but promised all the same she'd check on her. *MeeMaw probably just PRETENDS to be asleep*, she thought.

Simone made her way back up the stairs. She knocked softly on Bradley's door then a little louder when he didn't reply.

She turned the knob and slowly opened the door. She wasn't used to seeing his room with the light on. It was unnaturally bright. She glanced around the room, impressed with how clean it was—or at least *had* been before trophies and whatnot got thrown all around.

"Bradley?" She peeked in his closet. Where the fuck *was* he? She started to turn around to go check the boy cave but thought she heard something coming from the open window.

She poked her head outside and again said, "Bradley?"

"Mmm," was her reply.

Now she stuck the upper half of her body out the window and looked above her head. She saw where the hem of Bradley's jeans met his shoes. One leg was crossed over the other.

"How do I get up there?" she asked, trying to make her eyes adjust to the moonlight.

"Just stand on the windowsill and hoist yourself up."

Good grief! She was still in her cream-colored dress. But *he* was worth getting a little dirty for. Wasn't he?

She kicked off her shoes and did as he'd said. Where Bradley was reclining there was room for one more body—hers. First she kneeled on the edge of the ledge, then she swung herself around so that her butt made contact with the roof. She scooched up closer to Bradley, who was lying on his back, hands folded across his stomach. He looked at her then looked back up at the night sky.

Simone leaned back on her elbows for a minute or two, then lowered herself all the way down. Now she was lying flat on her back next to Bradley. There wasn't much space between them, and she could feel the heat, emanating from his body.

She turned her head to face his.

"You come out here often?"

He nodded.

She turned her head so she could also look up at the stars. For a long time, she didn't say a word, and neither did he.

Then she said, "Pretty."

"What."

"It's a pretty night," she said.

He sighed.

She let a few more minutes pass. Then she said, "Your mom filled me in on what happened."

She could hear his breathing get a little heavier. "Such an asshole," he mumbled.

"Bradley, your mother is not an asshole!" She turned her head to see if he "got" her little joke. But he wasn't smiling. So she changed tactics.

"I know. What an asshole."

Now he was making weird little choking noises, and Simone realized he was crying. She turned on her side and grabbed on to his arm with her hands and snuggled her face up against his shoulder.

He swiped his eyes with his other arm. It was hard for him to get the words out, but he did his best.

"All I want is my dad, Simone. I just. Want (he took a jagged breath) my fucking dad!"

She squeezed his arm a little tighter—snuggled a little closer. But she didn't say anything. It wasn't her turn to talk. It was Bradley's. And she would listen.

"I just want to be with him," he said. "When he and my mom split up, he said he'd come back for me— that we'd live together in his new house. But it was one excuse after another. Then he and Sheila had the twins, my two younger brothers, and he said when they got older he'd bring me over. But he never did. My brothers are gonna be *five* this summer. Five! Five fucking years he's made me wait." He wiped his face again on his sleeve. "And I don't even know them. I follow my dad on Instagram. My brothers are in T-ball, now. I told him I could help them with their swing. I could play catch with them. My dad and I *always* played catch." It was here he fell apart. He could barely spit out his next words. "I guess he plays catch with *them*, now."

Oh, this was breaking Simone's heart! She could hardly stand it. There was nothing worse than loving somebody *so* much and them not loving you back. And worse—to see the one you loved with someone else, like you were replaced. Poor Bradley! This wasn't *his* fault. He was just collateral damage. But how could she explain this to him? All he knew was that his little brothers were taking his spot in his father's heart. *Hmm.* Just like Jen was taking Simone's place in Travis' heart. It was just so mean. So cruel. And yet the offenders didn't give it much thought at all. *They just treat you like trash. Just act like it's no big deal.* Yeah, she could sometimes glimpse the remorse in Jen's eyes. She could tell Jen, at least, felt a *little* bad. But the worst part was how it all made Simone feel like she didn't belong anymore. Like she'd reached her limit. Like the universe was saying *time to spit you out—we don't have any more use for you. You are so old news.*

So when Bradley said, "You probably think I'm a big baby, crying over his *daddy*. I guess you can't possibly understand."

Now she sat up. She kept her hands on his arm and pushed at him a little as she spoke her words.

"But I do understand!" she said. "Oh my gosh, Bradley, I do!" Now *she* was crying and as soon as Bradley noticed her tears, he sat up.

"No one understands better than *me*," she said. "You feel so deserted and all alone. The abandonment is enough to just *kill* you."

It was quiet. Then—

"I've thought about it, Simone."

She almost gasped. *No!* She hoped he wasn't saying what she thought he was saying. But he was.

"Sometimes I just want to end it," he said. "I think about it a lot."

She put a hand on his face and made him look at her.

"No. You don't," she said.

"But I do!" He started crying again. He looked at her through his tears as though to say *I just want my life to be over* and she looked back at him, lips trembling, as if to say *I know…I know*. She pulled him close into a hug. He rested his chin on her shoulder.

"No, Bradley," she said, rocking him a little and rubbing his back. "You've got too much going for you. You've got your whole *life* ahead of you." *Unlike me! Oh my gosh, I'm the last person who should be counseling him right now!*

"It just hurts," he said, crying on her shoulder. "It hurts so bad!"

"Oh, Sweetheart. I know," she whispered. She rubbed his back some more. "I know."

They remained in their embrace for quite some

time, both of them sobbing. Sobbing in a way only the truly brokenhearted could understand. And it was during this mutual time of compassion that Simone knew what she must do. Even if it was the *last* thing she wanted to do. But she had to.

"I know this doesn't take the place of your fishing trip," she said. "But it would make me really happy if you would do me a favor."

They let go of each other. He looked at her like *what are you talking about?* She took in a deep breath.

"I want you to go to California with me."

Now he smiled a little. But he obviously thought she was just trying to be funny.

"Yeah? California?" he said.

She nodded. "I have plane tickets."

Now he laughed. "You do not have tickets."

She made a face. "*Yes* I do!"

"No way," he said, but she could tell he really wanted to believe that she did.

"I'll prove it," she said. "Follow me."

She carefully scooted her butt down to the edge of the roof and put her feet on top of the windowsill below. Bradley quickly followed suit, no doubt, so he could give her assistance if needed. She appreciated this, but even to her own surprise she monkeyed her way back in through the window with relative ease, despite her form-fitting dress. Bradley hopped into the room right after her.

She grabbed her purse from off his bed, still where she'd tossed it, and pulled out the two airline tickets she never did end up refunding. She waved them like a fan in front of her face.

"Wow!" he said. Then moments later, "What

day are we leaving?"

She looked at one of the tickets.

"Oh, fuck!" She looked at him. "Wednesday."

The next few days flew. When Simone wasn't at the office "doing April's job!" (because April's voice wasn't quite back to normal, yet) she was out shopping with Bradley. It was actually kind of fun. Didn't matter to her how much she raked up on her credit card. *Serves Travis right!*

So it was enjoyable to spoil Bradley a little. She practically bought him a new wardrobe. He was so sweet about it, too—never asking for too much. He'd pick the less expensive pair of shoes or pair of shorts, for example, and Simone would roll her eyes and say *really? I know you want THESE!* and she'd throw the "good" pair onto the counter and swipe her card.

Bradley seemed to be over the events of Sunday night. And quite frankly, so was Simone. As much as she'd enjoyed dinner with the Reynolds clan, she'd left with a bad taste in her mouth. The more she thought of it, the more she agreed with herself that these people were way out of her league and she had no business being around them. They conducted themselves to a higher calling, and this made her feel somewhat…inferior. Almost like she was a bad person. *And I don't need anyone making me feel bad. I can do that all on my own.* As much as she enjoyed the attentions of someone the likes of Desmond Reynolds, she would never—*could* never—think of him as anything more than a client.

So when Des called the office Monday morning with a question for April, Simone fielded it to

Meredith. On all *three* of his calls.

"What's the matter?" Meredith had asked her. "I thought you two kind of liked each other."

But Simone deflected by dumping more responsibility onto the shoulders of Heidi and Jodi, telling them to *suck it up*. They'd be on their own all week because April was sick and had to take care of her mother, anyway, now that Bradley would be gone.

Simone had learned her lesson about showing up at her own house before school hours, so she waited till Tuesday afternoon for her and Bradley to stop by. She wanted to box up the clothes (from her closet, at least) "and clear some space for Jen."

At this statement, Bradley had looked confused. "Wait. Isn't she like the *other woman*?" The *first* time he'd said that was when Simone had grabbed the box of crackers on top of April's refrigerator. "For Jen," she'd told Bradley, "because she's nauseous."

But Jen wasn't home when they got there. Maybe she was volunteering in Robby's classroom, who knew. Travis, of course, was teaching school. So it was nice to be there by themselves, and they actually accomplished a lot.

Before they left, she put a note on the counter:

> *Sorry to let myself in! Cleared some closet space, Jen. (Enjoy the crackers.) Off to CA for my mom's birthday. Talk to you when I get back, Travis.*
>
> *SS*

Not the most eloquent note, she thought, looking it over, *but I suppose I'm capable of leaving worse notes!*

Soon as she and Bradley made it home, they packed for the trip. April was so nervous about her "baby leaving home for so long—" *it's just a week, April, my gosh*, Simone had scolded her—"and on a plane no less!" Simone had just rolled her eyes.

"Yes, April, people fly. They do it all the time."

But whatever trepidation mother felt for son, Simone could tell that deep down April was grateful. Bradley's countenance had changed drastically since Sunday because now he actually had something to look forward to. An excursion to California was the perfect distraction from his asshole father.

It was nice, sitting next to Bradley on the plane. The hours passed—him sharing songs with her from his phone—her briefing him on all the people he would meet.

Seeing California through Bradley's eyes was a treat for Simone. Things she took for granted (like rush hour traffic, cars with no rust, and palm trees) were a novelty for him, and his questions had no end. Simone was glad she'd rented a convertible so they could drive with the top down. He seemed to really like that—his hair, blowing all wild in the wind.

They made it to her mother's house just shy of "dinnertime," which at this house meant "late afternoon." Ron was in the driveway, working under the hood of a car—it was probably Brady's. She'd heard that Bret, at least, lived on his own. *About time!* The boys were what, in their 30's now? Neither one of Ron and Leesa's sons was married. *Shocker.*

Ron smiled real big when they pulled up to the curb. He walked over but didn't hug his sister because he had grease on his hands. Simone didn't mind. They were never the touchy-feely type.

"Hey, Es!" he said.

"Hey, Ron," she said. She introduced him to Bradley. The screen door opened and Simone's mother stepped onto the porch. She looked the same as ever with her red hair piled high in a bun on top of her head. She supported her overweight girth (the aftermath of her weakness—sweets!) by holding the rail as she walked down the steps. *She's slowed down since I last saw her,* thought Simone, walking up to meet her mom halfway. They embraced for a long time as Bradley stood awkwardly by.

When Simone had phoned her mother to tell her she'd be coming out to California after all, her mom couldn't have been more thrilled. She didn't mind one bit that Simone was bringing a 17 year-old, troubled teen as her travel companion (although Simone hadn't breathed a word to anyone about Bradley's issues.)

So when her mom noticed him, standing shyly behind Simone, she gave him a big hug and said, "You must be Bradley. I'm Kate."

"Nice to meet you," said Bradley. "Thank you for having me."

"Oh, no problem at all," she said. "Come on in the house and meet Leesa and Brady."

So they left their luggage in the convertible for the time being so that they could greet the rest of the family.

"Hi, Tess!" said Brady, giving Simone a hug.

Later, when Bradley asked her *why does he call you Tess?* She explained to him how her father had always called her by her first initial, S. And Ron had always followed suit and called her "Es" as well.

"But my dad's full name for me was "the SS Beauty." She cleared her throat more from embarrassment than sentiment. "Nautical humor. My dad was a sailor. Also, my maiden name is Sylvester, so it kind of went together, you know? So when I married Travis—" she paused. Then taking a deep breath she continued. "I knew we were a match made in heaven because his last name is Sanders, and this way I could keep my initials. Hmm. What did *I* know!"

When Bradley still looked confused she said, "Anyway. To answer your question, when they were little, my nephews called me Auntie Es. Then when they got older I became Aunt Es, which sounds like Tess, so now they just call me Tess." But by now, she'd lost him. *Teenage attention span*, she told herself. Bradley was busy looking out the back window, which had a nice view of the beach. Barry Sanders had never been rich or anything, but he'd invested all his savings in this here beach house. He'd always said the fresh, ocean air made him feel so much better, health wise.

Once she'd gotten all caught up with Leesa, which was accomplished in a few sentences (they'd never had much in common) she and Bradley lugged their suitcases into the house. They would both be sleeping on the two perpendicularly touching couches in the little living room because all three bedrooms were occupied. She'd given Bradley the quick 1,300 square foot tour. He'd marveled at the pictures adorning the walls from Simone's cheerleading days.

"You were a rah rah?" he asked. She nodded as if to say *yeah, and I don't want to talk about it.* Although, those had been fun days.

"Who's she?" Bradley asked, pointing to another cheerleader next to Simone.

"That's Bren. You'll probably meet her. I'm sure she'll come to the party on Saturday."

He picked up another picture, displayed in a camo-themed frame. He raised his eyebrows when he said, "Rambo?" (Because Bren had addressed it: To Rambo.) Simone took the picture out of his hands and set it back on the console. She shook her head and they walked away.

Dinner was great. Her nephew did all the cooking these days, along with a bunch of taste-testing, apparently, based on his chubby waistline. He'd prepared enchiladas, one of his specialties, he told her. *At least he makes himself useful*, Simone thought. Course, to hear her mom go on and on about how wonderful he was—*he does this, he does that*—she was left with the impression Brady *couldn't* move out even if he wanted to—not with *that* kind of constant praise and appreciation from his grandmother!

Brady did have a job, but it was a "dumb" job, as Simone labeled it, if only in her mind. In her opinion, a dumb job (for a young man *his* age, anyway) was only part-time and did not require a bachelor's degree. *Definitely the product of his parents.* Because Ron still worked at Food Warehouse. Leesa cleaned houses—said she currently had seven clients. "That's like a house a day!" she reported to Simone. Simone just opened her eyes wide and nodded her head to share in Leesa's excitement, but inwardly she couldn't help but think *Sweetheart, you wouldn't last a day in MY shoes!*

She didn't even *want* to know what the plan was for the 80th birthday party. She thought it was a *little* strange that no one was picking her event-planning brain but figured maybe they were walking on eggshells around her. Since she'd arrived, no one had asked her one question about her doomed marriage or about Travis or Jen or *anything*. She'd at least expected Ron to tease her about it. This was always his way of lightening the mood. Except there really was no mood to lighten. Dinner was…pleasant.

Using a frozen yogurt run as an excuse to show Bradley the town, he and Simone hopped in the rental car after dinner and drove for several blocks. She showed him her high school and the grocery store where she used to work. She drove by the make-out park where kids went after dances and football games. She drove him past Bren's parent's house and pointed out the window upstairs and how they'd sneak out sometimes, via the Oak tree. They drove up the coast a ways, and Bradley drank it all in. Their last stop was her favorite yogurt place on their way back. Good thing she'd written down everyone's order or else she'd have forgotten by now. But this was her treat to the family albeit a small one.

The rest of the evening was spent watching "the evening shows" in the living room—with her mother and Ron, that is. Leesa and Brady were watching their own shows in Ron and Leesa's room, which formerly belonged to Simone's parents. But Simone knew her mother was probably so thrilled to have her son and his family live with her she'd probably *gladly* given up the master bedroom.

Simone's mother said her goodnights at 9:00. "Some things never change," Simone told her. She turned to Bradley and said, "She always goes to bed early."

Ron, on the other hand, had no problem occupying the living room couch a.k.a. Simone and Bradley's sleeping place, keeping them up, late—and they were still on Ohio time, too! But it wasn't so bad. Bradley looked like he was enjoying some of their childhood stories from "way back when." And when Ron hugged Simone goodnight and said, "It's really good to see you, Simone," she was so taken aback by the sweetness in his voice and the use of her actual name that she didn't respond. She just looked at him and blinked.

Simone had changed into sweats and brushed her teeth hours before. Now all she had to do was toss a blanket and pillow at Bradley. He asked her what the plan was for the next day.

"The beach."

Chapter Twelve

Thursday began with a long bike ride on the bike path. Ron and Leesa gladly loaned their beach cruisers to Simone and Bradley who pedaled out to an old, familiar spot near Belmont Shores. Simone wanted her Ohio friend to experience some nice waves and figured this location would be the best that day.

They stopped only for a bite to eat. By then the sun was out in full force. Stomachs contentedly full, they set up camp on the sand with their towels and mini cooler (of sodas and chips) and played Bradley's music on the borrowed JBL from Brady. *I guess Brady could have joined us,* she thought. But it hadn't occurred to her to include him. And anyway, he and Ron had plans to attend the Angel game in Anaheim at noon, and Simone had no intention of leaving the beach.

Here she thought this California trip would be good for Bradley, but it was actually good for her as well. Nothing felt better than to stretch out on the sand in the warmth of the sun, hearing above the music all the customary sounds which could lull a body to sleep: the squawking of seagulls, waves crashing, the wind-muffled conversations of fellow sunbathers floating through the ocean air. Of course, there was also the occasional *holy mac-anoly!* from Bradley. He said this every time he spotted yet another scantily clad girl his age, strutting what her mama gave her on the sand before him.

Simone smiled. "You like the beach?"

He gave her an exaggerated nod. "I like." He was reclining on his back, torso propped up by his elbows. Simone periodically advised him to wear more sunscreen but discovered Bradley didn't always listen to good advice.

"Come on, I want to teach you to body surf," she told him, standing up and walking toward the water. And if she had thought the bike ride over had put a perma-grin on Bradley's face, this *really* did the trick. They swam for at least an hour, maybe more. Bradley soon became an expert at diving under the powerful waves. Simone eventually tired out and left him to play by himself. She collapsed onto her towel, hoping to rid her fingers and toes of their prune-like appearance.

She checked her phone, thinking she'd see yet another message from April (who kept checking up on Bradley, annoying as that was.) Instead, she noticed she had a text from Desmond. *Meredith! She KNOWS I don't want to talk to him!*

His text simply said:

> Simone, it's me, Des. Could you please give me a call at your earliest convenience? I have a question for you.

Why did her heart always do this? It stopped working even at the sight of his name. *Another* reason why she shouldn't interact with him. She felt like calling Meredith and ripping her a new one, knowing *she* had probably prompted this text. Instead she responded to Des with:

> Hey, there, Des. Actually, I'm in

> California on vacation right now.
> I won't be back till next week.

Surely, he'd take the hint. Surely, whatever question he had could be easily answered by Meredith or Heidi or even Jodi. But Desmond Reynolds was nothing if not persistent.

> I'm in California, too.
> Whereabouts are you staying?

She was so surprised she didn't think before responding.

> Staying with my mom in Long
> Beach. She's turning 80 next
> week but her party is Saturday.

She hoped by saying this, he'd back off. But no. Not Desmond Reynolds.

> No kidding? I'm in Sunset. You
> should meet me for dinner.

She was surprised by her own reaction because now, all of a sudden, she wanted to see him. She wouldn't be able to put into *words* how she was feeling, other than that aura of his was drawing her close once again. All the same, she fought it.

> I've got April's son, Bradley, with
> me. I'm afraid I'll have to take a
> rain check.

She figured that solved that! But then:

> No, that's perfect. Bring him
> with you.

She lied and told him they had plans to go out to dinner that night with her family. He texted:

> How about tomorrow? I'm
> having my girls over for a
> barbecue. We'd love to
> have you and Bradley join us.

Wow. What could she say? She knew Meredith would kill her if she jeopardized this account. Simone sighed.

> That would be great.

He seemed so happy with her response—even offered to send a car, but she said *no, just send me your address*. Then she remembered to ask:

> What was your question, Des?

She smiled when he responded:

> Just got it answered.

*   *   *   *   *   *   *   *

The next day Bradley was so sunburned, she

couldn't possibly take him to the beach again, as much as she wanted to. That would be child abuse, she told herself. Not wanting to have to answer to April for 3rd degree burns and yet, not wanting her guest to be *bored* just hanging around the house with her and her mother all day, Simone gave Brady some money and asked him to take Bradley to a movie or something at the mall. Brady was happy to comply.

It all worked out rather well this way. Ron was at work. Leesa was cleaning a house, and Simone's mother was left to shore up the last minute party plans.

Simone offered to return a call to the party supply rental place, but her mother called the number and said, "Don't be silly! You're on vacation, and you'll be doing enough of *that* when you get back."

But when her mom's smile turned to a frown mid-conversation with the vendor in charge of tables, chairs, canopies and whatnot (the party would take place on the beach behind her mother's yard) Simone mouthed out *what's wrong?*

When her mother failed to respond, and when it didn't appear she was making any headway with the party planner, Simone took the phone from her.

"Excuse me, this is Kate's daughter, Simone Sanders. To whom am I speaking?"

Simone stared at her mother as she listened to what the employee had to say.

"I need to speak to your manager."

Simone continued to look at her mother, all the while shaking her head and rolling her eyes. Her mom started to say something, but Simone held up a finger, like *wait*. The manager had just gotten on the line.

"No no no no *no*," Simone said to this person.

"That's completely unacceptable."

Apparently, the company had overbooked (which unfortunately was something that happened *far* too often in Simone's line of work) and they were trying to not only downgrade to five fewer tables of lesser quality, but wanted to do all the set-up a mere hour before the guests were expected to arrive. This would never do!

By the time Simone got through with the phone call, she'd successfully reinstated the original order *and* got a photo booth thrown in at no additional cost as "compensation for the emotional stress" they'd just put her mother through!

Kate Sylvester smiled at her daughter. "Wow. That was fun, watching you in action."

Simone just "sharpened her claws" on her clavicle then blew at her fingernails, like *all in a day's work!* and the two shared a nice laugh.

"Simone, I'm *so* glad you're here."

And Simone believed her. Her mom looked *happy*.

"What are you planning to wear at your party?" she asked.

"I'm wearing the sundress you sent me, of course!" her mother replied.

Oh. Yeah, that's right. Jodi.

"Let's see it," she said.

"*You* know what it looks like!" said her mom.

"I mean, try it on for me." *Good save, Simone.*

Ten minutes later, her mother emerged from her bedroom, donning a really nice Liz Claiborne sundress, complete with accessories and a cute pair of sandals that matched the shade of blue in the dress.

Sheez, Jodi! How much did you spend?

"Mom, you look great!" she said.

"Thanks to *you*," she replied. "You always send me the nicest birthday gifts."

Simone looked down out of guilt. Then she pulled a Ron and made light of it. "Nothing but the best for my mother on her 80th birthday."

"Think of it as an investment," said her mom, loosening the strap of her sandal.

"What do you mean?"

"Someday when I'm gone you'll get it all back. Well. Maybe not the clothes—I'll give those to Leesa because they're too big for you. But you can have all my shoes and jewelry."

Really? Simone didn't want to comment except her mother went on to talk about the Trust she'd set up "in case something happens to me."

"I just want you to have an equal share in this house, Simone. You know it's paid for, and it's worth a lot of money, now." This was true. When her parents bought this house back in the 1970's for a whopping $375,000, they'd thought it was overpriced *then*. Now her mother could sell it for more than a million.

"I don't want you to think that because your brother lives here, it all goes to *him*."

"Mom—"

"I love you both the same, and when I die, I want everything to be divided equally."

"Mom, you're not going to die!" But even she knew how ridiculous this sounded even as she said it. Everyone was going to die eventually, right? *Some sooner than others*, she told herself.

"Simone, I don't know how many more years

you think I have ahead of me. I'm just trying to set things in order. Because I love you."

Simone tried to protest. She told her mom not to worry—to just leave everything in the Trust to Ron and Leesa and the boys.

"Really, Mom. I'm good. I don't need anything."

"But you're on your own, now," she said. "I want to take care of you, Simone. I want you to know that you are always welcome here." She tried to say more, but now she was choking up.

Simone walked over and gave her mother a nice, long hug.

"I know, Mom. I know," she said. And she believed it.

Simone was almost relieved when it was time for her and Bradley to take off for their dinner date with Desmond. When Leesa had come home from cleaning a house that afternoon, she'd immediately proceeded to clean her *own* house—*to get ready for the party.* Simone had felt bad, just sitting there doing nothing, so she'd picked up a dust cloth and helped her sister-in-law make everything look perfect. In the middle of their labors, Ron had come home and started sprucing up the exterior of the home, mowing the tiny strip of lawn out front and blowing and hosing down the deck out back. He'd even cultivated the dirt in all the flower beds. He was still at it when she and Bradley drove away.

When Bradley had come home from his and Brady's movie at the mall that afternoon, he'd looked tired, and Simone's mother had insisted he take a little nap in her room. Simone chalked up his fatigue to too much sun *and a normal person's activity level.*

Now they were both refreshed and ready for a nice evening out. Sunset Beach wasn't terribly far away. Simone took the scenic route, driving along Ocean Blvd. through Naples—the whole nine yards although it was more like nine *miles* altogether. They arrived in Sunset Beach in less than twenty minutes.

Bradley thought the three-story dwellings, "all smushed together" shoulder to shoulder "not much space between them!" were "pretty cool." Of course, Desmond's house was on the beach side of the street. It, too, was a three-story home. All gray. Looked like it was made out of concrete. And this seemed fitting. The structure was nice and strong and solid. *Just like Des.*

Parking *would* have been a chore had Des not texted her to "park in the driveway" when he'd sent her his address, or should she say directions. She thought it was cute how he was trying to take extra special care of her, but honestly, the GPS in the rental car would've been more than fine. All the same, it made her feel like she was a special, honored guest.

Des walked outside to greet them before they had a chance to take the walkway on the side of the house to the "front" door. Naturally, in *this* neighborhood, backsides and garages of homes faced the street, the fronts overlooked the million dollar view.

Simone was toting a chilled bottle of almond-flavored champagne, one of her favorites. As soon as they walked through the front door, Des popped it and poured her a glass. As he was doing this, his two daughters walked into the room, coming down from a spiral kitchen stairway. It was quite impressive, this kitchen. In fact, the whole house was beyond amazing. She never thought Bradley would ever close his mouth, so in awe was he of his surroundings. He was just taking it all in whereas Simone tried to play it cool and keep her focus only on Des and his two daughters.

"Simone, this is my oldest daughter, Delaney, and this is my Daria."

The girls greeted Simone and Bradley with warm hugs, much in keeping with the way the rest of Des' family had greeted her at Granny's house. Simone thought the girls were lovely. Absolutely lovely. She could tell they were every bit as classy as Dante the way they made her (and Bradley) feel so welcome, and once again Simone was feeling like she was royalty or a special celebrity.

Des poured Bradley a Coke. Delaney and Daria helped themselves to the champagne at Simone's urging. "I don't want to drink this by myself!" she had said when it became obvious that Des was not going to have any. Daria thanked Simone, telling her *Dad doesn't keep anything at the house, so this is a treat.*

And as if to answer the puzzled expression on her face, Des told her, "It's not my vice. I have an occasional, social drink. But I can live without it." So it sounded to her that this was merely a preference, and she was grateful she hadn't brought alcohol into the home of a recovering alcoholic.

"Let me show you around," said Des, and she and Bradley followed him into the living room adjacent to the kitchen. Everything was decorated to perfection. He'd chosen lots of grays with black accents—every now and then she'd notice a pop of white amidst green plants in either bronze or white tiled pots. All the furniture faced the massive front window. No TV was necessary in *this* room. The ocean outside was its own entertainment system.

"Is this a private beach?" Simone asked.

"Sometimes I wish!" said Desmond. "It can get pretty hectic here during the summer months. But I suppose that comes with the territory."

"It's part of the experience," smiled Simone, taking a sip of her drink.

Directly behind the big couch was a formal dining area. The tiled space, separating the kitchen from the living area ended with a bathroom next to a staircase, which they proceeded to climb to the second level.

"This is where we spend most our time," said Des. This room had more comfortable-looking furniture (a dark blue, velvet sectional) and a big flat screen TV. The balcony doors were open, allowing the salty air to come into the room. Simone inhaled deeply and closed her eyes. *So nice!*

This level had two guest rooms. "One for me, and one for my sister," smiled Daria.

"Do you visit your dad often?" she asked then quickly added, "Because I sure would if I were you!" Bradley nodded in agreement.

"Not as often as we'd like," said Delaney.

"They live in Calabasas," said Des. "So it's kind of a trek for them."

"Plus, I imagine running a kabillion supermarkets keeps you pretty busy," said Simone. The girls nodded in emphatic agreement.

"We're here for the symposium this weekend over at the Long Beach Convention and Entertainment Center," said Daria.

"It's a supermarket symposium," said Desmond. "This will be the first time in twenty years I won't be there."

"Dad's passing the baton to *us*," said Delaney, giving her dad a little hug.

"Yes," said Des, smiling with pride. "The baton is going to very capable hands." He looked at Simone. "My girls will do a fabulous job."

"No doubt they will." Simone smiled back at him. She was hoping Bradley was listening carefully and taking all this in. She thought it was good for him to be exposed to a family with such a strong work ethic.

But at the moment, Bradley was looking at all the pictures displayed on a credenza spanning the wall near the stairway. Simone glanced over, and Des' wedding picture immediately caught her eye.

"Is this Cynthia?" she asked, touching the top of the frame although as soon as she said it, she felt stupid. Of course it was Cynthia!

"Yes," he said.

"She's gorgeous, Des," said Simone. And indeed she was. Now she could see that Delaney was the spitting image of her mother, whereas Daria looked more like her father. But both Delaney *and* Daria shared the same, dark eyes and dark, wavy hair, and flawless dark skin as their beautiful mother. In the picture, Cynthia's skin almost glowed, especially where the neckline of her wedding dress dropped, exposing her shoulders and clavicle. She was staring up at her groom with eyes that said *I believe in you.*

You are my world. In turn, he was smiling down at her ruby, red lips as if he were saying *I will never let you go. You are mine.* It made such a powerful impression.

"Yes, she is," said Des. And for some strange reason, his agreeing that Cynthia was gorgeous hurt Simone's feelings. And even *she* didn't know why. Was she jealous of Des' ex-wife?

Mercifully, Daria intervened. "Our family took such a hit when my parents divorced," she told Simone. "Dad tried all he could to keep the marriage together."

Simone looked over at Des who nodded. And in some strange way, she felt closer to him in that moment. They had a shared experience. She, too, would have done anything to keep Travis if only he'd been willing. But he *hadn't* been willing. Obviously, neither had Cynthia been willing.

She continued to look at Des, and her silence was her polite way of saying *tell me more.* Her ploy worked because Delaney continued with the story.

"Dad was always a believer," she told Simone. "But when he rededicated his life to the Lord—"

"And got serious with his faith—" Daria interjected.

"She left me," said Des. And that ended *that* conversation. Or at least Simone didn't press them further. But she had a feeling she'd dig it out of Des, later, if she had the opportunity. Because right now, looking at Des and his daughters and this beautiful beach home, she couldn't fathom why any woman would leave him. Unless there was more to the story.

They proceeded up the stairs to the third level, which was all master suite. Des had one of those oversized beds that was low to the ground. It had an expensive-looking, black comforter and was adorned with all the appropriate pillows and an oversized throw at the foot of the bed. The room had no clutter whatsoever. A big, furry black area rug on the carpeted, gray floor served as the main focal point of the room. To the right was the master bathroom, which Simone imagined was spa-like in design, but she didn't step inside. As it was, she felt like she was already invading his personal space. Just seeing his bed caused her mind to wander and wonder what it would be like to wake up next to him. Which even she knew was ridiculous. He was her client! She gave her head a little shake and took a sip of her champagne then headed back out the door and down the stairs.

The girls produced a couple of platters filled with olives, cheeses, vegetables and crackers and brought them out to the deck in front of the main living area. Simone and Bradley were directed to have a seat on the nice, cushy lounge chairs in the enclosed area where patio met sand. By now the sun was starting to set, and how glorious it was to be there, right at this moment. Like Des had planned it this way.

He was now busy taking steaks out of the mini refrigerator next to the grill. He seasoned them with all manner of peppers and spices although they already looked as though they'd been marinating all day.

"You're in for a treat," said Daria. "No one grills like my dad!"

Even Bradley took an interest in the dinner to come, standing by Des and asking questions. But of course, *he'd* be interested. *Bradley really DOES like to cook.* Simone smiled, pleased with how well he and

Des were apparently hitting it off. Meanwhile, Simone engaged in lively conversation with Des' daughters, and by the time dinner was ready, they'd polished off the almond champagne.

The meal was everything she thought it would be. Come to find out, it was filet mignon—*from our famous meat counter*, the girls informed her. Des grilled everything, including the vegetables and roasted potatoes.

By the time they finished eating, they were stuffed. It was dark, now. When Simone started to stand up to take her plate into the house, Daria took it from her, saying *I got it, Simone*, and she and Delaney immediately started to clear the outdoor table. Much to her surprise, Bradley joined in. She stifled a smile because she could tell he liked the girls, who to him were more like "older women" in their early twenties.

"I think we should walk off this dinner," said Des. "Care to join me?"

He stood up and offered his hand. She slipped her small hand into his big one as he led her to the sand. She would have liked to continue on this way, but he let go once she'd slipped off her shoes and set them on the patio's brick mini-wall.

She wasn't sure how far they'd walked, but it felt like a long way. If she didn't know better, she'd say they'd ventured partway into Seal Beach.

"So tell me about yourself, Des," she said when things got a little too quiet.

He chuckled. "Well, let's see. You saw where I spent most of my childhood—near Granny's house. We lived on the next block over. A buddy of mine encouraged me to go to college with him out here in

California when he got a baseball scholarship—"

"What college?" Simone asked, thinking he'd say Cal Poly or UCLA or something. But no.

He said, "Long Beach State."

"Oh, really!" Simone found this fascinating because that's where she'd have gone had she not followed Travis to Ohio and become a Buckeye. "I had no idea you were a Dirtbag!"

This made him roar. "No! Not a Dirtbag. *He* played baseball. I played football. Actually, it was the last *season* of 49ers football."

He went on to tell her how the team was dismantled due to state budget cuts, but she wasn't listening to any of that. Her mind had started to wander. It fascinated her to think *wow. If I had gone to Long Beach State, I might have met Des.*

"So did you share a dorm room with your friend?" she asked.

"Yeah, for the first year I was out here," he said. "But we became good friends that year with another buddy of ours—Kirk, was his name."

"*Was* his name?" she asked.

At this, Des looked upset. She could almost see his mind as it reached back in time to some unpleasant memory.

"Yeah," he said, softly.

"Do you not want to talk about it?" she asked, trying her darndest to be sensitive, but now she *had* to know.

"No, it's okay," he said. They'd reached a big pile of rocks—large rocks, and Des sat down on one of them. Simone sat next to him. He looked at his folded hands on his lap as he spoke.

He went on to tell her that his friend, Kirk, was the start of his success in business. Told her how Kirk's parents had owned a little grocery store in Redondo Beach, but when Kirk's father had passed away, his mother couldn't run it by herself.

"And that's when Kirk had to step up and help her," he said. "He asked the two of us to come on board, so we did—my friend, Eric, and I. So we all moved in to Kirk's mom's place. And she was glad because we paid her rent and lived there all through college even though it was a tight squeeze, all of us crammed into that little two-bedroom house!" Here he laughed. Simone knew exactly what he meant, thinking of her mom's house. But hey, space was a luxury that many beach-dwellers (like her father) couldn't afford. But as any beach-loving Californian could attest to, space was easily sacrificed for location.

"At first, it was great," he said. "The three of us had a good handle on everything. But Kirk was a party-er, and he was starting to party a little too hard." He looked at the water out in the distance then back at Simone. "He started doing heroin."

She could only imagine the rest of the story. So it was no surprise to her when he told her how before long, Kirk's involvement in the running of the store deteriorated to nothing. That Kirk had overdosed one night and died—that his body was discovered under some pier in L.A.

"I'm so sorry, Des." She could tell he was still not over it. He looked as though he'd probably *never* be over it.

"We found out later it wasn't an accident," he said. "It was a suicide. Kirk had left a note—told everyone he was sorry, but his pain was too much."

Simone looked down at her lap. She was afraid if she looked Des in the eye she'd give herself away. That he'd see right through her.

"We had no idea, Simone. No idea he even *had* any pain.   Kirk was *always* joking and laughing. Partying." He paused then said, "He seemed to be living the life. I think what hurt the most was the fact he'd never told us anything. Who *knows* how long he'd been planning to do that."

Simone dug her toes into the soft, cool sand beneath her feet and made a small circle. She mumbled *that's awful, Des. I'm so sorry.*

"And I forgive him for doing that, but man, it was *hard*! You know? It was the absolute most selfish thing he could do. All it did was hurt the rest of us. I didn't think his mom would *ever* get over it. We tried to help her. She insisted we keep living at her house. But even *that* was too painful for her cause not long after, she sold her house and moved back east with her relatives. Eric and I put a down payment on the grocery store and made monthly payments on it for a while."

He let out a big sigh. "Then life just happened so fast. I graduated college, got introduced to Cynthia who had also just graduated with a business degree from USC, and we got married right away. Two years later, we changed our store's name to Sunset Supermarket, and from there we took off."

"Why Sunset?" Simone asked. "I mean, why not Redondo Beach Grocers or something?"

He smiled. "It was my dream to one day buy a house in Sunset Beach. So to keep the dream alive, that's what we named the store."

He told her Cynthia was the driving force behind their tremendous success. That she'd never liked Eric too much, and soon as they could, they bought him out. Then they invested in a second store in Torrance, then in another in Santa Monica....

"On and on it went," he said. "We eventually settled down in Sherman Oaks—"

"Wait, what happened to Sunset Beach?" Simone smiled.

"Happy wife, happy life?" said Des. And they both laughed. "But I didn't mind. I was happy, Simone. It really didn't matter to me where we lived."

"How long have you lived here in *this* house?" she asked.

"I bought this house a few years after Cynthia and I divorced, so let's see...about five years ago."

She didn't mean to pry—well. Yes, she did. So she repeated what the girls had told her earlier.

"She left you because you got stronger with your faith." And exactly what did that mean? That he went to church twice a week instead of once?

They stood up and started to walk back toward the house.

He sighed. "Cynthia and I were what the Bible would call 'unequally yoked.' In other words, *I* was a believer, she wasn't. My granny warned me to be careful, but I fell hard for that woman, Simone. We met through a mutual friend of ours, and I was just *bulldozed* by her passion and zest for life. To this day, she's just a cesspool of energy. And I don't know...I guess I thought she'd eventually come around."

"But she didn't."

"No. She didn't. I mean, she always went to

church with us—I always insisted we bring-up our kids as Christians. But I think my rededication scared her. I'd gone to a Harvest Crusade one summer with my son—"

"Oh, really?" she asked. Bren had wanted to go to one of those crusades the summer after their senior year, but Travis didn't want to, so they didn't end up going.

"Yeah," he said. "I went forward when they did the altar call—prayed with someone. And when I went home I thought everything would work out for me with Cynthia."

"But it didn't."

He shook his head. "At the back of my mind I thought we could sell the business and start doing more things for the Lord. I wanted to go out on the mission field. But Cynthia is so driven. She just wanted to keep *growing* the business, *growing* the business." They walked several steps in silence. "And then she met someone who shares the same mindset as hers." Here his voice trailed off a bit, "and she's been with him ever since."

She sensed this was as far as he'd go. That he wouldn't elaborate. That he wouldn't disclose another word about it. And she was right. She grabbed onto his arm and rested her head against it as they walked—just for a few seconds before letting go.

"It's nice to have someone to talk to. Someone who understands," he said. Simone nodded her head.

When they arrived at the house, it was after 9:00. Simone didn't want to outwear her welcome, so she said her goodbyes to Des and the girls—and even to Bradley. While she'd been walking, it had been determined that Bradley would spend the night on Des' couch and visit the supermarket symposium bright and early the following morning with Daria and Delaney. Simone did an exaggerated *oh really!* But Bradley looked so excited about it, she could hardly say no. And besides, Des promised he could get Bradley back to Simone's mother's house in time for the birthday party. She'd already told him the party would start at 3:00.

It was then she made the spur of the moment decision to invite *Des* to the party. *Why not?* She'd met *his* family, he may as well meet hers. And besides, *I owe him a dinner*, she told herself.

Des looked very pleased with the invitation. "You sure your mom won't mind a total stranger at her party?" He opened her car door for her and she stepped inside.

"Not in the slightest," she said, taking a moment to text him her mom's address. She looked up at him and smiled. "I'll see you tomorrow."

"Goodnight, Simone," said Des, closing her car door.

Goodnight, Des, she said, if only in her mind.

He was still standing in his driveway as she drove down the street and turned the corner.

Chapter Thirteen

Ron and Brady were heavily into their Xbox game when she got home that night. *Of course.* Her first instinct was to sigh and start making herself a bed on the couch so they'd take the hint and take their game elsewhere, but she supposed her mother and Leesa had already retired for the night, and *these* two knuckleheads would make too much noise. They got so excited over a dumb game!

So Simone shook her head and flopped down on the other side of Brady. Without taking their eyes off the TV screen they asked her where Bradley was. When she told them he'd be going to the supermarket symposium in the morning, Ron looked over and said *yeah?*

And during his split second lack of focus, Brady crushed Ron's player and won the game. Ron good naturedly said *dammit!* and the two laughed. Simone laughed, too. *You know…Ron's not a bad father*, she thought. *HE never abandoned his kids.* And he and Leesa actually had a decent marriage. It worked for them. And here they were, spending their meager savings on a party for their mother. She supposed it was the least they could do, living here rent-free all these years. Well. At least they paid the utilities and chipped in for food, but still.

Ron tossed his controller beside him on the couch. "I've always thought it would be fun to go to that," he told her.

"What."

"The symposium."

That's right. Ron has made a career out of Food Warehouse, she thought.

"Well, hey," she said. "I've invited a client of mine to the party tomorrow. He knows a thing or two about the grocery store business. Maybe you could pick his brain."

Before she could quite spit out Desmond's full name, Ron said, "Are you kidding? *That* guy's coming *here*?"

Apparently, Des' reputation preceded him. Either that or Ron really did know a thing or two about his own industry, go figure.

"Just don't tell mom," she said. "I mean, not that he's *coming* here but who he is." She wanted her mom's honest take on Des, unclouded by visions of wealth and prominence.

"You, too, Brady," she said, leaning into her nephew, causing him to topple on his side a bit.

"Yeah, cause I'm such a blabbermouth, Tess." he said, sarcastically. He went back to his game, or tried to, anyway, because now Simone was climbing on top of his side, giving him a Bill Murray type noogie. Try as he might, he could no longer play his game because all three of them were laughing too hard.

She supposed her brother's son wasn't so bad, either.

Early in the morning, she had an erotic dream. She dreamt she was in the little twin bed at April's house, under the sheets, wearing absolutely nothing. Then Travis appeared. He was telling her all kinds of nice things—how sorry he was for going after Jen. And at the mention of Jen's name, Simone all of a sudden had blonde hair, and she was in her twenties. Maybe this was her subconscious mind, telling her that the only way Travis would find her attractive was for her to look more like Jen. Then *he* disappeared, and the next thing she knew, Des was with her. He sat at the foot of her bed. He put her foot on his lap, the one that was poking out of the covers, and he gently began to massage it. He uncovered her leg a little more and ran his fingers up and down her shin. She held out her hands to him and he brought them closer, kissing them with his sensuous lips. She put both hands on the sides of his face and pulled him closer to her. He lied down on top of her, nuzzling his nose into the side of her neck.

And that was it. She woke up. It was one of those dreams where she so badly wanted to go back to it. But try as she might, she couldn't. Which was probably just as well because she had work to do.

Leesa was already out and about, retrieving the birthday cake and a few helium balloons. The party rental crew showed up nice and early *thanks to me!* and did their thing. Simone played the role of supervisor, directing everyone here and there. The photo booth was a nice touch. She was pleased to learn that their guests would get to keep copies of their pictures and that a duplicate set would go to her mother.

So all morning and into the afternoon, all five of them—even Brady—were busy bees, despite the preparations made in advance. When the taco guy eventually arrived, Simone knew it was showtime. Time to get dressed. Like her mother, she wore a sundress with shoes she could easily fling off her feet. She'd even thought to set up a shoe station where the deck stairs met the sand. This way guests could deposit their shoes in one place and not have to search for them after drinking too much booze. Ron had put together a makeshift bar so that their friends could *help themselves to their pleasures* all afternoon.

Once Simone was completely ready, she sat her mom down in the bedroom and did her face. *I'm not used to wearing this much make-up, Simone,* her mother complained, but when all was said and done, Kate Sylvester looked amazing. She smiled into the mirror and gave Simone a big hug.

Brenda was the first guest to arrive. Her husband was out of town, she said, so she brought her youngest daughter with her. Kyla was nine years-old now and had a beach bag in tow. She was the spitting image of her mother at that age, and feisty, too. Outside of a few extra pounds, Brenda looked the same as ever. She sure was excited to see her old friend, Simone.

"Hey, Rambo!" she said, giving her a hug. "Long time no see!"

Simone stopped smiling. She put her hands on Brenda's shoulders and thoroughly warned her *not* to utter that name in her presence ever again. She certainly didn't want Des to get wind of that! She had too many secrets to keep. So when Brenda threatened to call her Rambo all day long, Simone said, "Well, maybe I'll tell everyone what *you* did behind the bleachers at Homecoming."

At this, Kyla looked up at her mother. Brenda covered her daughter's ears with two hands and said, "Okay, *Simone*. You win!"

"I always win," smiled Simone.

She took Brenda out back and helped set Kyla

up with a big blanket nearby so she could play. There were other kids, playing on the beach that day, and she figured a daughter of Bren's was sure to make friends.

When Simone answered Bren's question of *where's Travis?* it was then she told her they were getting a divorce. She would have told her more (*it's funny how easy it is to just pick up where we left off*, she told herself, because it felt like she'd just been with Brenda *yesterday*) but more guests began to arrive. With promises they'd talk later, Simone helped her mother and Ron greet everybody.

In a sense, it started to feel like a reunion. Lots of Ron's friends from high school showed up. There were all kinds of neighbors, past and present. A couple of Simone's aunts and cousins came in from out of town, no less. When she looked around, the party area was full. She had no idea her mother was this popular!

To look at her, you'd never guess that Kate Sylvester was 80 years-old. Simone had always attributed this to good genes, but now as she observed her mother, interacting with all her guests, she decided that she remained "young" because she simply had a happy heart. And this inner happiness radiated to everyone all around her. Kate would never *once* think that *her* kids hadn't turned out right. In *her* eyes, Ron could do no wrong. Leesa was a surrogate daughter (thank goodness!) And Brady was sweet and helpful.

She even likes ME, thought Simone.

And Simone decided even Ron's younger son, Bret, was a good "kid," too. Simone chuckled when he walked out to the deck because she supposed in *her* mind, Brady and Bret were still snot-nosed brats. Not the case anymore!

Bret was quite tall and handsome, and he had a date with him—a tall, lanky blonde-haired girl he was introducing as his fiancé, Amanda. When Bret saw Simone, his face lit up and he gave her a big hug.

"Sorry I didn't come out to see you sooner, Tess! I've been working a lot of overtime." He told her he was living out in Ventura—still employed as a highway maintenance worker. He went on to explain the recent improvements he was personally responsible for on the 101.

He seemed so proud of himself, telling her that as much as he'd always enjoyed living here at the beach "with Gram," he just had to get out on his own. "Time to settle down!" He smiled as Amanda walked over and slipped her arm around his waist. He smooched her lips and said, "Meet my better half."

And for the first time ever, Simone really got to know her younger nephew, Bret. It made her feel bad that so much time had gone by between them. So many lost years. She had basically ignored Ron's kids. *And why?* she asked herself. They were *good* kids.

As she engaged in conversation with Bret and Amanda and mingled with all the guests, Simone kept looking around, waiting for Des to arrive. Every little outburst of laughter, every little sound, would cause her to look over in hopes of seeing him.

Before long, her wish came true. Bradley walked out to the deck, first, and he looked happy.

And then Des appeared. He spotted her immediately, out on the sand by all the tables. To watch him make his way out to her was like watching a President of the United States, making his way down the aisle at the Capitol on his way to deliver a State of the Union Address to the nation. Instead, Des was making his way over with a parcel he was carrying in the crook of his arm. He shook at least a dozen hands because he introduced himself to anyone in his path. Simone smiled. *Look at him.* She didn't know why, but she felt *proud* of him. Proud to know him.

With eyebrows raised, Simone's mother put a hand on her back and asked, "Who's *he*?" By now, Des had stepped down to the sand.

Simone placed a hand on Des' arm as he walked up and said, "Mom, this is my business associate friend I told you would be here today. Desmond Reynolds."

"Des," he said, smiling and giving her mother's hand an enthusiastic shake.

"Nice to meet you, Des. I'm Kate."

"Yes, her name is Kate," said Simone, feeling all gawky and nervous all over again.

"Happy birthday, Kate!" He handed her the box of imported Belgian chocolates he'd been carrying. The sheer gift wrapping alone screamed *I cost a fortune!* And yet, it was the perfect, subtle gift. *Nice touch, Des.*

"A man after my own heart!" said Kate, acting like she was trying to cover the box with her arms. "Hide these, Simone—I will not be sharing."

Des laughed, and Simone took this as her cue to exit stage left so that her mother and Des could get better acquainted. She passed Ron on the way into the house and grabbed his arm.

"Mom's talking to Desmond. Remember what I said." He tilted his head back like *no worries, Es!* She knew she could count on Ron to play it cool.

And later, he did. Ron and Des hit it off big time. Ron gave him a cold beer and called all his high school buddies over. They all looked like they were swapping funny stories. *Hopefully, none about me,* thought Simone. She was paranoid because it seemed Des constantly looked over at her, and their eyes would meet. He seemed to be finding his own entertainment, though, which she found refreshing. Over the years, she'd gotten used to Travis, who wasn't very social.

At long last, Ron got everyone's attention so he could say all manner of wonderful things about the "birthday girl," who sat beside him and smiled up at him like there was no tomorrow. And if that didn't warm Simone's heart to see her mother and her brother looking so happy, what her mom did next made her downright want to cry.

Kate Sylvester stood up beside Ron and said, "Thank you all so much for coming out today and making my birthday so special, my goodness! I just want to thank my son, Ron, and his lovely wife, Leesa—and Brady, too! (everyone laughed) for spoiling me this way." She had her arm around Ron, and she turned to smooch him on the cheek.

"I also want to thank my daughter, Simone, for coming all the way out from Ohio to be here today." Now everyone was clapping and woo-hooing. "Simone, you really made this day *extra* special. Thank you, Honey."

It was then her mother walked all the way over to her and gave her a big bear hug. Simone held back her tears as all manner of thoughts flooded her brain.

What if I had spoiled this beautiful party? Am I really that selfish? Maybe Heidi and Jodi are right.

Maybe I AM a Stone Cold.

But no sooner did the thoughts come than she let them fly away. She didn't have time to get weepy right now. Not with Desmond standing nearby. Thankfully, out of the corner of her eye she saw Leesa, fast approaching the cake table, gesturing for Kate to come over. A few attempts were made to light the candles, but here at the beach, gusty winds made something like that an impossibility.

Ron got everyone started on the "Happy Birthday" song. When their mother faux-blew-out her unlit candles, everyone laughed. One of Simone's uncles shouted, "Oh, no! Senility's set in!" and this caused another wave of laughter.

Des came up close behind Simone. The feel of his hand on her back made her all googly inside.

"You have a nice family," he told her.

She nodded. And for the first time ever, she thought *yes. I do.*

"And what a great day for a party!" he said. "I was going to take my cake over by the water and enjoy the sunset. Care to join me?"

She nodded. Des grabbed two plates from the table where Leesa and Bren were furiously cutting slices of cake, plopping them onto plates and jabbing each piece with a plastic fork. Once again, the wind made this a necessity. Paper napkins had to be weighted underneath the plates.

They found a nice spot to sit on the sand not too far from the water's edge. It really was a beautiful day and now an equally beautiful evening. Just as she'd suspected, Bren's little Kyla had made a few friends and was busy creating a castle a few feet away with two sunkissed sandmates.

"I hope Bradley behaved himself last night," she said, taking her first bite of cake.

"We had a good time," said Des.

"Oh, yeah? What did you do?" she asked.

"We had a really nice talk."

"Oh, yeah? About what?"

"About life," he said. He looked over at her. "Bradley's got some challenges."

She nodded. "I know."

"I told him I know his father."

"You do?" She didn't mean to ask right after her second bite, mouth full, but what a small world!

Des laughed. "Not his earthly father, Simone. His heavenly father."

Oh. But before she had a chance to feel stupid, he continued.

"I basically walked him through the Bible, from Genesis to Revelation. Told him everything I know. And in all of that, I showed him how much his father in heaven loves him no matter what."

She just nodded and handed Des the rest of her cake. *Okay. That's cool, Des,* she thought. *Anything to calm that kid down.*

"And then I prayed with him. And we talked about his future."

"I'm so glad, Des," she said. "Bradley needs something to do with his life. I'm glad he got to listen to a real role model. Someone who's made it in life."

Des looked out at the waves. "Well. I'm not just talk, Simone. I back my words with action. I told him I'd help get his job back at the store. Laid out some preconditions for him." He looked at her and gave her a little nudge. "I think he understands."

"I think that's great, Des." She didn't quite understand what that meant, but she soon would once she returned to Ohio.

"Did you have a nice birthday, Mom?" Simone looked at her mother. It was way past the birthday girl's bedtime—almost 10:00! She and her mom and Leesa and even Ron, Brady, and Bradley were busy with the post-party cleanup.

"Yes, it was wonderful!" she said. "More than I ever expected. Thank you all so much!"

Simone had to ask. "What did you think of my friend, Des?"

"Oh, he's *nice*—and handsome!" Kate smiled at her daughter and made her eyebrows go up in one quick little movement, a gesture not lost on Simone.

Oh, no. Was she that obvious? Could people see on her face how attracted she was to this man? And as if to confirm not just to her mother (and an eavesdropping Ron and Leesa) but to herself as well that she was in *no way* deluding herself that this relationship could ever cross over into something more, Simone said, "He's my *client*, Mother."

She smiled. "Yes, I know. He told me he's retiring soon and that his son is starting a Sunset Supermarket in Ohio and you're helping them plan a grand opening on Memorial Day weekend."

Her mom was looking at her again. She looked like she was up to something.

"And?" said Simone.

"Oh, nothing," said her mother. Kate stumbled a little over a plastic chair. Simone had the party rental place so paranoid, they'd said they wouldn't retrieve their tables until close to midnight. *Just in case.* Simone had agreed if only to be persnickety, full well knowing this party would be put to bed long before then if she knew anything about her mom.

And as if to validate her thoughts, Leesa said, "Mom, why don't you get to bed? *We'll* clean all this up for you, okay?"

"Good idea!" said Simone. "It's been a long day. You go turn in for the night."

"You know, I'm not even going to protest," said Kate with a laugh. She picked up her shoes and advanced up the steps of the deck. She thanked her children once again for a wonderful day.

The photo booth guy appeared on the deck. Bradley or Brady must have let him in through the house. He immediately began to unplug everything and prepare for loading.

Simone raced up the stairs and saw that the designated table for photos was completely full. A sheer, Plexiglas sheet blocked the wind from blowing all the pictures away. "Are these what people left behind?" she asked him. Then in broken English he reminded her that these were all for her mother to keep.

Simone looked at all the pictures, all the while laughing at some of the poses—"Ron, check this out!" She showed him the one of Bret and Brady being ridiculous.

Then her wheels started turning. If it was the last thing she did, she would give her mother the perfect birthday gift.

Chapter Fourteen

"There's something to be said about a short commute." Simone was talking to Meredith, who was only half listening. She was staring intently at her computer screen as Simone stood in the doorway to her office. "If I can, I'll come back later, but I think everything's under control."

"Mmm." Meredith barely looked up.

She's probably working on the next "big client," she told herself. Just as Simone was about to close the door and walk away, Meredith said, "You know he made a special trip for you."

At first, Simone thought she was talking about one of the grand opening vendors who must have come to the office while she was out on the west coast.

"Who?" she asked, pivoting back around.

"Who do you think? Desmond. He went all the way to California. Just for you."

Simone shook her head. "Well, it's true, Meredith, that we met a couple times while I was *there*," she said. "But he didn't go out there for *me*! His daughters were in town that weekend for a symposium, so he went out to see *them*."

Meredith shook her head. Simone couldn't tell if her boss was moody that day or just out of it because she had no expression on her face. No tinge of some devilish grin as if to take credit for playing matchmaker. After all, *she* was the one who had encouraged Des to contact her.

"No," said Meredith. "He went there to see *you*. He told me." She took a sip from her coffee mug then set it back down on the desk. "He also told me I shouldn't *tell* you that!"

She knew Meredith wouldn't make *up* something like this, so it must be true. She wanted to play it cool, though, so she slowly closed the door.

But oh, this new revelation made her want to shout for joy. She practically skipped to her car. *So Des is into me! It's not my imagination, either. He's so smooth, too, if he really did make the trip just for me.*

And for the first time in weeks, Simone got her mojo back, as she told her reflection. She checked her face in her rearview mirror, and she liked what she saw. Of *course* Des liked her. Why wouldn't he? And now that she was on to him, she wouldn't hold back. Now that the emotional playing field was level, she determined to *really* make him like her.

For the first time in she didn't know how long, Simone felt like she could conquer the world.

She didn't even mind anymore that she had to see Travis. They were meeting at a Greek café near the house, soon to be their *former* house. Travis had asked a realtor to join them, and today Simone would sign the necessary documents to put the house up for sale. She'd told Travis he and Jen could go ahead and live in it. *She* certainly hadn't cared back when she'd planned to die. And now that she had something to live for, she cared even less. As far as she was concerned, her life with Travis was all a tainted memory. An illusion of something that had never really existed. And *Travis* certainly never cared much for the house. He'd always complained it was *too big* and *too white*.

For the most part, their meeting wasn't as painful as it probably should have been. Who knew?

Maybe she was still basking in the afterglow of her California vacation. She'd been home for two days, and even April had commented that "something's different about you."

Maybe it was because she was humming all the time. Or maybe it was because she'd asked April to help her make a scrapbook. Simone wanted to create a memory book for her mother with all the photo booth pictures she'd discreetly confiscated from her mom's party. It's not like her mom was missing them—*she probably has no idea she even gets to have her own copies.*

So when Travis asked her how she was doing, looking at her like she'd crack then crumble if he said the wrong thing, she said, "I'm great, Travis. How are you?" Then she added, "How's Jen?"

This must've taken him off-guard because he shrugged a little and said Jen's morning sickness was getting a little better. Of course, he didn't thank her for leaving Jen the crackers!

The realtor's eyes looked like they were watching a tennis match, going from Travis to Simone and back again, which made Simone want to laugh.

Signing the listing agreement wasn't too painful, either. If she was completely honest with herself, Simone would say that it brought her a sense of closure.

"If it's okay, I'll come by this weekend and remove all the stuff I want," she said. "Which won't be much. Just my clothes and personal things."

"We can have an estate sale," Travis told her. "We can split the profits from the furniture. Unless there's a few things you want to keep."

But my, isn't he accommodating! She thought about this a second then decided *no. No point.* She was comfortable at April's house, and that's where she would stay. For the time being, anyway.

"I don't really want anything, Travis," she said. Then to have a little fun with this, she added, "I don't want any reminders of our life together, seeing it was all a lie."

At this, their realtor coughed and made some excuse about having to rush off. She shook their hands and collected the papers and left. Her two clients watched as she passed their booth outside their window and rounded the building, out of sight.

Travis turned his attention back to his soon-to-be-former wife. "Simone. It wasn't a lie."

"Well. *Whatever* it was, I'm over it," she said. Point blank she asked, "Did you file the divorce papers?"

He nodded. "Actually, since you didn't want to contest anything, we were able to do a dissolution of marriage. It's a lot quicker—takes about a month."

She stared at him. Didn't speak. And it worked. He started to squirm a little.

"And I've already paid for it, so no worries about *that*," he said. "It wasn't too much."

She continued to stare. He continued to squirm.

"Soon as it goes through, I'll mail you the papers. All you have to do is sign them and mail them in."

She nodded, slowly.

And that concluded their meeting. He held the heavy glass door open for her, and without looking back, she got into her car and drove away.

She arrived back at April's to a great big commotion. Not quite as serious this time as the one with Bradley, but it was every bit as noisy. And on top of all the voices, talking all at once, a little clinking sound could be heard, coming from the kitchen. It sounded like Bradley had a friend over because she could hear him laugh every now and again.

"No, Mom, I will not!"

Uh oh. April never called MeeMaw "Mom." Something was up.

The Old Lady Club plus April were congregating at the dining room table. It was Wednesday and for whatever reason, April was home early from work.

"Simone, tell them to stop their nonsense!" said April, pleading with her eyes.

Simone played dumb. "What are you talking about?"

"They want me to go on a date with someone!"

"*Who*?" she asked, still playing dumb.

"Carter Hamilton from church," she said. "They think I like him, and they've arranged a date for me with him this Saturday!"

MeeMaw winked at Simone and Simone asked, "Well, what's the matter with that?"

"Oh, I don't know!" said April. "Because it's *wrong* on so many levels?"

Simone wanted to laugh in the worst way.

"But he's agreed to it, Dear," said MeeMaw. "Just think of it like a blind date."

"Mom, the last person I dated was Tim!"

"Yes, Dear, I know," said MeeMaw. "That's why you need our help."

MeeMaw's friends were all nodding in agreement.

"I'm not going," said April. "Just call the whole thing off." She stood up and pushed in her chair as though she were positioning herself to storm out of the room, if need be, if only to make a statement.

MeeMaw and her friends frowned and made little gasping noises. One of them said, "Help us out, Simone. Tell her to go!"

"I think you should go," said Simone.

"Whose side are you *on*?" asked April.

"Oh, good grief, April! What is wrong with you? You need to get out of this house *once* in a while. Just go!"

"No."

Suddenly, that smooth-sounding, rich voice she was beginning to know so well came from the kitchen. Then Des appeared in the doorway.

"Everything okay in here, ladies?" he asked.

Simone smiled. She scanned his body head to toe. She'd never seen him dressed this casually. He was wearing old, ripped jeans with a faded burgundy t-shirt. He even had on tan work boots.

"Des!" she said. "What are *you* doing here?"

Now Bradley joined him in the doorway. Des tilted his head in Bradley's direction and said, "Oh, not much. Just taking care of some preconditions." He winked at Simone as though she ought to understand.

"We're fixing things up around the house," said Bradley.

This was just so weird. Back at her mom's house, Des had told her he'd be flying back to Ohio that week—she hadn't realized it would be this soon.

"Today we're working on a new faucet for the kitchen sink. But I'm afraid I'm a little rusty."

It was now she noticed that the collar of Des' t-shirt had a big wet spot. This was what Bradley must've been laughing about in the kitchen.

"Isn't he sweet to do this, Simone?" April asked. And now she knew why April was home early.

"Oh, it doesn't have much to do with *me*," said Des, "as much as it has to do with Bradley. *God* loves him unconditionally, but before he starts working for Dante, he has to satisfy some preconditions, first."

Bradley just stood there and smiled.

Des nudged him. "And I expect you to be ready on time Sunday morning, bright and early."

"He's making me go to church," said Bradley.

April couldn't contain herself. She clapped her hands together. And even MeeMaw uttered a *praise the Lord* under her breath.

And once again, Simone felt anger, like the second Bradley stepped out to do something (anything!) good, his mother always had to ruin the moment by being stupid. So she decided to deflect the attention over to April.

"Now if only Bradley's mother was as smart as Bradley, she'd listen to good advice." Simone folded her arms and leaned against the wall. This was starting to be fun—putting April in the hot seat.

"And what advice might that be?" asked Des.

"We've set her up on a date this Saturday with a *nice man*," said MeeMaw, "but she won't go!"

Des raised an eyebrow. "How come, April? You don't like him?"

MeeMaw answered *for* her. "Oh, she likes him,

alright. She's just bashful."

"Embarrassed to *death* would be a more accurate description," said April.

"Okay," said Des. "So aside from *that*, what's your main objection?"

April put both hands on the sides of her head like she was overwhelmed beyond belief. "I haven't been on a date since I met Bradley's father!"

"So?" said Des. "When's the last time you rode a bike?"

Simone was trying not to laugh out loud. But this was fun, watching the volley between them.

"Gosh, I don't know," said April.

"And you don't think you could hop on a bike right now and ride it?" he asked. When April's face showed doubt, he said, "What if it had training wheels? Could you do it, then?"

"I don't know what you're trying to say," said April, sinking back down into her chair.

"What if you took another couple with you? Would it be easier for you *that* way?" asked Des.

"Oh, I think that's a wonderful idea!" said MeeMaw although April shook her head.

"Simone, you'd tag along with her, wouldn't you?" asked Des.

She opened her mouth to speak but Des said to April, "Simone and I could join you guys."

April thought a moment, and much to Simone's surprise she said, "Well. Okay, that could be do-able. Would you go, Simone?"

Would I! she wanted to proclaim. But she was far too cool for that. She merely said, "Well, actually, I think it makes a lot of sense, April. Des and I could sort of scope him out for you—"

"See if he's worthy of you," smiled Des.

April looked around at all the expectant, smiling faces staring back at her. Even Bradley had an amused look on his face.

When she said *oh, alright!* the room erupted in cheers. MeeMaw uttered another *praise the Lord!*

"I fail to see why we have to go to this much trouble," complained April. That's all she'd been doing all afternoon—complaining about the upcoming double date. "What if we don't even like each other?"

Simone rolled her eyes. "It doesn't matter! You are *long* overdue for a makeover, April."

They were driving home in Simone's car from the never-ending shopping trip from hell. It had been like pulling teeth to get April to try on clothes at Rancher's Roundup because she seemed to have an objection to everything Simone had picked out for her.

Not my color. Not my style. Too young. Too tight. Too short.

It was determined (by Des) that the date would transpire at a brand new, country-western bar in North Ridgeville. Simone had suggested they go to dinner and a movie, but Des thought it would be more fun to throw some dancing into the mix.

"You two-step?" she'd asked him.

"Yeah, I two-step!" he'd responded.

Would this man ever cease to amaze her? She didn't know many two-stepping, African-American men out there and told him as much. He confessed that he'd always been a fan of country music.

"It's wholesome," he'd told her.

So in good faith, Simone had picked up a DVD so she and April could practice a few line dances before the big date. Des told her they would arrive at Boots (MeeMaw loved the name!) a little early and take the two-step lessons together, saying that it wouldn't hurt him to have a refresher course. "I haven't been western dancing for many years," he'd told her.

So Simone was excited. She only wished April could share in her enthusiasm. Simone had found *herself* an outfit right away. She'd splurged on a light brown, suede skirt with fringes above the knee. This she would wear with a pair of old cowboy boots she already owned (but never wore, so they looked new.) Not sure what to wear *with* the skirt, she'd bought several different tank tops in different colors.

Finally, April agreed to buy a black pair of Wranglers and a long-sleeved, shimmery red shirt with fringes on the two front pockets. She said all the boots she tried on felt uncomfortable. "Good grief, April! You've got to have the most sensitive feet on the planet!" So she talked her in to a comfy pair of black suede shoe boots.

"The pant legs of your Wranglers are so long, they'll give the illusion you're wearing boots."

And that was that. For *that* day, anyway.

The next day, Friday, she treated herself and April to a manicure at her favorite salon. Saturday morning, she set April up with her personal hairstylist. This was April's biggest objection.

"How long have you worn your hair this way?" Simone had to practically growl at her to make a point. When April shrugged, Simone said, "Just as I thought. It's time for a change, Friend!"

Simone paid extra for April to get her hair straightened. Now, instead of her customary, frizzy bangs, April sported a part on the side of her head with her bangs brushed to one side. She looked like a brand new woman.

"Oh, my!" April said, smiling into the mirror. "I want to kiss you!" she said to the stylist.

"Save your kisses for your date," said Simone. She laughed at April's shocked expression then ushered her home. *Now* she needed to do her face.

"Trust me, April."

If she thought it was a pain to do the clothes and the haircut drill with April, this was the worst. She'd even asked her, "What, is wearing make-up against your religion or something?"

April shook her head. "I just don't like it," she said.

"Well, it likes you!" said Simone, admiring her handiwork. They were in MeeMaw's room so MeeMaw could join in on Simone's fun.

"What do *you* think about make-up, MeeMaw?" asked Simone, thinking MeeMaw would more or less have an Amish point of view.

But MeeMaw said, "If the barn needs painting, paint it!" At this, Simone *roared*.

She laughed even harder when MeeMaw said, "Ugly ain't spiritual."

"*Mee*Maw!" said April, but she, too, couldn't help but laugh. Simone thought *finally, April's having fun with this.*

As for Simone, she was ecstatic. For the first time in weeks, she felt alive. And happy. Like everything was good and well in the world. Even *she* was surprised by her heightened, emotional state.

And laughing right there in MeeMaw's bedroom, little did she know that somewhere during the upcoming, magical night ahead, during the double date, during all that country-western dancing, Simone Sanders would let herself fall madly in love with Desmond Reynolds.

Chapter Fifteen

"It's not like he *did* anything," she told her mother over the phone. It was such a nice day, Simone was enjoying her Sunday afternoon conversation on the front porch. She swiveled on the patio chair, feet up on the railing.

"Sounds like he didn't have to," said her mother. "You sound absolutely smitten, and I couldn't be happier for you, Simone."

And if she could smile even bigger, she did just then. In almost a squeak because she was so excited, she asked, "Do you think this is going way too fast? Is Des what you would call a rebound relationship for me?"

After all, the ink on her divorce papers wasn't even dry, yet. She hadn't even *received* the papers, yet.

"Based on what you've told me," said her mom, "I think it's all perfectly normal. If I hadn't had the pleasure of meeting him, yeah, I might think you were crazy!" They both laughed. "But he sounds so committed, Simone. I mean, really, *really* committed to you."

Her mother was right. Des *was* committed. More strongly than mere words could express, he'd already shown her in so many different ways that he was devoted to her. That he wanted a relationship with her. And they hadn't so much as shared a kiss.

And despite the *absence* of the standard, goodnight kiss, the double date had gone *way* better than planned. Even April had said so.

Des had hired the Rolls Royce guy to pick up

himself, then April's date, Carter, and then finally April and Simone. Both men had presented their "dates" with flowers. Even MeeMaw got into the action, acting like April was still in high school and off to prom. With Bradley's help, she'd walker-ed herself out to the foyer to send everybody off.

Des looked dashing in his Ropers and Wranglers, *my oh my!* What *was* it about cowboy clothes that were so damn sexy? Or maybe it wasn't the clothes at all. Des could have worn a toga, and Simone would have been just as impressed.

April seemed bashful at first with Carter, but once Simone coaxed a couple of drinks into her, she lightened up, considerably. She was actually pretty funny. The whole date was lighthearted and fun, from dinner at the steak house to the two-step lessons and of course, all that dancing.

Des was amazing. *Rusty, my ass!* thought Simone a time or two. He was able to swing her around and dance beside her at times—skillfully leading and guiding her all about the dance floor. She caught on pretty quickly, but even if she hadn't, all she had to do was follow his lead. His capable, strong hands—one on her waist and the other holding her hand—made her feel so comforted. So wanted.

And he was right. He *was* a social drinker. He only had three beers all evening, but that was enough. He really didn't need it. Des gave the impression that he could have fun in any situation, with or without liquid encouragement.

April and Carter hadn't danced as much as she and Des danced, preferring instead to talk at the booth and get to know each other better. Although, Simone and Des did their share of talking as well. Mostly, they talked about Bradley. Simone learned that Des' "preconditions" set forth for Bradley (before he could work at Dante's store) included making repairs around the house and going to church on Sundays.

"Anything in life worth having is worth working for," Des told her. And the way he looked at her after saying this convinced her that *he* was playing for keeps. All she heard was *I love you madly, Simone.*

And while she knew this comment was directed to *her*, she played dumb and said, "April can't thank you enough, Des." She really *had* seen a difference in Bradley. Gone were the days of sleeping all the time!

"I want him to go back to school," said Des.

"At least get his GED, right?" she asked.

"And beyond." Simone raised her eyebrows when Des said he'd be willing to send Bradley to college, "*if* that's the route he'd like to take."

Wow, you really do back up your words with action, she thought. But she didn't say anything. She chose instead to bask in her partner's presence…his gorgeous eyes. His sexy scent. His warm body. *Mmm.*

She wanted nothing more than to kiss him all that night. Wanted to kiss him passionately, right there on the dance floor. She felt like he wanted to do the same, but for whatever reason, he held back. And all this accomplished was to drive Simone *wild*. She even tried some of her subtle tricks to get him to *make a move, already!* But Desmond Reynolds was far too solid to fall for any of her shenanigans. And she dared not try her more aggressive moves with him because her instincts told her he was not one to toy with. He was *nothing* like Travis. Simone could *not* push Des around. And much to her surprise, she didn't want to. Manipulating this man was the last thing she wanted to do. *Been there, done THAT!* she told herself. Nope. This time around, she would let the object of her affection pursue *her*, so she'd know it was for real.

So as she told her mom, "It's not like he did anything. He didn't *make* me fall in love with him. I just am."

And she no sooner reported to her mother that she'd been invited to Granny's that evening for Sunday dinner with Des' family than MeeMaw's entourage pulled up in the driveway. Simone concluded her conversation with, "Keep an eye out on the mail, Mom—I'm going to mail you a special package this week." She was just about finished with the mini scrapbook o'photo booth pictures she and April had been diligently working on for the past few days. Her mother just chuckled and said *all right, Simone. Enjoy your dinner, tonight.*

Simone walked up to the minivan in the driveway and asked, "Where's April?" Supposedly, April had gone to lunch after church with the Old Lady Club that day.

"She went to lunch with *Carter*." MeeMaw's face gave away her excitement. Simone had to laugh at *all* the adorable, smiling faces in the car. *They are so proud of themselves,* she thought as she helped MeeMaw get out of the car.

"April wanted me to tell you that Bradley's with Desmond this afternoon." Simone already knew this, so she nodded and said *well, MeeMaw, I guess that just leaves you and me.*

They both turned to wave a final goodbye to

the departing minivan.

Simone surprised even herself by thinking there was nothing she'd rather do at this moment than spend some quality time with MeeMaw.

She helped her change out of her Sunday dress and into her usual nightgown and slippers. She fluffed the pillows on the headboard and turned on MeeMaw's favorite channel—her 24 hour religion network, as Simone labeled it.

She sat in the chair by MeeMaw's bed.

"Did you like the church service this morning?" MeeMaw asked her.

More than you know! she wanted to say. At the conclusion of their "double date" the night before, Des had invited her to church with Bradley and him that morning, and she'd willingly accepted. She'd enjoyed being seen with Des and even more than that, sitting beside him in the pew. Every time the pastor asked the congregation to pray, Des had grabbed hold of Simone's hand. She could have sat and held his hand all day! But she knew he and Bradley had plans to help Dante after church. Surprisingly, she'd *liked* church that morning. She'd even paid attention this time to the actual message—something about the importance of reading God's word.

"You gotta read it to believe it," smiled MeeMaw as they continued to discuss the morning sermon. "It's *all* in here." MeeMaw reached over and lovingly patted the cover of her Bible, resting on the nightstand.

"*What's* all in here?" said Simone, smiling back at MeeMaw.

"All the answers to life's problems," she said.

Well, I'm not too sure about THAT, thought Simone. Wasn't the Bible antiquated and outdated? How on earth could something written so long ago be relevant to modern times?

All the same, she nodded in agreement with MeeMaw so as not to offend her. Then they both turned their attention to the preacher lady on TV.

Ironically, she was preaching along the same lines as the pastor at Lamb's Book. "You have to study the Word for yourself," she said. "God's word is alive and powerful and sharper than any two-edged sword," she said.

Simone hated to admit it, but she was entranced by this woman. As much as she wanted to pretend that she was merely "enduring" the program for MeeMaw's sake, nothing could be farther from the truth. She was captivated.

Fifteen minutes into it, she turned to discuss this phenomenon with MeeMaw. But MeeMaw had fallen asleep. Her head was tilted back a bit, and her sweet little mouth was wide open.

Normally, this would be the perfect "escape" for Simone. On any other day, she'd have tiptoed out of the room, saying *sayonara* to the preacher lady on TV. But not today. Today Simone sat glued to her seat.

The preacher woman ended her message with, "Take the challenge. Read God's word. I promise, you won't be disappointed."

The woman smiled at the camera, and that was that.

Simone glanced at MeeMaw's Bible, still resting on the nightstand. She looked at MeeMaw and determined by her heavy breathing that MeeMaw was out for the count.

Simone silently picked up the Bible and opened it to the very back, to the book of Revelation. That's the book MeeMaw's friend had read from on that infamous day long ago at the pancake restaurant. As the preacher lady had suggested, Simone wanted to see the words for herself.

She skimmed the book, chapter by chapter, not quite comprehending much of it. It painted such a dismal picture of so-called future events, and a lot of it was hard for Simone to understand. But eventually, she found herself in chapter 20. She read:

> *And I saw the dead, small and great, stand before God; and the books were opened: and another book was opened, which is the book of life: and the dead were judged out of those things which were written in the books, according to their works.*

Perhaps MeeMaw was right. God's word *was* alive and powerful because it was making Simone's *heart* pound, especially when she read the last verse.

> *And whosoever was not found written in the book of life was cast into the lake of fire.*

And *why* was her heart pounding? These were the exact words that were read to her at the pancake restaurant. The words hadn't bothered her this much *then*. Or maybe they had! Perhaps they'd been brewing in her subconscious in all the weeks leading up to today. Maybe that's why they were suddenly having such an impact on her.

Then she remembered how Des had asked her if *her* name was written in the Book of Life. And Simone honestly didn't know. But she *wanted* to know. If there was the remotest possibility that the Bible was all everyone claimed it to be, and if there really was a book called the Book of Life, Simone wanted *her* name to be *in* it. So she closed her eyes and prayed.

She'd never done this before. She didn't even know if she was doing it right. But she just approached it the way they did at church. She just closed her eyes and talked to God. She asked Him to put her name in the Book, if it wasn't there already. "And if my name is blotted out, please rewrite it," she whispered.

She had a long conversation with the Lord. And then she sat quietly and waited. And listened.

And when the tears began to roll down her face, she knew that she'd been heard. Somewhere deep down within her, she knew her name was recorded in the Book. She felt a peace she'd never felt before.

And somewhere, deep within her spirit, Simone Sanders knew she would never be the same.

It was hard to believe the grand opening was now only a few days away. How time had flown! Simone had worked side by side with Des every step of the way. They'd been inseparable. When they weren't at the office, they were out having fun. It seemed they were developing a great routine: country-western dancing on Saturday nights, church on Sunday mornings, and dinner at Granny's on Sunday evenings.

When he wasn't with Simone, Des spent time with Bradley, who was now working nights at Dante's store. He had Wednesdays off, and since this was MeeMaw's day to hang with her homies, as he affectionately called them, Des had gently suggested *that* be the day that Bradley honor his mother with lunch.

So as of the past couple of Wednesdays, it was Bradley's new habit to bring lunch to the office for April and her colleagues, something he made himself, of course. Heidi and Jodi always went out to lunch, so they didn't partake. But Meredith did. She always shut herself into her office, anyway, so this was April's way of including her. Simone told everyone that Meredith's isolation was merely *her way of coping with all the stress* although she personally didn't understand it. Meredith had nothing to worry about. Obviously, the "big client" was happy. Obviously, the client was enamored. *With me*, she'd think with a giggle. What could go wrong? All the same, despite the reclusiveness of the "big boss," April's new habit on Wednesdays was to transform the conference table in Meredith's office into a picnic of sorts for the three of them plus Bradley.

"There's a bunch of mail for you on the dining room table," Jen told her. The way she said it, with a hint of dread in her voice, caused Simone's instincts go on high alert. She played it cool, though. She just nodded and continued packing her things.

She and Bradley were making their last trip to the house. Even Simone was surprised at how very few "things" she had that she considered special. Or at least, special enough to keep. She scoured each room of the house—took a couple items from the kitchen. But mostly, she took from the master bedroom. And even if Travis *had* left the pictures of all their vacations up on the walls, she wouldn't have wanted them. That was all in the past, now. And this weekend, the realtor was hosting an Open House.

When they carried the last few boxes to the Sunset Supermarket van in the driveway, which Dante was loaning Bradley to drive himself to and from work until he could buy a car of his own, Simone went back through the open front door, straight to the dining room.

She saw the envelope in question and gathered it along with all the other mail into her hands. Jen was standing in the foyer, now.

"Well. I guess this is it," said Simone. "I probably won't see you again until the house is sold." Although, she couldn't imagine why Jen would need to accompany Travis to sign escrow papers or anything like that. Maybe she was just trying to be polite to Travis' baby mama?

Jen smiled. She looked like she wanted to say something. Like she wanted to apologize. *But why?*

In her former days, Simone would have used this moment to make Jen squirm a little. But she was far too happy, now. She had too much good going for her. She was *content*. She was *busy*. In fact, she was planning to run more errands after she and Bradley had a chance to unload the boxes back at April's house.

Simone took two quick steps toward Jen and gave her a little hug.

"Hey. It's all good," she said. And honestly,

she believed it. And while she couldn't bring herself to say the words, she really did hope that Jen would be happy with Travis.

Again, Jen smiled as though she was too moved to speak. She nodded her head quickly, and Simone turned and walked out the door.

She read "The Dissolution" while waiting in the doctor's office. Everything seemed to be in order. Travis had kept his word and kept everything fair. The house would be sold and the money would be divided. The joint *bank* account would be equally divided. No spousal support. Once this was signed, it was final.

"The sooner the better," she whispered, hoping no one in the waiting room heard her. She scribbled her signature in all the highlighted places and sealed the papers into the pre-addressed envelope.

"Simone?" said the nurse, standing in the doorway.

Simone gathered her belongings and followed her into the examination room. She answered all the preliminary questions, peed in a cup, and removed her clothing. She put on the customary robe and sat on the examination table.

When the doctor walked in and asked her the reason for her visit (because this wasn't merely the annual well-woman appointment), she said, "I want to make sure I don't have any sexually transmitted diseases."

He keeps a good poker face, she thought. Her doctor nodded and got right to work. The nurse drew blood, and that was that. She'd know in a few days if she would have the green light to be intimate with Des.

As she'd told her mom a few days before, "If I picked up some kind of STD in Hawaii, I can't pass it along to Des." No. She couldn't risk doing that.

Oddly, she was able to talk freely with her mother about her escapades with Finn. It was like her mother didn't blame her for behaving the way she had in Hawaii. Of course, she didn't mention to her mom that her ultimate goal had been to come home from Hawaii and kill herself. But the betrayal by Travis alone was enough to justify her actions as far as her mother was concerned. No judgment. *Wow!*

So days later when the doctor's office called, Simone could hardly contain her glee when she learned that she was completely healthy. She was so excited, she scheduled a different kind of appointment for Saturday afternoon. For fun she took April with her.

"What are we doing *now*?" April asked. As always, they'd be going with Carter and Des to Boots later that evening.

"Ever had a bikini wax?" Simone asked.

When April started to protest, Simone grabbed her by the wrist and said, "April. You and Carter are getting closer, right?"

April nodded. Yes, it was true. The two were hitting it off.

"Well. You need to be prepared," said Simone.

"Prepared for *what*?" asked April.

"For sex."

When she said it, April looked *horrified* and for the rest of the afternoon, Simone couldn't stop laughing. And as much as she teased April for naively thinking that adults "wait for marriage," especially at *their* age, April insisted she was merely "going along" with Simone's "shenanigans."

And poor April! Simone signed her up for a *Brazilian*, and every time she heard April's screams, coming from the room next to hers, Simone clutched the pillow on her salon table to her face to smother her laughter. She could only imagine the overgrown landscape the poor esthetician had to work with! *April's Nether Region*, they were calling it. "The dark abyss," Simone told her own beautician.

She heard, "Simone, I hate you!"

"Beauty is pain!" Simone yelled in the direction of April's room. *When* she could breathe.

But that night, those words couldn't have rung more true. Beauty *was* pain *and worth every penny!* When she and Des went to Boots all by themselves (because April was still hurting and opted instead for dinner and a movie with Carter) Simone was grateful for having taken all her precautions. Of course, she didn't tell Des she'd seen a doctor. However, she did tell him she was commemorating the end of her marriage to Travis with a few drinks. She told him it was official: her marriage to Travis was over.

Des seemed to understand that she needed extra attention that evening. He just smiled his lopsided grin and laughed when she ordered a few more vodka martinis than usual.

Des drank nothing that night. It was as if he knew he had to be the designated sober one. It was Simone's night to cut loose and act crazy.

But Des was stone cold serious.

And when Craig Morgan's "Wake Up Lovin' You" came on, Des *was* playing for keeps. He led

Simone to the dance floor and looked down into her face like she was his everything. Her only defense was to look right back up at him. To never let his powerful grip on her ever let her go. There were people all around and yet, no one else existed. All she could see amidst the blurry lights in her peripheral vision was Des' gorgeous face. Her feet felt the vibration of the music and Craig Morgan's soulful, powerful voice, traveling into her inmost being.

And then Des kissed her. They clung to each other in the middle of the dance floor and for the first time, Simone understood the concept of two becoming one. Their souls intertwined, marked outwardly only by their interlocking lips. Des gently lifted her off her feet and held her in his arms like he would never let go. Simone closed her eyes and allowed herself to get lost in this man. In this incredible man. *Des, I love you*, her spirit told him. And though no words were necessary, Des pressed his mouth to her ear and said, "I *long* to wake up loving you, Simone."

She opened her eyes and looked into his face. "Take me home, Des," she said. And what she meant was *tonight is the night.* She had every intention of waking up in Des' arms, even if it was in the twin-sized bed in April's guest room. Just like in her dream.

Unfortunately, Simone didn't quite get to live out her fantasy. When the song ended, Des had to practically carry her out of the building.

"Everything's still spinning," she told him as he walked her up to April's front door a bit later.

April met them on the porch. "I've got her from here, Des," she told him. Simone couldn't even kiss him goodbye. She just gave a little wave over her shoulder. Des chuckled and said *goodnight, Simone. I'll call you in the morning.*

She was too out of it to comprehend April when she said, "We'll see about that!" Nor did she remember much about April, walking her up the stairs, taking off her boots, and covering her with a blanket as she lay her head on her pillow.

It wouldn't be until hours later, when the morning light shown through her window that Simone would smile and remember the love she'd felt for Des on the dance floor...the love he'd obviously felt for *her*.

Oh well, so it didn't quite work out to plan, she thought. So she continued to lie in bed, rolling around a *new* plan in her mind.

She would wait *one* more day—till the night of the grand opening—to give herself to Des. She would plan a special celebration of their love, of all their hard work together on the new store. She would *surprise* him. And she would be stone cold sober this time.

She smiled and rolled on her side, hugging her pillow, oblivious to reality. Oblivious to the nature of life.

Because in that moment, Simone was convinced that nothing could ever go wrong for her ever again. She was *far* too happy to remember that in real life, sometimes even the best laid plans fall apart.

Chapter Sixteen

At last, the day arrived. All the tireless efforts of the good people of Com Corp, all the activity surrounding the grand opening of the first ever Ohio Sunset Supermarket, would finally come to fruition.

Simone and April were up the morning *of* when it was still dark outside. Even Bradley seemed to perceive the significance of this monumental event and came down the stairs, all sleepy-eyed, as the two women were sipping their coffee in the kitchen. Of course, Bradley would have to stay home and take care of MeeMaw, but even that seemed a huge contribution to the day ahead.

"The reporters will be there first thing for the unveiling," said Simone.

She thought it would lend a dramatic touch to place a white satin sheet fringed in red, white, and blue over the Sunset Supermarket sign. She envisioned a picture of Dante's smiling face in all the newspaper and internet articles that would ensue as he pulled down the sheet, revealing his very own store. And in case the reporters didn't quite capture it, Simone had hired her own trusted photographers as well.

She'd really outdone herself this time. She'd pulled out all the stops. Not one detail was left untouched, and though Heidi had been appointed as "manager in charge" of the festivities, Simone had mentored her, every step of the way. And it had been fun. Especially knowing how pleased Des was.

Des had been *more* than impressed (by all the reports given to him) on a thrice daily basis by his breakfast, lunch, and dinner companion, Simone.

"Course, he's so enamored with you he'd be happy if you'd only hired the popcorn people and face painters," April kept telling her.

Simone smiled and thought *she's probably right*. Des had her feeling so secure in his love for her, she felt like she could do no wrong in his eyes, even though he still hadn't uttered the *I love you* words, yet.

Neither had she. But she would.

She had it all planned out. Between the lingerie she'd purchased special (after the good news she'd received from her doctor's office of no sexually transmitted diseases, hallelujah!) and the Brazilian wax she'd laughingly endured Saturday afternoon with April, she was ready to express her love to Des in the fullest way possible.

He'd of course been staying at Granny's house all these days, but at the close of the grand opening, his plan was to drive back to Dayton with his parents and spend a few days with *them* before heading out to California for the birth of his first grandchild. He had already asked Simone to accompany him for the big event, which in Des' mind was even greater than Dante's grand opening. Which Simone didn't quite understand, thinking shouldn't *someone* hold down the Sunset Supermarket fort? After all, it was so new! In *her* mind, babies were born every day. Des could easily Facetime his son and daughter-in-law when the baby was born and visit later. Meanwhile, Dante's store could be running smoothly under Des' capable direction.

But no. She was learning that this was not the way the Reynolds family operated. Family was of the utmost priority as far as *they* were concerned. And while she didn't quite get it because it was still such a new concept to her way of thinking, she knew Des wouldn't miss this baby's birth for anything.

So she just went along with the excitement surrounding the upcoming arrival of a brand new Reynolds, and at her insistence, she'd purchased her own plane ticket. She and Des and Dante would fly to California the following weekend. All this time, she kept up the farce that she would stay at her mom's house, but she knew that once she and Des slept together, beginning tonight after the grand opening, Des would insist she be with *him* (all alone) in his house on the beach. *Yes, I'm that good!* she laughingly told herself.

It was definitely time. Their relationship had advanced to the point where intimacy was the logical next step. Simone knew this would seal their love. And oh, she couldn't wait!

Just thinking about Des' tender, loving care for her sent her imagination spinning. He was so in tune with her, forever noticing every little thing she did...every little movement, every little detail on her body. They couldn't watch a *movie* together without him bringing her hand to his face and delicately running his fingers along the contours of her bones and knuckles. He'd encircle her wrist with his hand and comment *how petite and soft* she felt to his touch.

He'd kiss her goodnight and run his fingers along the outline of her chin and clavicle. He told her one night that her collarbone was his favorite part of her body, and on occasion he'd kiss one part of it, then another.

When they two-stepped together at Boots, sometimes his big, strong hands would span her rib cage, and again he'd comment that she was *so little*. She laughed one time when he said, "I could almost break you, Simone."

She enjoyed his sexual innuendos—enjoyed everything about him. And while she realized he was only human, she had him elevated so high on a pedestal—he was almost god-like to her. She often *thought* of him as her African god. *And I'm his goddess*, she would tell herself.

April smiled at Simone over her coffee. "*You* don't appear nervous at *all*," she said.

Simone poured out the remaining contents of her mug into the sink. She shrugged and said, "No. I guess I'm not."

"You're up to something," said April.

"Yes, April, I am," she said. She walked over to Bradley and covered his ears with her hands. "I'm going to take Des home tonight and make him mine."

April bit her lower lip. Bradley shook his head, sheepishly, and walked out of the room.

"I'm going to follow him to Dayton after the grand opening and knock on the door to his hotel room—"

"Won't he be staying at his parent's house?" April asked.

Simone shook her head. "No. Apparently, they have a two-bedroom condo, and they sleep separately. Des calls them a couple of old fuddy duddies."

"Oh," said April, laughing along with Simone. Then she added, "What about their couch?"

"He's tried that, but he's so big, it's not the best

night's sleep for him," Simone told her. "He says it's just better to stay at The Rivers." She smiled slyly. "Room 411. That's his favorite."

"What are you planning to do?" asked April.

Simone opened the refrigerator door to show April the champagne that was chilling. "I'll keep it on ice all the way there," she said. "I'll pick up the chocolate-covered strawberries I've ordered when I get there. But aside from that, it's basically me in a teddy underneath my dress."

April's eyes opened wide. Simone knew *April* would never do something like this. *No, not her!* But before she'd allow any kind of judgment to fall, she quickly told herself *but I'm not April.*

"Well. I guess you know what you're doing," said April.

"I know exactly what I'm doing," said Simone. "And don't wait up for me tonight."

It was as if God was smiling that Memorial Day. Never had an event run as smoothly for Simone as this one. Even the set-up was seamless. Everyone arrived on time, from the party supply rental truck to the food vendors to the entertainment. Even the port-o-potties were all set up and ready to go.

In the future, Dante's Sunset Supermarket would be open 24 hours a day, but today it was still under Grover's schedule of 9:00 a.m. to 10:00 p.m.

Flyers with a printed itinerary had dotted local neighborhoods and flooded social media in the weeks leading up to today. Thank goodness there was extra parking on the streets, and even the kind people at the church next door were allowing free parking as well because the Sunset Supermarket parking lot had all but transformed into a county fair.

Even Meredith looked chipper. It was like the vampire had come into the light and turned human, contrasted to all the time she'd been spending in her office of late, which even for Meredith was more than usual. Jodi had compared her one day to a chicken that was brooding and referred to Meredith's office as a nesting box.

But today, Meredith was shining in all her glory. Literally. She'd even dressed the part, right down to her designer red, white, and blue scarf. It didn't matter that it was blazing hot that day. Meredith dressed as professional as ever in her bold, blue blazer and red heels. *No* one would see *her* sweat. No. Not Meredith. She smiled and acted excited to shake hands with every customer who walked by the Com Corp booth. Simone had invited several local establishments to set up shop, as she called it, in the parking lot that day, including the local car wash and donut store. *Anything to generate community support*, she'd told Heidi.

And even though Heidi complained of severe monthly cramps that morning, Simone told her to suck it up—it was all part of the territory. *You can whine later*, she told her. When Meredith overheard their conversation, she pulled Heidi aside, and Simone figured she'd lecture Heidi as well. After all, Simone had learned everything she knew from Meredith. But out of the corner of her eye, she saw Meredith pull something out of her purse—a plastic pill bottle. She assumed it was some kind of ibuprofen. Whatever it was, it did the trick because Heidi was smiling no less than 20 minutes later as though nothing bad at all was happening with her ovaries. *Leave it to Meredith!*

Dante sure smiled nice for the cameras at the unveiling. That was at 10:00 a.m. From there on, Com Corp had something planned every hour on the hour. The local high school band performed a bunch of patriotic songs at 11:00. At noon, a group of veterans were honored with special buttons hand-delivered by local law enforcement. Of course, speeches were made. Des made the final speech.

"And to show our appreciation for all that our veterans do, Sunset Supermarkets is dedicating a wall to commemorate the men and women in uniform who serve our country selflessly, day in and day out." He gestured to Dante, who then walked over and handed him a plaque.

"The first plaque on our wall honors a World War II veteran who happened to be the father of a very dear friend of mine." He held the plaque up high and said, "In memory of Barry Sylvester, former Naval PT boat operator and World War II veteran."

Des smiled at Simone who was standing off to the side of the platform. Her eyes welled with tears. All she could do in that moment was mouth out a *thank you* to her Des. This dedication had Kate Sylvester written all over it. She must have planned this with Des at her birthday party! *Now* she remembered the little chat she'd had with her mom about Des and how she'd been so mysterious at the time.

"Come on up here, Simone."

It was at this point, walking up to stand next to Des (who gave her the biggest hug ever) that Des introduced her to the audience as the "mover and shaker" over at Com Corp. He then thanked Com Corp for a job well done and asked Meredith, Heidi, and Jodi to wave and be recognized as well. The crowd politely clapped for all of them, and Meredith couldn't have looked more pleased.

Des and Simone walked off the platform, arm in arm. Simone admired the plaque and with more tears thanked Des for honoring her father this way.

"He was an amazing man," Des told her. "He *must* have been to have a daughter like you."

He even walked her into the store and hung the plaque on the wall himself right in front of her. She gave him a big hug and a kiss and whispered *I will thank you properly, later.* But the unsuspecting Des had no clue. He just smiled.

The rest of the afternoon passed quickly. Simone realized—and her team emphatically agreed with her—that the best idea of all was the hiring of a dynamic DJ. This guy had most everybody up on their feet, dancing, thanks to the *second* best idea of the day—the beer wagon. Des had objected to it at first, but Simone had reasoned with him that *no* one would show up on Memorial Day if alcohol wasn't part of the program. "It's just not American," she'd jokingly told him. He'd reluctantly deferred to her better judgment, but the compromise was *beer only.*

"I'll do even better than that," she'd told him. "Free *root* beer floats to all the kids." Not to mention complimentary hot dogs. Of course, people were free to order other selections from the food trucks.

She was delighted to see Josephine out and about with Robby, no less. They walked up to her at some point in the afternoon. Robby's face was all done up with red, white, and blue stars from the face-painting booth.

"Jen's smarter than I thought," said Simone, giving Josephine a nudge. "Free babysitting, eh?"

But before Josephine could say anything in her own defense, Simone changed the subject. She really didn't care. Honestly. And if Josephine wondered why the change of heart (and why so happy?) all doubt was dispelled when Simone introduced her to Desmond. When Des wasn't looking, Josephine gave Simone an exaggerated nod. Simone nodded *her* head, too, and that said it all. She almost said *and feel free to tell Travis*, but she refrained.

But just when Simone didn't think the afternoon could have gone any better, she got one *more* little surprise at the close of the day. Right around sunset, she happened to look up at the Sunset Supermarket sign on the front of the store. The way the sun's rays were shining, at first all she could see reflected were the two capital S's from Sunset and Supermarket. So to her it looked like a big SS. And though she had jokingly told her mother *oh, I could never marry Desmond* (because his last name didn't start with an S) in that moment, it was as if she were getting a big, divine wink from God. It was as if God were telling her *see? You still get to have an SS.*

Simone smiled, thinking about this, all throughout her three-hour drive to Dayton. She'd played along with Des when he'd kissed and hugged her goodbye near the close of the grand opening celebration just after sunset, telling her he was going straight to his hotel because he was *wiped*.

"*You're* wiped!" she'd told him. "Try wearing heels all day!"

But it was all a ruse. Soon as Des left, *she'd* left. She'd sped home to April's, flung off the offending shoes, and showered. She needed to be fresh as a flower for her first real night of love with Des.

Her bag was already packed and waiting in the foyer. She grabbed the champagne out of the fridge, stuck it in the ice in her cooler, and off she went. Even MeeMaw looked a little stunned by how rapidly Simone kissed her cheek goodbye on her way out the door. Bradley just yelled, "Don't do anything I wouldn't do!" from his boy cave upstairs, and Simone laughed. Of course, April was still at Sunset Supermarket with Heidi and Jodi, supervising all the cleanup. Meredith, of course, had left hours before.

"That's the beauty of being the *big* boss," Simone had told her team. *And that's the beauty of being ME*, she told herself. *I'm second in command, and I do what I want. And I want to do Desmond. Tonight!*

The drive didn't feel as long as she'd expected. Her Lexus was comfortable to begin with, plus she enjoyed song after song from her new playlist of country music, including the beloved Craig Morgan song. She even listened to a sermonette on YouTube from MeeMaw's preacher lady. Simone had been listening to a *lot* of her sermons, lately—mostly ones about how much God loved her. She was starting to believe it.

A little after 9:00, she picked up her chocolate-covered strawberries from the all-night bakery in Dayton. She knew it was corny, but she'd asked the bakers to first dip the strawberries in chocolate then drizzle them with white-chocolate stripes. She would have fun, later, explaining to Desmond that this symbolized their relationship, at the core of which was the color of the red strawberry, representing their deep love for one another.

"Cheesy, perhaps. But meaningful," she told her reflection in the rearview mirror after parking in the hotel lot. She reapplied her lipstick.

She had no small load to carry, but she managed. She slung her bag and purse over her shoulder and rolled her mini cooler behind her, box of strawberries and champagne safely tucked inside along with an ice bucket and two long-stemmed glasses.

She was wearing a plain, white sundress—form-fitting with an oversized, golden "easy access zipper" (she called it) down the front. Underneath, she wore a white, lace teddy and nothing else. Her feet, semi-recovered from the day's activities, now donned heels even higher than before. *Des will like these. A lot!* she'd said to herself on the drive over, giving her shoes (which she'd placed on the passenger seat next to her) a little pat.

She was quite impressed with the hotel, beginning with the courtyard and then the lobby. It was elegant, yet homey. How could that be? *So Des!* she thought. She'd once had a conversation with him about how could a guy like him be *so* down to earth? With his millions, he could live large if he wanted to.

"I don't need that," he'd told her. "I live comfortably and I do what I want, but extravagance? Why? When there are so many people in need out there…." He didn't get into it, but Simone got the strong impression he was a benevolent soul.

She was able to find her own way to the elevator and up to Des' room on the fourth floor. When she was sure no one was around, she set down her items at her feet, bent over and gave her hair a big fluff. She gave the door three firm raps.

Seconds later, she heard the lock unclick, and then she saw Des' beautiful face as he cracked open the door.

"Simone!"

He was definitely pleasantly surprised to see her standing right there in front of him. He had the same expression he always had whenever he saw her. His eyes lit up and he smiled ear to ear.

"Hi, there," she said as he opened the door wider. She pressed up against him and threw her arms around his neck. He responded by locking lips with hers. She thought they'd never stop kissing because as always, it just felt sooo good.

"What are you *doing* here?" he asked her.

In a sing-song voice, she said, "Surprise!"

He laughed. When she leaned down to grab the handle of the cooler, he asked, "What have you got *there*?"

"Presents," she said, making her way past him into the room. He grabbed her bag and purse and brought them into the room, letting the door close behind him.

"I was almost falling asleep," he said.

She could tell. Three pillows, smushed against the headboard, were slightly indented in the middle where Des' head had been. The covers were pulled down, and the TV was on low. One small lamp was on, giving the room a cozy feel. Des was still dressed, but his shoes and socks were off his feet.

Simone set-up her "presents" on the little table by the window then turned around to face Des. He had set her bag and purse on the floor by the bed. He was still smiling.

"I can't believe you're here," he said.

"Where else would I be except wherever *you* are?" she asked him. "Can I pour you a drink?"

Thankfully, she'd thought to bring the champagne glasses; otherwise, they'd be plastic-cupping it. The only thing she *hadn't* thought of were a couple of candles.

Des quickly walked over to the table and skillfully popped the cork off the bottle.

Simone pulled back the sheer curtain on the window and said, "What a great view!" She could see why he liked this room so much.

"I know," he said. "This is where I stay whenever I'm in town." He poured the champagne and handed Simone a glass.

"Thank you," she said, trying to sound sexy.

Much to her surprise, he poured himself a glass as well. They clinked their glasses together and Des said, "To a job well done, Miss Director."

"To Ohio's first Sunset Supermarket and to Dante," said Simone in return. After they both took a sip, they sat down on the two cushy chairs by the table.

When Simone crossed her legs, Des said, "You're looking mighty fine."

She smiled and took another sip of her champagne. He was so easy!

They went on for a bit, talking about the grand

opening and what a great day it had been—*even the weather*, said Des, and Simone said *I ordered it special, just for you.*

"I have no doubt about *that*," he said. And then he just smiled at her, not so much drinking his champagne as he was drinking *her* in with those sexy green eyes of his. He shook his head and said *damn.*

"What." But Simone *knew* what. He was appreciating her assets. She knew perfectly well what he was thinking. He was thinking the same thing *she* was thinking. All the same, it was fun to play coy like this. To make a little game out of the upcoming sexcapades that would follow—no doubt sooner than later, based on the degree of hunger she was sensing from him.

They stared at each other for a bit, not saying anything. Then Des broke the silence.

"What's in the box?" he asked.

"I brought dessert," she said.

"Oh yeah?" He eagerly leaned forward.

She set down her glass and opened the lid of the box. She picked up one of the strawberries, and he looked like he was a little kid in a candy store.

"Those are my favorite!" he said. "How did you know?"

The fact was she *hadn't* known. It had just seemed like the perfect thing to bring. So she attributed her good guessing skills to being on the same wavelength as her beautiful man. She and Des were definitely meant for each other.

She stood up and brought the strawberry over to him. She sat on his lap, her legs in the middle of his, and put the strawberry up to his lips. He closed his eyes as he took the first, sensuous bite.

"Mmm, you know what I like," he said, taking another bite.

Yes. I do, she thought. *Yes, I do*.

Simone took the third and final bite. She swallowed, licked her lips, then licked Des' lips, and thus began another never-ending kiss.

Des squirmed a little, and as he shifted position in his chair, it jostled Simone to such an extent that she stood up.

"Want another strawberry?" she asked. The champagne was going straight to her head and she felt deliriously happy. No doubt she was in for the best night of her life.

"I'm good," said Des.

Simone glanced around the room. "Trash can?" She didn't want to set the messy strawberry stem on the shiny, wooden table.

Des gestured toward the desk, but Simone was already walking in the direction of the bathroom.

"My hands are sticky," she said, over her shoulder.

This hotel was so quaint, it had a little arched doorway from which one could see a long counter top up against the mirrored wall straight ahead. To the left was the actual bathroom—quite spacious, at that. To the right was a big, walk-in closet. She could see that Des' shirts and pants were already hanging from the quality, wood hangers. Two pairs of his shoes had been placed neatly on the bench below.

Simone tossed the strawberry stem into the wastebasket and ran her fingers through water, streaming from the bathroom faucet. By now, Des had followed her and was standing in the archway.

"Thank you for the dessert," he said, standing with a hand on either wall. He leaned forward, supporting himself by his arms, and she walked over and smooched his lips.

"That was only a strawberry," she said. "Not the dessert."

He looked a little puzzled.

Oh, Des! she wanted to say. She knew he was a man of God, but...did she have to spell it out? Was he *completely* out of practice? *How many years have you been divorced?* she wanted to ask him. Surely, he hadn't remained celibate all this time. Not such a fine specimen of a man as *he* was! She sighed. *So be it.*

She leaned back against the long counter and unzipped her dress, all the way down till it became detached. She grabbed the lapels and slipped the dress off her shoulders, down her arms, and then let it drop to the floor. There she stood, wearing nothing but her white, lace teddy and insanely high-heeled shoes.

She wanted to laugh at Des' expression, *but that wouldn't be romantic, Simone,* she told herself. She hadn't intended for things to move *this* quickly, but obviously, the guy needed a little help. In *her* mind, she'd imagined *Des* unzipping her dress. She'd imagined *Des* being the one to make the first move. But whatever. It didn't matter. What mattered was the love they shared and the expressing of that love—both verbally and physically. The sequence of *how* it happened certainly didn't need some predetermined, premeditated formula. Love was love.

"This is the dessert, Des," she said. He just stared and she thought *good grief, do I need to take off my lingerie myself, too?* When he continued to gape at her, she thought *yeah, I guess I do!*

She reached for the spaghetti strap on her left shoulder, but before she could pull it down, Des walked over and put his hand on top of hers. She smiled and grabbed his face with both hands, pulling him in for a kiss.

But he didn't return her passion. He pulled away, mid-kiss and held both of her hands in his.

"Simone, we need to stop," he said.

"Why?" she stood on her tippy-toes and kissed the side of his face.

"Because you're going to tempt me to do things I shouldn't do, and I just can't take it."

"Des." Now she smiled and rubbed her lips together. "Don't worry. I'm not married anymore. I signed and sent in the papers for my divorce." She called it "divorce" because that's what it was, wasn't it? Plus it sounded more official than "dissolution." She leaned forward and put her head on his chest. "I'm not someone's wife anymore." She looked up into his eyes. "I'm all yours."

His eyes softened when she said this. But all he did was look at her. He didn't say anything.

So *she* said it. "I love you, Des. I love you with all of my heart."

He pulled her close in a big embrace. He stroked her hair.

"I love you, too, Simone," he whispered. He kissed the top of her head. "I love you, too."

Now they were getting somewhere! Simone put her hands on Des' shoulders and leaned back just a tiny bit. Now her expression was serious.

"Then show me, Des," she whispered.

"Simone." He looked up at the ceiling, as if he were pleading for divine help. As if he were looking at an angel or even at God Himself, staring down at him from the crown molding of the hotel wall.

Simone knew he was having a crisis of conflict. She really wished she didn't have to make him compromise his principles this way—good grief, she'd had no idea! Leave it to Des to be the only man in America who had the will power to put God above sex! *She* knew he wanted her. *She* knew this was hard for him. But more than anything, she *needed* this. She needed *him*. Inside of her. Right. Now. She'd waited long enough, and she'd come all this way. She would not take no for an answer.

"Please, Des," she said. "I just want to be with you."

"And I want to be with you," he said.

"Then what's the matter?" she asked.

"Simone, I think of you as my *wife*," he said.

"Well, good!" She smiled and even laughed a little.

"But you're *not* my wife," he said. "Not yet."

Now she let go of him. She couldn't believe this. "Des, you've got to be kidding me," she said. "Are you trying to tell me that we can't make love unless we're married?"

But he *wasn't* kidding her. He nodded.

"Do you know what century this is?" she asked. Now she was starting to feel angry.

"Jesus is the same yesterday, today, and forever," he told her.

"Don't preach at me, Des," she said, snatching

up her dress from off the floor. Who did he think she *was*, the devil? Last Sunday at church the pastor read in the Bible where the devil tempted Jesus three times, and all three times the Lord responded with the word of God.

"*I* don't know!" she said, jamming her arm into the armhole of her dress. "Maybe I should feel flattered!" She jabbed her other arm into the other armhole. "Maybe you really *do* want to marry me. Maybe you really *do* want the fairy tale that I'll wait patiently for our wedding night—whenever *that* might be!" Weren't people supposed to wait awhile after a divorce before getting married again? What if it took a long, long time before she was emotionally ready? What if it took a year? Or two years? "Well, guess what, Des? In case you haven't noticed, I'm not a young, virgin maiden. I thought you would *want* this. I thought you would want *me*!" She was trying not to cry.

Des looked like *he* wanted to cry. "I *do* want this. I *do* want you," he said.

"Then *prove* it!"

When he continued to just stand there, not saying anything, she snapped. "Unless, of course, there's some *other* reason why you don't want to do me. Maybe you have someone else in your life."

Des shook his head. She knew he didn't, but she just wanted to be mean and say this. Then she wanted to be even *more* mean.

"Maybe it's because you don't have any game!"

She started to put her zipper together at the hem of her dress, but she didn't get very far. Before she quite knew what was happening, Des lifted her up off her feet. With one hand, he swept the vase of flowers and whatever other accessories were on the ledge behind her onto the carpeted floor below. He set Simone on top of the counter, grabbed the under part of her thigh, and wrapped her leg around his waist. All the while he kissed her lips, long and hard, thrusting his tongue deep into her mouth. His other hand found its way to the inside of her lace bodice, making a little ripping sound as he took firm hold of her bare breast. Simone closed her eyes, overwhelmed by the sensation. The back of her head was now resting against the mirrored wall, and Des' hand traveled up her body, making its final resting place on her chest below her neck. He kept his pelvis smack up against her crotch, but he pulled his head back a ways, ending their kiss. She opened her eyes, and he was staring right at her. He cupped her neck with both hands, thumbs on her ears. She closed her eyes as he kissed her chin. He kissed her cheek and then her earlobe. He was breathing very hard, and so was she.

Then very distinctly, in that voice she knew and loved, lips pressed to her ear, he said, "I got game."

And then he backed away. He grabbed a pair of shoes off the bench in the closet. Once in the archway, he turned to face her. She was still sitting on the counter, head spinning, completely stunned.

"You stay here tonight, Simone."

"Where are *you* going?" she asked, stepping down to the floor.

"I'm getting another room. I can't talk right now. We'll talk tomorrow."

She heard him grab something off the

nightstand—most likely his wallet and phone—after which she heard the door open then shut.

Her first reaction was to smile. She'd enjoyed their interaction. If this little snippet they'd just engaged in was any indication of the kind of lover *Des* was, then he was everything she'd imagined him to be and more.

Her *next* reaction was to think about what kind of man Des was. She *had* to respect him. *Had* to admire him. He was a man of scruples. He had integrity. He was true to his character at all times, even when standing in front of a half-naked woman in a hotel room. What kind of guy could walk away from *that*?

But then, hours later, seemingly out of nowhere, her thoughts took a much different turn. A somber turn. They took her where she least expected.

Because it was her final reaction that snapped her back to reality. And the more she thought about it, the longer she reclined on the bed in Des' hotel room, staring at the ceiling, the more she convinced herself that this would never work. *They* would never work.

She wouldn't *let* it work.

And at some point in the wee hours of the morning, sometime after 3:00 a.m., Simone Sanders knew what she had to do.

She got dressed, grabbed her belongings, and headed back to North Olmsted.

Chapter Seventeen

She arrived back in her own neck of the woods at about the time April should be waking up for work. Not wanting to explain anything to *her* just yet, Simone decided to kill time at the Greek restaurant. When she'd met with Travis there for the listing agreement, she'd noticed it was a 24-hour diner that boasted "the best breakfast in town." But Simone was too upset to order breakfast. She just sat and drank several cups of herbal tea till she was sure April had left the house.

She knew Bradley was upstairs, sleeping, when she eventually tiptoed in. Nowadays when he slept in, he had a good reason. He worked night shifts at the supermarket so that during the day, he could still be around the house if MeeMaw needed him. Simone often thought about hiring a caretaker if only a couple days a week—just to free up some time for Bradley. Yes, he was maturing by the day, but a kid needed to be a kid. Her consolation for procrastinating was how well the *cleaning* service she'd paid for was doing thus far. If she'd thought April's house was clean *before*, it wasn't. And April couldn't thank her enough.

Technically, Simone could make it to work on time. She could even arrive early, like April. All she'd have to do was change into a non-wrinkled outfit and comb her hair. Her make-up was relatively untouched from not sleeping all night.

But she just didn't have the energy. She was drained. She was mentally, physically, and emotionally drained. So after emptying her poor bladder after stalling the past hour with all that tea,

Simone crawled underneath the covers of her bed and fell asleep.

But not for long. A couple hours into her snooze, her phone woke her up. Des was calling her. But she ignored it. She didn't even have the energy to listen to the voicemail which followed.

She did, however, call April. *I should at least let someone know I'm not coming in today*, she thought.

"I wasn't *expecting* you'd come in today," said April. "I imagine you'll be enjoying the day in Dayton with Desmond."

"Actually, I just got home." Okay. So it was a little lie. When April sounded surprised, she added, "It was just a turn-around visit. I never meant to stay." Another lie.

April asked, "How did it go?"

"How did what go?"

"Your little surprise."

"Actually, April, I'd rather not talk about it."

Did she imagine it, or did April make a little gasping noise? Not wanting to give her any time to ask more questions, Simone quickly changed the subject. "Is Meredith pissed I'm not there?"

"Um…no," said April. "She's not here, either."

"Really?" This was odd. "Where is she?"

"She's visiting her kids for a few days. I guess her daughter from Canada is visiting Meredith's son in New York, and her other son is going to meet them, so Meredith thought she'd fly out to see them while they were all together. It was kind of last minute."

"Hmm," was all Simone had to say about it. Made sense. It was about time Meredith took a vacation. *She'd* worked hard like all the rest of them on the grand opening, so why not? She deserved it.

After April assured her it was a slow week, relatively speaking, Simone used Meredith's absence as an excuse to stay home. And April didn't argue, but she did sound concerned.

"Don't worry about me and Des, April," she told her friend. "I know what I have to do. It's all good."

But the way April said goodbye sounded like she wasn't at all convinced.

"Hey, Simone, it's Des. I take it you went home. Look, I'm real sorry about last night. I want to talk to you. Could you give me a call? I don't feel right, and I want to hear the sound of your voice." There was a pause. "I love you, Simone."

She listened to this voicemail several times. Then when the second voicemail came in a couple hours later, she listened to that one.

"Hey, Simone. I don't blame you if you're still mad at me." He chuckled a little. "I'm mad at me, too!" He blew out a deep breath. "Baby, I want you to call me. Please. Let me make this up to you. Please. I love you."

An hour after this one, she listened to the third voicemail. It sounded more urgent.

"I'm coming to see you tomorrow so we can talk, Simone. This is killing me. I need to see you." A pause. "Please forgive me, Simone. I love you. I'll see you tomorrow."

Well, now I'm definitely going to work, she thought, walking out to get the mail—*if only to avoid him!*

She had to admit, she was flattered that he was pursuing her so relentlessly. She supposed a better person would let him off the hook…would text him and say *it's okay, don't come all the way out here. Stay with your parents.*

That had been his original plan, anyway. He was slated to spend Tuesday through Friday in Dayton, catching up with his folks, then Saturday he and Dante and Simone were supposed to fly out to California together.

Except Simone had canceled her flight that morning, right after listening to the first voicemail. Perhaps a nicer person would text Des to let him know this…to let him know he shouldn't expect her.

But that was just it. Simone *wasn't* a nicer person. She wasn't even a *nice* person. She was just a Stone Cold with nothing more inside of her than a stone cold heart.

Not Des. Des was a *good* person. He had a big, *soft* heart full of love for humanity. *His* heart brimmed up and spilled over with compassion and grace and kindness and all things good. And *as* such, he deserved someone who was more his match. He needed someone who would bring out the best in him— someone who would promote him and nurture him and be his spiritual equal.

All *Simone* could ever be to him was a temptress. What he felt for her was only pure, chemical reaction. He was attracted to her, no doubt about it. He was drawn to her. But her physicality was just a decoy. Once he peeled back the mask, once the proverbial honeymoon was over, he'd see that he'd made a terrible mistake.

Or maybe he wouldn't. Maybe he'd get used to her and get sucked in to her turmoil. Instead of influencing *her* to be a better person, maybe he'd compromise his values to appease her. Maybe over time, he'd hang onto her because that was just the easy thing to do. Maybe she'd beat him down the same way she'd beaten Travis down.

But who was she to bring *Des* down like that? To drag *him* into her deep, dark world? Into her selfishness?

After what had happened last night, which in her mind translated to Des' rejection of her grand seduction, she'd formulated a clearer outlook on the situation. Here she thought Travis was horrible for seducing Jen. Heck, she was no better!

And Des was just too good. He was too pure.

"And he loves the Lord," she'd whispered with trembling lip to her reflection in the bathroom mirror before she'd left Des' hotel room.

She had to leave him. She had to let him go.

Simone Sanders loved Desmond Reynolds *so* much it made her heart ache. She loved him so much, she had to set him free. Her mind was made up. There was nothing he could do to change it. So why answer his calls? Why talk to him at all?

Of course, she knew she could only stave him off for so long before having to confront the issue. She knew he wouldn't give up on her—not without a fight. He'd already said he was coming to see her.

Okay, fine, she told herself as she grabbed the mail out of the box. She noticed the *big* envelope in the pile was addressed to her.

She tossed the mail on the credenza in the foyer but took the *big* envelope up to her room.

This was the official document. The dissolution of her marriage to Travis Sanders. Of all days to arrive.

It's amazing the effect the printed word can have on a person's mind. It was so impactful. So official. So important.

Ironically, a few days prior she might have easily shrugged this off. She might have even mailed a copy of it to Des just to say *look! I'm free! Let's go for it. Let's get married and live happily ever after!*

But looking at the papers in her hand was like staring at a major reality check. How had she ever thought in a million years she could give Des a happily ever after? Wasn't this here document proof of that? Simone couldn't even give an ordinary guy like Travis a good life. How could she have ever entertained the possibility that she, Simone Sanders, could *ever* be worthy of someone like Desmond Reynolds?

Oh, it would be so easy to continue on with the façade and keep Desmond in the dark about her true nature. But she would not. She loved him too much.

She would set him free.

True to his word, Des came to town special the next day, just for her. His timing seemed a bit predictable and strategic—he showed up at the office at lunch time. It was "Bradley Lunch Wednesday" as they were starting to call it. As was her habit, April had set up the conference table in Meredith's office with a table cloth and paper goods. And though Meredith wasn't there, they knew she wouldn't mind if they invaded her office space. Heidi and Jodi *might* have joined them for once, but Simone had made the atmosphere a bit tense first thing that morning after a comment Jodi had made.

"Hopefully, she'll hatch that egg before she gets back," Jodi said, referring to Meredith and her newfound "broodiness." She then said, "We ought to call her Meri-broody."

And Simone couldn't stop herself. She blurted, "I guess that's a nicer nickname than Stone Cold."

Even April got an *oh crap!* look on her face when she heard Simone say *that*.

Jodi tried to apologize. "That was before I got to know you better, Simone," she said, back-pedaling. "Now that I know you better, I regret having said that."

Even Heidi owned up to her part of it. Which was all quite nice, but evidently, space was needed between the apology and the awkward moment. So Heidi and her guilty friend, Jodi, had high-tailed it on out to lunch together as usual.

Bradley lightened the mood when he walked in, brandishing lunch. April had just finished declaring how proud she was of her son for all of his recent accomplishments.

"It's all on account of you and Des," she told Simone. "I don't know where we'd be without you."

Simone just shook her head and didn't comment. Soon enough, April would figure out that "Des and Simone" simply didn't exist. Simply *couldn't* exist. Not in *that* way.

Today, Bradley brought cornflake crusted chicken fingers and Ranch dressing with a side of breadsticks.

"So much for my figure!" April winked.

Since she'd been dating Carter, April had lost almost ten pounds. *See what love does to a person?* Simone would tease her. But April insisted she and Carter were still in the getting-to-know-each-other phase of their relationship. *Too early to call*, she'd respond with a smile, but Simone knew better. April had a spring in her step.

Which was probably why April didn't seem to notice the tension in the air when Des walked into the room.

Of course, Des didn't let on that anything was the matter. He walked over and gave Simone a kiss on the cheek, as usual. He gave April's cheek a kiss, too. He fist bumped Bradley and said *long time no see* even though it had only been a week since they'd worked together at the store.

Thankfully, Bradley did most of the talking, making his mother laugh about certain crazy customers who came to the store, like the old lady who always, always, always insisted she'd given the cashier a twenty instead of a ten.

Throughout Bradley's lively lunchtime narrative, Simone could feel Des' eyes on her. She looked at *him* once or twice. But all she could see was sadness on his face, and this made *her* feel sad.

When Bradley packed up and left for the day and April returned to her cubicle in the room down the hall, Simone and Des remained seated in Meredith's office. Des rolled his leather swivel chair closer to Simone's and put both hands on her legs. Her first instinct was to place her hands on top of his, but she stopped herself. She had to try to make this easier on him. She had to call upon her inner Stone Cold.

"I've just been sick, Simone," he told her. "I hope you can forgive me. I never meant to hurt you."

"You didn't do anything, Des," she said.

"You got *that* right," he said. "A beautiful woman came to see me, and I didn't do a *damn* thing." He squeezed her hand, now. "I want to make it up to you."

And this was exactly what she had feared. Des loved her so much, he would compromise his standards for her. She suspected this was what happened in the Garden of Eden when Adam agreed to eat the forbidden fruit along with Eve. Maybe Adam had loved Eve so much, he couldn't let her fall from grace without him, all alone. But *she* couldn't let *Des* fall.

"No," she told him. "I don't *want* you to make anything up to me."

"It was such a surprise. I wasn't ready."

"You don't have to explain, Des." She gave her chair a push away from his so they were no longer touching.

"I just envisioned something *more* for us, Simone," he said. "I want to *marry* you. I want you to be my wife."

She shook her head and looked at her lap.

"I know it's happening so quick," he said. "We've only known each other what, a month?" He laughed. "But Simone." He grabbed the arm of her chair and wheeled her over to him. "Can you look at me, please?"

Slowly, reluctantly, she looked into his eyes.

"I know what I know. I'm not a kid. I've been around the block. I don't need to think about this to know marrying you is right. And I know *you* know it, too."

She shook her head. Oh, how easy it would be to just agree! To just say *yes, Des, yes. I do know.* How easy it would be to let this man love her...to be his wife. But she couldn't! She loved him too much. It really *was* cruel to be kind, so she would be mean. Brutally mean.

She would tell him the truth.

"I highly doubt you've been around the block, Des. If anyone's been around the block, it's me."

He started to say something, but she wouldn't let him.

"Do you know what I did when I found out my husband was having an affair?"

"I'm sure whatever you did, it was justified," he said. "You don't have to tell me. It's none of my business."

"No, it *is* your business, Des, because did you know before I even went to your hotel I had to get myself tested?"

Now his eyes looked *really* sad.

"Yeah. I wanted to make sure I didn't have a sexually transmitted *disease.* Cause you don't deserve that, Des. I could *never* do something like that to you."

He shook his head. "Simone, I don't care about your past," he said. "I only care about our future."

"But don't you understand?" she said. "How could we have a future with all the dishonesty?"

"What dishonesty?" he asked.

"I haven't come clean with you," she said. She all of a sudden became fidgety. Maybe it was because she really didn't want to disclose any of this. But she had to. While she spoke, she swiveled her chair right then left, right then left.

"When I was *still* married to Travis, I went to Hawaii. And on my *birthday*, I had a one-night stand with a twenty-one-year-old *kid*, Des. He was *twenty-one*." She said it twice for shock value. She hoped he'd make the connection that Finn was only four years older than Bradley!

"You were hurt," he said. "You were seeking revenge. You needed someone to make you *feel* good. I don't judge you for that, Simone. I know exactly how that feels."

"You do?" she asked him. "Did you ever screw a total stranger? Especially when you were married?"

He shook his head.

"No, I didn't think so," she said. "Because who *does* that? Who *does* that, Des? Certainly not *you*. Only the desperate do something like that."

She wasn't quite getting the shocked reaction out of him that she thought she would. So she took it up a notch.

"This kid and I did it *all night long*, Des. All night long. He did things to me that I wanted *you* to do to me last night. But you have morals, Des. *You* were able to say no because that's who you *are*."

"I'm not perfect, Simone."

"Well, you're pretty damn close," she said. She stopped swiveling a minute to cross her legs and interlock her fingers on her lap.

"Not *even* close," he said. He was speaking softly, like he was talking someone off the ledge of a 20-story building.

"Oh yeah? If it had been the other way around and *you* were the tramp, would you have told me?

Cause I wasn't going to tell *you* at *all*."

"That's okay, though," he said. "You don't even need to tell me *now*."

"But now you know," she said. "Now you know I'm a ho. And I forced myself on you last night, and you deserve so much better than that."

"Simone, if I got what I deserved, I'd be burning in hell."

"Stop preaching at me, Des." She'd heard the pastor at Lamb's Book say this exact same line.

"I don't mean to preach at you, Simone—"

"And that's another thing," she said, standing up. She tried to make her way over to the door but he grabbed her by the wrist. Not hard, but it made her look down at his hand. "I wouldn't make a very good wife for you. We'd be unequally yoked, as you say. You need to find someone better suited for you."

"I want *you*, Simone."

She wrenched her arm free and walked to the door. Turning to face him, she said, "Des. We're done. I don't want to talk to you anymore. Please leave."

She held the door open for him. At first he just sat there. Then with a tear in his eye, he stood up and walked over to where she stood. He placed his hand gently on her shoulder and softly said, "I'm not going to give up on us. I love you too much, Simone."

And that, she thought, *is precisely the problem.* With stone cold eyes, she said to him, "Don't waste your time. It's over."

Des waited till the following evening to contact her again. He asked if he could meet her someplace where they could talk.

Simone refused. Then he threatened to come over to April's house until she convinced him that it would only upset MeeMaw. Of course, it *wouldn't*— MeeMaw was quite enchanted by Des—but she told him MeeMaw was already under *enough* distress about the break-up, which Simone had finally revealed to April, who had then told MeeMaw.

"But I still want to talk," he said.

Simone closed the door to her room and sat on the bed. She put her phone on speaker because April was out to dinner with Carter, Bradley was at work, and MeeMaw was downstairs, watching TV in her room. No one would hear their conversation.

He kept telling her he loved her. It nearly broke her heart to know she was breaking *his* heart like this. But she had to. She also knew she had to take it to another level.

"*How* can you love me, Des? You know nothing *about* me."

"I know what I know," he said.

"You know what I *want* you to know," she said.

"I know that you're the woman of my dreams," he said.

"Yeah! More like woman of your nightmares."

"All I see when I look at you is beauty, Simone. Inside and out."

"Really?"

"Really."

"It's all an act, Des," she said. "You know how you like family? Well, I don't. For many years I completely *ignored* my family. To this day, I barely even know my nephews."

"You could have fooled *me*," he said. And she

knew why he said that. At her mom's party he'd gone on and on about how much her nephews admired her.

"I *did* fool you," she said. "I don't like *kids*, either. That's one reason I moved to Ohio. I didn't like it when my mom watched Brady and Bret."

"But you were young, Simone," he said. "Of course you weren't feeling it with the kids at the time."

"No, Des, I wasn't," she said. "And you know what else?" *Here goes,* she thought. *This will chase him away like nothing else.* "I despised kids *so* much that when I was eighteen…I had an *abortion.*"

Now there was silence on the other end of the phone. No doubt Des had to process this.

"I didn't even like my *own child,*" she said.

The silence continued. Then finally, he said, "Simone, I'm sorry."

She wanted to say *sorry? Sorry about what?* What was *he* sorry about? But the words wouldn't come out. She was crying now and didn't want him to know. Didn't want him to know how after all these years—right *here,* right *now*—in this unexpected moment of truth, at *50 years of age,* her heart was *bleeding* for a child she never got to know. For a baby she'd never gotten to love.

The pain was too much.

As if to console herself, she pressed on with full disclosure. Des *had* to know the real her. He had a right to know what she was made of. What he'd come *this close* to embracing. To spending his life with.

"You know…I guess what goes around *comes* around," she said through her tears. "No *wonder* my husband left me. It was payback. I deserved it."

"Don't say that, Simone." If she didn't know

better, she'd say *Des* was on the verge of crying.

"But I did deserve it!" she said. She laid back on the bed and held her phone above her face. "I deserved everything he did to me because I never gave him a choice. I never gave him a chance to say no, don't do that, let's raise our child—we'll be fine. Only I didn't. I went ahead with the procedure. I didn't even *tell* him until afterwards."

"You were young. You were scared," he said.

"Then how do you explain what I did a few years *after* that? I got my tubes tied so we could never have children together. But Travis *wanted* children. And I didn't give him a choice." She put the back of her hand over her eyes.

"Simone, you can't change any of that," he said. "It's all in the past. God forgives you."

And this struck something deep inside of her. *Did* God really forgive her? How could it be? Because she realized in that moment that she didn't forgive *herself.* That she *couldn't* forgive herself.

"Simone, are you okay?"

She knew he couldn't see her, but all the same, she moved her head continuously from right to left in one big *nooo* as she silently cried her tears. He said it again, more softly this time.

"Simone, are you okay?"

It took all she had within her, but after taking a deep breath, she was able to form two sentences before hanging up.

"I'm going to bed now, and I don't want to talk anymore. Please don't call or text me."

She let the phone drop to the floor. She rolled onto her stomach and buried her head in her pillow and sobbed. And sobbed.

   She fell asleep, still whispering *I'm sorry*.

Chapter Eighteen

You'd never have known anything was wrong with her. The way she showed up to work on time. The way she walked into the office. The way she greeted those she passed on her way to her desk. With eyes completely dry, no one would know she'd shed enough tears the night before to fill a swimming pool. The way she moved, the way she talked, the way she sat right down and got to business, no one would ever guess just hours later she'd deliver such a devastating blow.

And when the oversized bouquet of flowers arrived, complete with love letter attached, one might have thought reconciliation was in the air. Even April smiled and sighed—most likely a sigh of relief—at the sight. And when the second bouquet arrived at lunch time, well. This was just confirmation that all was right with the world again.

Simone allowed her office mates to believe in the fairy tale. To believe that happily ever afters really existed.

Cause they'd find out. Eventually.

Simone read his letter for the third time.

> *Simone,*
>
> *The flowers are a pale representation of your beauty. But I send them as a manifestation of the love I have for you. You've indicated that you don't deserve "someone like me," but Simone,*

nothing could be farther from the truth. If you could only know how much I love you...if you could see inside my heart of hearts...you would see a man who is broken without you. I want you by my side. I can't let you go, Simone. I want you. I need you. I will never leave you. Please give me another chance, Simone. I love you.
Des

When the third bouquet arrived after lunch, along with a similar letter, she'd had enough. She needed to put a stop to this. Once and for all. She grabbed her phone out of her purse and called him.

He sounded so happy when he picked up, like the sound of her voice was medicine to him. She acknowledged her receipt of the flowers when he asked her if she got them, but never once did she say she liked them or that they were pretty. She didn't so much as thank him much less give mention to the heartfelt words he'd written in his letters. She remained as business-like as possible when she asked him to meet her, face to face.

She would speak to him one last time. And she knew just the right place to do so.

She asked him to meet her in the main, grassy courtyard of the community college where Travis worked.

She arrived first and sat on an isolated bench, far away from backpack-toting, summer session students who were either scurrying across campus, trying to get to class on time, or nonchalantly strolling to *kill* time. Des had sounded a bit surprised that she'd want to meet at her ex-husband's place of employment. But it was the *perfect* place to speak her truth. It would make more of an impact on her words, and maybe once and for all, Des would move on and forget about her.

When she saw him in the distance, her heart jumped like it always did.

She didn't stand up when he approached the bench. She knew he wanted to kiss her, or at the very least give her a hug. But no doubt Des could read her eyes which were shouting *don't touch me.*

"It's so good to see you," he said, sitting down, leaving a foot of space between them on the bench.

Simone held a relaxed posture, one arm resting on the back of the bench. She looked at him a few seconds before speaking.

"As you may have already guessed, I'm not flying out to California with you and Dante tomorrow," she said.

"I really wish you would," he said. "I want you to be there with us."

She shook her head. "No. It's a time for family. You need to be with your family."

"Simone, *you're* my family," he said. "You're my *world.*"

Why did he have to make this so hard?

"Des, I don't belong in your world—"

"You do."

"No. I don't. And I'm going to tell you why."

He leaned forward a bit, she assumed, to show her she had his full attention. He looked like he was breathing hard, almost like the actor in a horror film who'd just stumbled upon a dismembered body. It was as if he knew that what she was about to say would alter everything. And this was Simone's deepest hope. This was her best shot.

"The night of our first meeting for the grand opening—when Com Corp met you at The Fajita Grill?"

He nodded, still breathing hard.

"Almost didn't happen," she said. "At least, *I* almost didn't show up that night. Would you like to know why?"

He put his lips together and opened his eyes a little wider as his affirmative reply.

"Because that was the night I was going to kill myself."

She gave him a moment to digest this. He continued to look at her, not saying anything, like he instinctively knew she had more to say. Like by responding with words he'd jinx it and she wouldn't proceed.

"And I was going to do it right here. On this campus. In Travis' office."

"But you didn't," he said.

"But I was going to," she said. "I had every intention of ending my life that night. You know why?"

His silence spurred her on.

"Because I wanted to make him pay, Des. I wanted Travis to pay for what he'd done to me. *That's* what kind of person you've fallen in love with."

He mumbled something, and she said, "What."

"He's not worth your life," he repeated, clearly

this time.

And though she hadn't thought of it this way before, she agreed with him. No. Travis *wasn't* worth her life. *Was anyone?*

"The fact is," she said, "what you need to see is that you've allowed yourself to become involved with the type of person you least respect. I'm just like your friend who overdosed, Des. And just like Kirk, I'll disappoint you every time."

Des was getting all choked up, now. She didn't know if it was due to thoughts about his dearly departed friend or what she'd just revealed to him or both. He could barely get out his next words.

"Simone, the *pain* you must have felt to consider doing that. It breaks my heart. I never want you to feel like that again."

But she had to keep on. "That was only going to be my *second* attempt."

Then she told him all about her original plan but how she'd encountered Jen that morning. Des mumbled a faint *praise you, Jesus* as she was talking. He was *really* crying, now, not holding back.

"I can't believe you were almost taken from me." Des had his elbows on his knees, hands on his forehead. "Thank *God* it didn't happen."

"But if it did, you'd have never known me," she reasoned. "You'd have gone on, living your happy life without me."

"I *wasn't* happy, Simone," he said. "I mean. I wasn't complete. I had no one to share my life with."

"You have your kids. And now a grandchild," she said.

"But not you," he said. "You brought my

energy back. You made me remember what life is all about."

"What *is* it about, Des?" she asked. Because she couldn't fathom any kind of importance she might have, any kind of value she might be to him.

"Relationship," he said. "It's not about stuff or status. It's about relationship. It's about me and God and me and you and *yeah*, my kids. I *love* my kids. But *damn*, Simone. I love *you*!"

Now her tears flowed. She whispered, "How could you?"

"Do I need a particular reason?" he asked. "Can I explain something in words that can only be understood right here?" He tapped on his heart with the palm of his hand. "This—" he tapped it again then reached over and put his hand on *her* heart, "goes with *this*. And that's what I *know*, Simone. I know what I know." Her hand betrayed her as it grasped on to his. This encouraged him to pull her close in a long embrace as the two cried on each other's shoulders. Des rubbed her back and swayed with her, back and forth, back and forth. He grabbed her face in his huge, gentle hands and kissed her passionately on the lips, tears streaming down his face, tears streaming down *her* face. Over and over he said *Simone, oh my Simone.*

She couldn't take it anymore. She pushed him away and said, "Des, stop. I'm not doing this. It's gotta stop."

When he tried to come in again for another kiss, she stood up. Their hands were still clasped, and he looked up at her, pleading at her with his eyes. She was breaking his heart, and she hated herself for doing it. But she had to do it.

"This is goodbye, Des," she said. "I'm leaving, now."

"No, Simone, don't," he said. "Come with me. Come to California with me. Your mom's expecting you. Everyone's expecting you."

"No, Des."

"Then I'm not going without you. I'm staying *here* with *you*."

Now she was scared. She interpreted this to mean that she was on suicide watch or something. Like he felt obligated to ensure she didn't do something drastic.

"Listen to me, Des," she said. "You don't have to worry about *me*. I'm not going to do anything crazy, I promise. But even if I was *planning* to, you couldn't stop me. Do you hear me? *No* one could stop me. And you're the only one I've told about this, and I swear, Des, the secret stops here with you. If you *really* love me…." She grabbed his chin and made him look her in the eye. "If you really love me, you'll keep this between the two of us. You won't tell my mom. You won't tell *your* mom. You won't tell *anyone*. And if you really love me… " it was hard to get the next words out…"you'll stay the hell away from me."

His shirt was getting splotched as the tears dropped from his cheeks.

"Go, Des. Go to your family. I mean it. I'll be fine, I promise. But I *won't* be fine unless you go."

He slowly nodded his head. He brought both her hands up to his lips and kissed them. He kissed them until she'd backed so far away he could no longer touch her. She imagined he was still sobbing on the bench as she walked across the grass. But she didn't turn around to find out. She kept on walking and didn't look back.

Her phone rang on the drive home. She wiped the last tear from her eye and said, "Oh, crap." It was her mother.

"Hey, Mom," she said, trying to sound normal.

"Hi, Honey! I was waiting all *week* for you to give me a call, but I'm just dying to know…did you like the plaque?"

"Yeah, Mom, I did," she said.

And then she couldn't get a word in edgewise. Her mother went on and on about how sweet Des was and how he'd come up with the idea for the plaque and surprising Simone with it at the grand opening and how she and Des were talking about her dad at the birthday party and *oh, how wonderful you've found such a nice man, Simone.* She was praising Des about as much as she'd praised Simone when she'd called her last week to thank her for the "beautiful scrapbook" she'd received from her.

"He loves you so much," said her mom.

"Did he call you and tell you this?" She almost barked the words, already feeling angry at Des.

Her mom laughed. "No, of course not! I haven't spoken to him since I met him at my party. No, he didn't tell me he loves you, Simone. He didn't have to. It's written all over his face! I *saw* how he lights up every time he looks at you." And as if this wasn't bad enough, she added, "Don't let *this* one get away, Simone. He's a keeper."

She sounded so excited. So high on life. How could Simone disappoint her? She'd broken enough hearts for one day. Why add her mother to the list?

"I can't wait to see you tomorrow, Simone. Do you have an ETA on when you think you'll pull up to the house? Will Des and Dante be with you? I'd like to fix dinner for everybody. Well. I'd like *Brady* to fix dinner for everybody." Her laugh was borderline giddy.

No. She would let her mother go on a few more days, believing that all was well with her and Des. She would lie.

"Look, Mom. Change of plans. I was going to call you later to let you know that I'm not coming out tomorrow."

She made something up about Meredith being out of town and the office needing her and that she'd be post-poning her flight.

"It's all good, Mom," she said, trying to act like it really *was* all good.

But it was *far* from good. And though she concluded the conversation with the feeling she'd made her mom okay with everything, Simone felt sick to her stomach.

She'd spent the rest of that evening and the next several days a zombie. And because she didn't hear from Des, not so much as one little text, she knew beyond a doubt that Des really loved her. And *she* really loved *him*. And it hurt *so bad.*

It hurt so bad it was crippling.

She felt herself slowly slipping back down into a long tunnel of darkness.

She wanted to die.

*   *   *   *   *   *   *

The day at Com Corp began like any other Wednesday.

You'd have never known anything was wrong with her. The way she showed up to work on time. The way she walked into the office. The way she greeted those she passed on her way to her desk. With eyes completely dry, no one would know she'd shed enough tears the night before to fill a swimming pool. The way she moved, the way she talked, the way she sat right down and got to business, no one would ever guess just hours later she'd deliver such a devastating blow.

And then the dark cloud burst.

It was almost lunchtime. April went into Meredith's office to set up the conference table. She was in there for what seemed like an extended length of time, *and* she'd shut the door behind her. Shadows could be seen, moving behind the opaque window on the wall next to the door. At times the movements were abrupt, almost like a dance. At times they were slow.

Of course, nothing intelligible could be heard. Just the low murmurings of two female voices, conversing back and forth with one another, same as what anyone *ever* heard, coming from that room. Heidi and Jodi certainly thought nothing of it. They said their polite goodbyes to whomever happened to be standing nearby on their way out of the building. Before the front door closed behind them, they mentioned something about checking out the new food truck across the street.

Most everyone else in this part of the building had already left, and those who hadn't soon followed the leader out the door. Simone and April and Meredith were the only oddballs who ever ate lunch *in* these days, but on Wednesdays it was so delicious. And free! And made with love by Bradley.

But this was no ordinary Wednesday. This particular Wednesday would forever be marked as special. As different.

As deadly.

She would make sure of it.

Because what no one knew…what no one was able to detect earlier that morning when she'd listened to her messages…when she'd rifled through the filing cabinet to find the manila folder she was looking for…when she'd calmly assigned everyone their individual tasks for the day…was that she wasn't in her right mind.

But how *could* they know? She never told anyone *anything*. All that anyone ever knew was what they thought they saw. And what they saw, day in and day out, was someone who seemingly had it all together. Someone who had life by the balls and was in control of her destiny. Someone who "took it all in stride" and "spit right back into the face" of any challenge too tough to bear. They saw someone who rarely got upset. Rarely played her emotional cards. Without realizing it, what they saw day after day was a *real* Stone Cold.

Except today she was out of control.

When she heard April scream, Simone ran over and burst through the office door. The sight that met her eyes made her legs shake and her knees knock together.

Meredith was standing behind her desk up against the far wall, holding a *gun* to her head! April was on the opposite side of the conference table closest to the opaque window.

Meredith looked more startled than Simone *felt*. Her eyes darted to Simone's form, standing in the doorway. She slowly lowered the hand that was holding the gun so that the barrel now rested on the desk.

Simone's first reaction should probably have been to run out of the cramped room and out of the building yelling *FIRE!* Or something like *somebody help! Call 911!* But oddly, she didn't do this. Once she got her bearings, she wasn't *too* fazed by the gun. Maybe it was because this was *Meredith*. Meredith, whom she'd known for so many years. *Meredith* wasn't dangerous! And obviously, she needed serious help.

"Meredith, would you like me to call anyone?" she asked, softly, taking a tiny step back and holding up a finger as if to say *be back in a jiff—let me go grab my phone.*

"Don't you leave me, Simone!" said Meredith. "Come in right now and sit down." She gestured with the gun for Simone to sit down at the table. Simone quickly complied. April's face was white as a sheet. She looked petrified, and she and Simone exchanged a brief, helpless glance with one another before turning their full attention back to their boss.

"Meredith, why don't *you* sit down, too?" Simone suggested. "Tell me what's wrong."

And like a small child, lip quivering, Meredith nodded her head and said, "Okay... okay."

Simone employed a *new* tactic. In the most authoritative yet non-scared-to-death voice she could muster, she said, "And let go of that gun! Good *grief,* you're making me nervous!"

Whatever it was about the way she'd said it, it worked. Meredith set the gun on top of the wooden desk, causing it to make a *thump* sound. She grabbed her coffee mug and with hands shaking, brought it up to her mouth and took a small drink. April remained where she was, pinned between the conference table and the wall with the window. Simone could hear her, breathing. She couldn't imagine *April* would know how to act under pressure. So it was all up to Simone. It was up to *her* to calm Meredith down.

Meredith was clearly frazzled. Even her eyes were crazy, looking from Simone to April then back to Simone again. She kept twisting the rings on her fingers and the bracelets on her wrists like this was a newly acquired, nervous habit of hers. Every now and then she'd pick up a pen or a pencil then put it right back down, or she'd tap the stack of papers piled high on the corner of the desk. Her face no longer had its usual luster. She looked like she'd aged about ten years since she'd returned on Monday from her out-of-state visit with her kids. She'd told everyone she'd had a wonderful time, but who knew? Maybe the family was having a serious problem or experiencing some awful tragedy that Meredith couldn't quite cope with.

"What's going on, Meredith?" Simone asked. "Is everything okay? Are the kids alright?" Meredith nodded. "The grandkids alright?" She nodded again. "Are *you* alright?" At first Meredith nodded her head yes. But then she started to cry and vigorously shook her head no.

"No!" She said it kind of loud, then even louder, "*No!*" She was bawling now. "No, I'm *not* alright. I'm *never* alright!"

Simone started to get up, but this only caused Meredith to push herself back a ways from her desk and yell, "Don't you come near me! You stay there!" And Simone slowly sat back down.

"We just want to help you, Meredith," said April. *She* was crying now, too. Simone shook her head at April in surprise like *let ME do all the talking. Stop!* But April hadn't noticed, and even if she *had*, she'd probably *cluelessly* keep talking. Because April was April.

Just as she thought, Meredith snapped at her trusted employee of so many years. "Oh, *do* you, April!" she yelled. "Or maybe you just want to go out with your *boyfriend*!"

April looked confused.

"When's the last time you even *called* me, April? Huh? Answer me that!"

April looked over at Simone as if to beg for help. It was all so confusing. It wasn't like April and Meredith ever hung out together. Meredith always disappeared at the end of the day, and everyone just chalked her up as independent. They just thought she kept her work life separate from her private life. And *Simone* got that. *She* never hung out with anyone at the office—not before moving in with April. So this all sounded just so bizarre.

Simone tried to change the subject. "Meredith, what can I do to make it better?"

"And you!" Meredith leaned forward, attempting to support her upper body with both hands on her desk, but she slipped forward, knocking a pencil holder and some of her papers off the desk. She didn't even seem to notice. "As if you're any better! You're the *worst*, Simone. The *worst!*" She yelled it.

"I don't know what you're talking about." Simone said it softly, hoping to bring the tension in the room down a few decibels.

"Just when I thought you were a *human*, you pulled your I'm-so-perfect crap on me. You lose your husband then three seconds later wham! You meet prince charming and *ride* off into the sunset." She did a little hand gesture with this last statement then seemed fascinated by the back of her own hand.

Just when Simone didn't think things could possibly get any worse, they heard Bradley's voice.

"Sorry I'm late—" he started to say but abruptly stopped in his tracks at the door. His eyes went straight to the gun on Meredith's desk. He looked at his mom and then at Simone. "Is everyone okay?" he asked.

"Yeah, we're just *peachy*," said Meredith. "Set the damn food on the table. What took you so long?"

The side of Bradley's lip rose as if to say *huh?* But he did as Meredith said. He slowly walked closer to the table and set down the two paper grocery bags he was carrying.

And as if she *weren't* holding everybody hostage on their lunch hour, as if they'd merely been talking about 4th of July plans or something, Meredith asked him, "What did you make for us today?"

She stood up and grabbed the gun off her desk. She sidestepped her way over to the grocery bags on the table and peered inside one of them. Or tried to. She almost lost her balance.

To add to the craziness, Bradley softly

answered, "Sub sandwiches. Chips. Brownies."

"Mmm. Sounds like the perfect last meal," said Meredith.

"Meredith—" Simone started to talk.

"Of course, it's not quite what *you're* getting used to, Simone, with that new boyfriend of yours. I bet *he* takes you out to some really *nice* places!"

She hadn't told Meredith she'd broken up with Des. Outside of April, she hadn't told *anyone* at Com Corp. As far as all her coworkers knew, she and Des were still going just as strong as ever.

Before Simone could say anything, Meredith went on with her rant.

"How nice, Simone, that you've found such a quick replacement for your ex-husband. Some of us aren't so lucky!"

As she spoke, she started waving the gun around. Not intentionally. Maybe she'd forgotten she was even holding it. Because Meredith seemed drunk.

Everyone just sat there, watching her move and sway. She went into a big spiel about Simone living the perfect life and how everything always fell into place for her all the time.

"*You've* never struggled. You're *never* lonely!" said Meredith. She sidestepped back to her desk. She hovered over her chair before finally plopping down onto it, as though this took lots of concentration and skill. Then she started to cry.

"It's okay, Meredith," said April, actually making her way around the table, trying to get over to her.

"Mom. Don't," said Bradley.

But for now, she was okay. Meredith was too

caught up in her own thoughts to notice April. *Her* gaze was upon Simone.

"You only knew for *two seconds* what it's like to have nobody love you! But not *me*, Simone. I've known for fifteen *years* that nobody loves me!" Her sobs were heartbreaking. "*Nobody* loves *me*."

"Yes, they do!" said Simone. "We *all* love you. And your kids love you so *much*, Meredith. *You* know that. You were all just together last *week*!"

Meredith shook her head. "They have their *own* families now. They *never* come out to see *me*."

Her stomach moved with every cry. April was now getting closer—almost at arm's length from the desk. Simone didn't blame April for trying. It was hard not to want to reach out and console a woman who was so distraught.

Then suddenly, Meredith noticed April approaching. She pointed her finger at her. Then at Bradley.

"And *your* son brings you lunch!"

Then everything happened so fast. April took another step toward Meredith, but Meredith sprang to her feet. She tottered backwards a step then rebounded off the wall behind her and nearly fell down in the process. When she regained her balance, with a shaky hand she pointed the gun directly at April.

And quick as lightning, Bradley leaped over the table and grabbed Meredith by her gun-bearing arm. They struggled for a few seconds before the shot was fired.

Their two bodies made a sickening sound as together, they hit the floor.

Chapter Nineteen

"Bradley!"

April was by her son's side in no time flat. Simone had never seen her move so fast. Didn't know she *could* move this fast.

Simone darted out of the room and raced down the hall to her desk but for the life of her couldn't find her cell phone. That's because it was still in her purse. She'd never taken it out that day. She was getting used to not hearing from Des, now, so why keep her phone out? Why have it out as a constant reminder of his absence from her life?

She picked up her desk phone and somehow her shaking fingers punched in 9-1-1.

She wouldn't be able to remember let alone repeat to anyone what exactly she'd told the operator if anyone had *asked* her to, so gripped by fear was she. Her whole body was shaking. She thought she heard the operator calmly say something about a squad car and an ambulance and was she able to stay on the line.

"Mm hmm," Simone said, taking the phone as far away from the desk as the cord would allow. The wall obstructed her view, and she couldn't see anything going on in the next room. All she could hear was April's hysterical voice.

"Oh God, please let him be okay!" Simone closed her eyes and whispered this into the phone.

"Are you okay, Ma'am?" the operator asked. "Are you in any present danger?"

"Um. No, I don't think so," she said, eyes frantically looking all around. The operator continued to ask Simone for an updated assessment on the situation, but Simone wasn't able to tell her much. So then the operator asked her questions of a more personal nature, like how long she'd worked at Com Corp, etc. Simone assumed this was to help distract her and calm her down. In a strange way, it was working. Little by little, she could feel her heart rate get a little slower. It was no longer pounding clear out of her chest cavity.

The operator assured her that help was on the way, and before long, Simone heard sirens approaching. She asked if she could hang up, now, and she did so with the operator's blessing.

Heidi and Jodi were following the paramedics into the main foyer, looking a bit stunned. They said from their bench across the street they'd seen the ambulance, pulling up to Com Corp and rushed over to see what was wrong. They spoke in hushed tones as a few cops stormed into the building. They entered Meredith's office right on the tail of the paramedics. They didn't let anyone follow them inside, not even Simone, even though she tried. It felt like they were in there for an eternity, but it couldn't have been more than a few minutes.

First, Meredith was wheeled out on a stretcher. Her eyes were closed and Simone couldn't tell if she was merely unresponsive or dead!

And then they wheeled Bradley out. Like Meredith, he had on an oxygen mask and was all strapped in to a gurney. His eyes were slightly open, and he looked at Simone, then at Heidi and Jodi before his gurney was pushed out the front door.

April followed closely behind. She was being

escorted by one of the EMT's, who had an arm around her waist. She was crying hysterically as she followed her son out the front door and into the ambulance, no time at all to look at anyone.

"Is there someone here in charge I can speak with?" asked the female officer who had arrived in the first squad car. Simone could now see other squad cars and even a news truck pulling up outside of Com Corp.

"That would be me," said Simone, stepping forward.

The woman officer and her partner asked for Simone's name and job title and a retelling of the events leading up to "the shooting," as they were calling it. To hear it in words like *that* made it seem all the more dreadful.

"Who got shot?" Simone asked, trying not to sound as frantic as she felt. It had all happened so fast.

"The male," said the woman officer.

Simone put her hands over her mouth. "Oh dear God!" she said and cried.

Not Bradley! This couldn't happen to Bradley! Not *him*. Not her special friend! He was just starting to get his *life* together. And he was a *good* boy. Just like April always said. Only *good* things should happen to good boys!

Which was why she broke down even more as she began to tell them her version of the story, how Bradley had only been there, bringing lunch for everyone. How Bradley had been shot, protecting his mother.

Heidi and Jodi immediately walked over and rubbed Simone's shoulders. They, too, were in tears.

"I didn't think Meredith was planning to *hurt*

anyone," said Simone, surprising even herself that she'd still defend her boss after all that had happened. "She was planning to end her own life."

And on and on her statement went. Heidi and Jodi reaffirmed that Meredith had seemed perfectly normal that morning. Granted, she'd spent a lot of time alone in her office that day, but didn't she always? There wasn't anything unusual about *that*.

"I have to get to the hospital," Simone told everyone, but it came out sounding distant, like she was talking out loud to herself. "I have to be with April. And with Bradley."

And if they'd thought to detain her from accomplishing this, her tears prompted at least one of the other officers in the room to say *we'll take you there.*

There must've been a million people in the emergency room, but Simone was oblivious to any of them. They, on the other hand, may have watched in fascinated wonder as an attractive woman wearing a designer dress and heels clicked by in the midst of two armed policemen all the way to the front desk, immediately gaining entrance through the swinging doors at the back of the room. But Simone didn't see any of them.

She was too upset. She'd said nothing the whole way over and scarcely noticed the sirens were on and that the cop driving the squad car was running through red lights all the way to their destination.

All she could think about was Bradley. And April. And MeeMaw! *Oh my gosh, MeeMaw!* she thought. This would just about kill her. Had *she* heard anything? Surely, she'd be returning to the house with the Old Lady Club about now if they weren't there already. She checked her cell to see if there were any messages.

No. None. Simone heaved a sigh of relief. No news was good news. *And bad news could wait!* She'd wait for more details before troubling her sweet MeeMaw with any of this.

The attending nurse pulled back the curtain and Simone saw the backs of April and Carter, whom she was impressed to see had arrived at the scene so soon. *He's a good man*, she thought, *to be with April in her time of need.* They were sitting on the only chairs in the space, facing a half-asleep Bradley. Bradley had a huge bandage wrapped around his arm.

April turned around at the sound of the curtain rings, sliding on the metal bar overhead. "Simone!" she said, getting up on her feet. The nurse closed the curtain behind them.

The two women embraced, and Carter stood up as well, most likely out of awkwardness. The space they were in was small and cramped.

"How is he?" asked Simone in a whisper.

"I'm goooood," said Bradley, opening his eyes a little wider. He was obviously feeling loopy.

"The bullet grazed his arm. They gave him a sedative to relax him. They bandaged him up pretty quickly." April was talking *so* fast.

Simone walked over to him and put her hand on his "good" arm. She uttered a silent *thank you* to God for answering her prayer, grateful as could be that Bradley was all right.

For lack of anything meaningful to say to a

teenage boy who'd just been shot, all she said was, "Hey."

"Hey," he said, smiling a little.

"You scared the crap out of me," she said.

He laughed. It was the kind of laugh a person laughs when they've been delivered from imminent destruction.

"I ain't bringing lunch to you guys no more," he slurred, closing his eyes.

"Yeah, you go and joke about it," said April. And somewhere during the ongoing *recount* of the afternoon's events delivered by his mother (as if Simone and Bradley hadn't been there to witness it personally and were just hearing about it for the first time) Bradley drifted off to sleep.

"Does MeeMaw know?" asked Simone.

April nodded. "Yes, I already called her."

Simone said, "I'll go home and check on her."

But then she thought *how?* She didn't have a car. Then, as if reading her mind, Carter offered to drive her.

April told them they were planning to admit Bradley for the night because he might still be in shock. Simone was grateful to hear this because indeed, it *had* been a traumatic experience to say the least. And Bradley could have been seriously injured or killed. Thank God he was fine!

When April insisted she was planning to stay *with* Bradley all night, Simone asked what she could bring her, later, from home. April was able to mention a few items before they heard some activity a few feet away.

Simone pulled the curtain aside, and they saw

the attending nurse, a couple of doctors, and the two police officers who had escorted Simone to the hospital, speaking to each other in low voices.

Simone and April stepped closer to hear what they were talking so seriously about. Come to find out, the officers had gone in to Meredith's room (she had a real room with real walls) to question her about her actions back at Com Corp, but they couldn't get any answers. So now they were speaking with the emergency room staff.

Simone soon found out that the reason the officers couldn't get any answers and the reason why the hospital staff had wheeled Meredith into a special room was because Meredith had passed away en route to the hospital.

"But *she* wasn't shot!" said Simone. Maybe she said that because *she* was in shock, too, just like Bradley.

Meredith? Dead? It just wasn't registering.

At least April appeared coherent.

And even though Meredith had nearly killed April's only child, had almost taken away her only beloved son, with *tears* in her eyes, April asked, "May we see her?"

On the drive back to the hospital later that night, Simone went over and over the events of the day in her mind. She still couldn't make sense out of any of it. It seemed so surreal. *So* unexpected. So left field.

Had she known Meredith was suffering from depression all these weeks, she'd have reached out to her. That's what the doctors' initial thoughts were, that Meredith was depressed, but no one wanted to speculate too much at this juncture. This preliminary assessment was premised on the prescription medication Meredith was taking, based on what was found in her office and in her purse—medication that was typically used to treat the disorder.

If I hadn't been so selfish! Simone wasn't sure she'd ever be able to forgive herself. She'd been so caught up in her *own* grief and misery, she hadn't noticed Meredith's. And apparently, Meredith's condition had been far more serious than her own.

Carter had first taken Simone back to Com Corp so she could retrieve her car. Thankfully, the news van had already left. Heidi had aptly answered the reporters' questions to the best of her ability, and apparently, the story had aired on the early evening news. So it was all the latest buzz. Nothing like this *ever* happened in the quiet town of North Olmsted!

Josephine had practically blown up Simone's phone with questions, questions, questions, so Simone had dutifully called her back and appeased her former neighbor with reassurances that she'd come out of the crisis unscathed.

She'd hoped the news hadn't reached her mom! Because she'd even gotten a text from Travis.

> Simone, glad to hear you're okay. If there's anything I can do, let me know.

She'd replied:

> Thanks, Trav. I appreciate it.

She was moved that he'd reached out to her. Who knew? Maybe there was hope for him after all.

Jodi had already contacted Meredith's family with the bad news (the second she'd received the grim update from April.)

MeeMaw's friends were still with MeeMaw when Simone had arrived at the house (where it had quickly become her job to reassure everyone that Bradley was fine.)

But Meredith was not.

Seeing Meredith, lying on a gurney, lifeless, was not a sight that would soon disappear from her mind. She and April both had burst into tears when they saw her. April had even grabbed on to Meredith's hand and told her she forgave her. But Simone couldn't say *anything*. It was just too sad to see her. She'd just stood and stared at Meredith as the tears rolled down her face. She felt so sorry for her. Meredith thought nobody *loved* her. What a horrible thought to harbor day in and day out. Especially when it wasn't true. And even if it were, *God* loved her.

After the Old Lady Club had finally left, Simone had helped MeeMaw to bed. She admired how MeeMaw always handled everything with such strength and compassion. When she'd vowed to keep Meredith's family and loved ones in her prayers, Simone believed her. She knew MeeMaw was a self-proclaimed "prayer warrior."

With many assurances from MeeMaw that she would be fine for the night, Simone had felt it was okay to leave the house for an hour or so. She'd grabbed what few things April thought she might need plus a toothbrush for Bradley before making her way back to the hospital.

She planned to visit for a little while with April and Bradley, but when she walked into Bradley's hospital room, she knew that mother and son would be fine without her.

They were both sound asleep in the dimly lit room. April was curled up next to Bradley on his hospital bed with her arm around his waist. Bradley was snoring softly. It was such a sweet picture. If she weren't in such a public place, no doubt Simone would have cried like a little baby at such a sentimental sight.

She thought *what is happening to me?* She was turning into such a sap!

So she just set their things on the chair by the bed, mouthed out a goodnight to her two dearest friends in the whole world, and returned back home to MeeMaw. But the person she really wanted was Des.

Simone was at the hospital the next morning soon as she was able to get there. She was going to bring April and Bradley home. All Bradley's reports were good, and he'd handled the news about Meredith like a trooper, according to April.

They were just about to leave the hospital room when Bradley said, "Crap, I left my toothbrush in the bathroom!"

"I'll get it, ding-a-ling," Simone said, ruffling the top of his messy mop of hair. He and April exchanged a smile and proceeded to walk out of the room, arm in arm.

When she flipped on the bathroom light, she gasped. *Des* was standing in the middle of the room. He smiled, and she couldn't help but smile back.

And then her smile turned into a frown as the tears flowed down her cheeks. They stepped toward each other, and right there in the middle of the bathroom, they clung to one another. For the next several minutes, in a silent embrace that said more than words could ever hope to communicate, they held onto each other like they were the last two people on earth.

Simone all of a sudden felt so weak. The past 24 hours she'd been so *strong* for everybody. But now her muscles melted. And this was okay. Because now her support was here, and all she needed to do was lean into her Des.

"I took the red eye soon as I heard," he said, walking with Simone out of the hospital room.

He told her that around 8:00 p.m. California time, a doped-up Bradley had sent him a text. Des had immediately called back but mostly talked to April.

"So April knew you were coming?" she said.

"Don't be mad at her. I told her not to tell you. Then when I made it here before *you* did, Bradley wanted me to surprise you."

Simone didn't mind. She didn't mind at all. But then she gasped.

"Des! What about the baby?"

"Kim's scheduled to be induced today," he said.

"You're going to miss the birth of your first grandson!" she said, looking concerned, now.

He just pulled her closer. "I'm right where I need to be," he said.

She looked up at his profile as they boarded the elevator, moved beyond belief. She knew how important it was for Des to be there when Dante's baby was born. And yet, he'd chosen to be with *her*. Even after she'd pushed him away!

She probably should have insisted he head back to California. She probably should have assured him she was fine. But she really didn't want him to go.

"You must be exhausted," she said, thinking he'd go to Granny's or even April's house so he could take a nice, long nap. But he insisted he wasn't tired.

In fact, he helped Simone all that day and all the following days that week. He helped her take care of all the millions of details that surround a tragedy such as this, like talking to the family and boxing up personal effects from the office and planning the best memorial North Olmsted had ever seen.

Simone had told Meredith's daughter, Courtney, that she would handle all the arrangements. She knew Courtney and her brothers were flying out to handle Meredith's estate not to mention their mother's *company*, and Simone knew *that* would keep them busy enough! All three of Meredith's children expressed to her their deepest appreciation.

Of course, Simone had help. She delegated tasks to Heidi and Jodi and April, just like she would with any other event. Ironically, *poetically*, Meredith's last hurrah was *almost* as big a deal as the grand opening for the Ohio Sunset Supermarket.

Simone had a full week to plan, and she pulled out all the stops. It was therapy for her to immerse herself in so many details. It was also her way of honoring her boss. *Indeed*, Meredith had taught her everything she knew about event planning. *Indeed*, she'd helped make her successful in the industry, and Simone would forever be grateful.

Just like her protégé, Meredith didn't have an extensive friend collection, so Simone substituted friends with vendors and clients they'd done business with over the years. She made sure to feature each company in the slide show. She shared a guilty laugh with Des about it as they were putting it together.

"Meredith would appreciate this," she told him.

"What, you mean using her memorial as an occasion to garner more business?" Des smiled.

"Des! I would *never* do *that*," she joked back with him. "It's how we show our *appreciation* to our *clients*." *Yep. Meredith taught me everything I know!* she told herself. She told Des, "If Meredith were here, I know she would wholeheartedly approve."

Des shook his head but smiled, looking at his cherished Simone the way he had the very first day they'd laid eyes on each other in the checkout line. Like she was a five-year-old, doing something cute.

When all the work was finished and she and Des were sitting side by side in the second row at Meredith's outdoor memorial service, Simone could finally breathe.

It was a beautiful ceremony. No mention was made of Meredith's prescription drug addiction. That's what Simone and the employees at Com Corp had learned from Meredith's daughter, Courtney. And because everyone was aware of it, why magnify it? It certainly didn't *define* Meredith. She was so much more than her addiction. But as Courtney reported, Meredith had suffered from depression half of her adult life. For the most part, she was always able to grin and bear it—to put a mask on and keep herself busy. Which was probably why she'd turned Com Corp into such a huge success.

But then there was the divorce. And when the last child flew the coop, Meredith took more and more medications to ease her pain. As the autopsy report revealed, she'd practically played Russian roulette, making deadly combinations of prescriptions (and mixing it all up with alcohol—which come to find out had filled her coffee mug on her desk.) Of course, all the various prescriptions had not been authorized by her physician, who was unaware Meredith had *other* doctors on her payroll as well. And then sadly, Meredith that fateful Wednesday had taken too *many* of her meds, and her body simply stopped working on the ride to the hospital.

It was just so sad to see Courtney and her brothers, crying over their mother. Meredith's older son and his wife tearfully said they would be taking over Com Corp until they could sell it.

"We had such a nice time when she came out to New York," Courtney told Simone and Des, who sat at the family table during the reception after the ceremony. "But looking back, it was almost our mom's way of saying goodbye to us."

What *April* didn't quite understand was why Meredith would choose to end her life at the office. *Doesn't that seem like a selfish thing to do? To traumatize all of us like that?* she'd asked Simone. Simone had only shrugged. The counselors whom Simone had hired (on the Com Corp payroll) to come into the office had explained to everyone that sometimes a person who takes their own life will do it in a place that feels comfortable to them. And Meredith considered her office a home away from home, so *that* made sense. But Simone didn't want to get into any of her own explanations with April as to how a person just really isn't in their right mind when they do such a horrific thing as that. Because Simone didn't want to ever give *herself* away. Only Des would know her deep, dark secrets. *Des* was the only person she completely trusted. He knew *everything* about her—and loved her, anyway.

Des seemed to feel safe enough with Simone to ask her if she still thought *she* could ever go through with something like that in the future.

She emphatically assured him *no. Not at all.* She had too much to live for. There were too many lives to touch. Too many people to help. She was here for a reason. In her heart of hearts, she knew God had gone to great lengths to pursue her. He had orchestrated every distraction, had divinely put every person in her path to show her the way.

No. Life was too valuable. Even sitting there during Meredith's ceremony, she couldn't help but think that Meredith was missing out. She was missing out on the gorgeous weather that day. She was missing out on her grandbaby's cute, little noises and facial expressions. She was missing out on so much!

Meredith will never laugh at a funny movie ever again.

Meredith won't get to see her little grandchild grow up into a fine, young man.

Meredith won't contribute to society, anymore, or help any of us with our Com Corp events.

Simone's other contemplation, sitting there at the memorial, was that life goes on. Even in the midst of a sad situation, on a day that was hard and heavy and so difficult to bear, the sounds of laughter could still be heard. People had plans. People had dreams. So for Simone to have thought that the whole world would come to a screeching halt if she ever died seemed outrageously foolish to her now. Family and loved ones would be sad, yeah! *But they'd get over it. Life always moves on.*

Her *final* contemplation she couldn't bear to dwell on. She barely dared to think it.

Is Meredith's name in the Book of Life?

So rather than go there, knowing she couldn't do anything about it *anyway*, she immediately snapped back to more productive thoughts. Thoughts about *life*, not death. She vowed from here on out to live free of regrets with people. *Every* moment of life was precious. And in the days leading up to the memorial, Simone had decided she and Des would do life *together*. Side by side.

She knew they'd exchange marriage vows at the end of August on a beach somewhere in California, surrounded by family and friends. She knew when they *finally* had sex for the first time on their honeymoon (she loved Des enough to wait for the wedding night) it would be nothing short of phenomenal. Because she knew Des was right. God would bless their marriage in leaps and bounds, simply for honoring Him this way.

She also knew Des would live his dream of doing mission work, beginning with a drug recovery outreach on the beach near their home. Simone would insist! And she knew *she* would continue to *learn* and to *grow* in her faith and to really *love* people, beginning with her family and Des' family and of course, her *new* family... April's family.

While the few remaining guests offered their condolences to Courtney and her brothers, two committed lovers slipped off unnoticed to a park bench not far from the main canopy to watch the sun set. This was their favorite time of day.

The beautiful man sitting beside her squeezed her hand with his. She smiled at him and rested her head on his shoulder.

Yep. She just knew what she knew.

If you or someone you know is experiencing thoughts of suicide, please get help.

The National Suicide Prevention Lifeline offers 24/7 support (free and confidential.) Call 1-800-273-TALK (8255)

About the Author

Shayne Ferguson's husband, children, family members and friends often ask her *where do you get your ideas for your stories?* And her standard reply is, "I really don't know." Naturally, she borrows and modifies snippets from her own experiences—her background, memories, impressions, don't we all—but Shayne describes story-writing as something spiritual, almost like it comes from some other plane. Because as she goes about her daily life, inspiration unexpectedly hits. Upon hearing of a suicide in her own community, this author had sadly contemplated the enormity, the tragedy of the loss, knowing that *every* life touches another. *Everyone* is needed. Her resulting questions surrounding the event coupled a year later with an ordinary trip to the grocery store (where the character Des was born), best explain the manifestation of *Stone Cold*. In all of her books, Shayne's faith inevitably comes into play. She can't seem to write a novel without including the One who inspires her the most and who consumes the majority of her thoughts, the One who'd shed His blood for her over 2,000 years ago. One of these days, she'll try writing a completely secular story just for fun, just to see if she can do it. But for now, even though God is woven into the fabric of all her plot lines, Shayne's *Rated R for Real* novels are intended to entertain. Few things give Shayne greater joy than to provide her readers with a good read. And if her books can inspire? Then that's a plus. Hope you enjoyed *Stone Cold*.

Printed in Great Britain
by Amazon

39213328R00189